GALAXY'S EDGE
EDITED BY MIKE RESNICK

ISSUE: 1   MARCH 2013

CONTENTS

Mike Resnick, Editor
Shahid Mahmud, Publisher

Published by Arc Manor/Phoenix Pick
P.O. Box 10339
Rockville, MD 20849-0339

Galaxy's Edge is published every two months: March, May, July, September, November & January

www.GalaxysEdge.com

Galaxy's Edge is an invitation only magazine. We do not accept unsolicited manuscripts. Unsolicited manuscripts will be disposed of or mailed back to the sender (unopened) at our discretion.

Each issue of Galaxy's Edge is issued as a stand-alone book with a separate ISBN and may be purchased at wholesale venues dedicated to books sales (e.g., Ingram) or directly from the publisher.

ISBN (Amazon Edition Only): 9781976853234

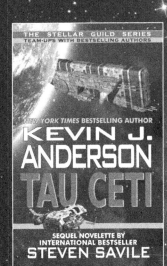
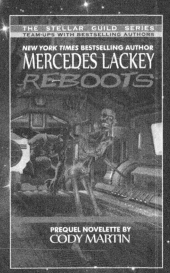
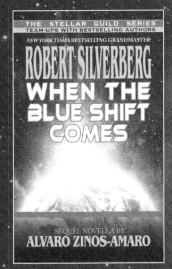

THE EDITOR'S WORD

by Mike Resnick

Welcome to the premier issue of *Galaxy's Edge*. We'll be coming around every two months with a mixture of new stories and reprints, reviews and columns. Almost all the reprints will be by very-well-known authors; most of the new stories will be by less-well-known (but not less talented) authors.

We're very proud to be the latest addition to the pantheon of science fiction magazines, which have a pair of histories—one long and glorious, the other just as long but inglorious (and infinitely more interesting).

You think not?

Let me share some of it with you before the last of us Old Guys (and Gals) pass from the scene and there's no one left to remember the Untold History of the Science Fiction Magazines anymore.

The Shaver Mystery

In 1938, Ray Palmer, an undersized hunchback with a pretty thorough understanding of his readership, took over the editorship of *Amazing Stories*. At the time, John Campbell's *Astounding Science Fiction*, featuring the best of Heinlein, Asimov, Sturgeon, Hubbard, van Vogt, de Camp, Simak, and Kuttner, ruled supreme among the magazines—but then Palmer came up with a gimmick that changed everything: the Shaver Mystery.

He ran a novel—rather generic, rather poorly written—called *I Remember Lemuria!* It was all about these creatures called Deros that lived hidden away from humanity but were preparing to do dire things to us. Nothing special in any way—

—except that Palmer swore to his readers, who consisted mostly of impressionable teen-aged boys, that the story was *true*, and that Richard Shaver was forced by the Powers That Be to present it as fiction or no one—including Ziff-Davis, Palmer's bosses—would dare risk publishing it.

Sounds silly, doesn't it?

Well, the *really* silly part came next: while Palmer was running another dozen or so "Shaver Mystery novels"—each worse than the last—from 1945 to 1948, his circulation skyrocketed. *Amazing* passed *Astounding*, spread-eagled the field, and became the top-selling science fiction magazine, not only of that era, but of *any* era.

I'll tell you a little story about the Shaver Mystery. Back when I was editing men's magazines in Chicago in the late 1960s, I used, among others, a very talented artist, slightly older than myself, named Bill Dichtl. One day we got to talking, and found out we were both science fiction fans, and Bill told me about *his* adventures with the Shaver Mystery.

He was a 14-year-old subscriber to *Amazing* in the late 1940s, living in Chicago (where *Amazing* was published), and one day he got a mysterious phone call, asking if he would like to help in the secret war against the Deros. Of course he said he would. He was given an address to go to that Friday night, and was warned to tell no one about this assignation.

So on Friday night, Bill sneaked out of his house and dutifully went to the address, which happened to be the building that housed the Ziff-Davis publishing empire. He took the elevator up to the appointed floor, found himself in a darkened corridor, saw a single light coming out from beneath a door at the far end of it, walked to the door, saw it was the room number he had been given, and entered. There was a long table, and maybe a dozen other earnest teen-aged boys were sitting at it.

Bill took a seat, and they all waited in silence. About ten minutes later a little hunchbacked man entered the room. It was Ray Palmer, of course. He explained that the Deros would soon be making their move against an unsuspecting humanity, and it was the duty of the boys in that room to spend the rest of the night warning as many people as possible of the coming struggle so they wouldn't be caught unaware.

He had lists of thousands of addresses, which the boys dutifully copied onto blank envelopes. He had thousands of folded and stapled "warnings" that they stuffed into the envelopes. He had thousands of stamps that they licked and stuck onto the envelopes. They finished at sunrise, and Palmer swore them all to secrecy and thanked them for helping to save humanity.

Bill had stuffed a copy of the warning into his pocket to give to his parents, just in case they had somehow been omitted from the mailing list. On the subway home, he opened it and read it—and found out that Palmer had duped the boys into mailing out thousands of subscription renewal notices.

By 1949 Palmer was gone. He started *Other Worlds*, hired a gorgeous Cincinnati fan, Bea Mahaffey, to edit it for him, and even brought Shaver along. (To this day, some people think Palmer *was* Shaver. They were wrong; he was actually seen with Palmer by some fans and pros. Someone purporting to be Shaver wrote some letters to Richard Geis' Hugo-winning fanzine, *Science Fiction Review*, in the 1970s, but no one ever saw him or followed up on it.)

Palmer's gimmick at *Other Worlds* was to get readers to pressure Edgar Rice Burroughs, Inc. to hire his discovery, "John Bloodstone," as the legal successor to Burroughs. ("Bloodstone" was actually Palmer's pal, hack writer Stuart J. Byrne, who had written a copyright-infringing novel, *Tarzan On Mars*, that Palmer wanted to publish.) ERB Inc. refused, and that was the end of that, and pretty much the end of *Other Worlds* (though you can still find illegally-photocopied copies of *Tarzan On Mars* for sale here and there).

Palmer's final stop was at *Fate Magazine*, begun in 1949, where he got rich one last time off a gullible reading public.

As for Shaver, not a single word of the million-plus that he wrote remains in print.

The Prediction Issue

The November 1948 issue of *Astounding* was typical of its era. It was not the best issue that John Campbell edited that year, nor was it the worst, and like all other issues of *Astounding* prior to 1950, it was far superior to its competitors.

Astounding's letter column was (and still is) "Brass Tacks," and in that particular issue there was a cute letter by a Richard A. Hoen who, like most fanboys, went over the most recent issue story by story, explaining in goshwowboyoboy fashion what he liked and disliked and why. Robert A. Heinlein's "Gulf" was pretty good, though not quite up to *Beyond This Horizon*, opined Mr. Hoen. He ranked it second best in the issue, just ahead of A. E. van Vogt's "Final Command," with Lester del Rey's "Over the Top" coming in fourth. He wasn't much impressed with L. Sprague de Camp's "Finished," which was fifth, and he absolutely hated Theodore Sturgeon's "What Dead Men Tell," ranking it last. Mr. Hoen also had words of praise for the cover painting by Hubert Rogers.

Only one problem: he was ranking the stories in the November 1949 issue, and of course none of them existed. It was a cute conceit, everyone got a chuckle out of it, and everyone immediately forgot it.

Except Campbell, who went out of his way to make it come true.

The November 1949 issue of *Astounding* featured the first part of Heinlein's serial, "Gulf"; Sturgeon's "What Dead Men Tell"; de Camp's "Finished"; van Vogt's "Final Command"; and del Rey's "Over the Top." And of course it had a cover by Rogers.

There was only one place the prediction fell short. Mr. Hoen had ranked a story called "We Hail," by Don A. Stuart, first. Don A. Stuart was Campbell's pseudonym when he was writing works of ambition (such as "Twilight") rather than space opera, and was taken from his first wife's maiden name, Dona Stuart. Well, Campbell didn't write a story for the issue—but in its place he ran the first part of "And Now You Don't," the three-part serial that formed the climax of Isaac Asimov's Foundation Trilogy. I don't imagine anyone had any serious objections to the substitution.

So when you hear writers like me say that science fiction isn't really in the predicting business, just remind us of the November 1948 *Astounding*.

The Magazines are Officially Noticed

Science fiction tends to cry and carry on because no one pays any attention to it, that it's a ghetto beneath the notice of the New York Literary Establishment and most of the Powers That Be in academia.

And yet science fiction has been officially Noticed (and more than once) by the United States Government, and that was long before that government started naming weapons and defense systems after rather silly science fiction movies.

Back in the Good Old Days of the pulps, more often than not the cover art showed a partially-clad (or, if you prefer, a mostly-unclad) girl, usually at the mercy of aliens who seemed more interested in ripping off the rest of her clothes than doing anything practical, like killing or communicating with her.

The thing is (and I refer you to the two introductory articles in my anthology, *Girls For the Slime God*), only one magazine actually delivered the salacious stories that went hand-in-glove with those cover illos, and that magazine was *Marvel Science Stories*. The first issue, back in August of 1938, featured Henry Kuttner's "The Avengers of Space," a rather pedestrian novella to which I suspect he added all the sex scenes after it had been turned down by the major markets. Then out came issue number two, and there was Kuttner with another novella of the same ilk: "The Time Trap."

What was the result?

Well, there were two results. The first was that Kuttner was labeled a debased and perverted hack, and had to create Lewis Padgett and Lawrence O'Donnell, his two most famous pseudonyms (but far from his only ones) in order to make a living, since it would be a few years before the top editors wanted to buy from Henry Kuttner again.

The second was that the United States government, through its postal branch, gave science fiction its very first official recognition. They explained to the publisher that if the third issue of *Marvel* was as sexy as the first two, they were shutting him down and sending him to jail.

And with that, *Marvel Science Stories* became the most sedate and—let's be honest—*dull* science fiction magazine on the market. It died not too long thereafter, the first prozine to be slain by the government.

But the government wasn't quite through Noticing the prozines. Move the clock ahead five years, to March 1944, which was when *Astounding*, under the editorship of John Campbell, published a forgettable little story called "Deadline," by Cleve Cartmill.

It became one of the most famous stories in the history of the prozines—not because of its quality, which was minimal, but because it brought the prozines to the official notice of the government for the second time.

We were embroiled in World War II, and in early 1944 the Manhattan Project—the project that resulted in the atomic bomb—was still our most carefully-guarded secret.

And Cartmill's story, which used knowledge and facts that were available to anyone, concerned the construction of an atomic bomb that used U-235.

Cartmill was visited by the FBI and other select governmental agencies the week the story came out, each demanding to know how he had managed to steal the secrets of the bomb. He pointed out that his "secrets" were a matter of public record. He was nonetheless warned never to breach national security again, upon pain of truly dire consequences.

The government representatives then went to Campbell's office, where he explained to them, as only Campbell could, that if they were not uneducated, subliterate dolts they would know exactly where Cartmill got his information, and that *Astounding* had been running stories about atomic power for years. They tried to threaten him into promising not to run any more stories of atomic power until the war was over. Campbell didn't take kindly to threats, and allowed them to leave only after giving them a thorough tongue-lashing and an absolute refusal to censor his writers.

So the next time you hear a writer or editor bemoaning the fact that science fiction doesn't get any notice, point out to him that there were actually a couple of occasions in the past when we got a little more official notice than we wanted.

Vietnam and the Magazines

Nothing since the War Between the States aroused more passions on both sides than did the Vietnam War. In 1968 Judith Merril and Kate Wilhelm decided to do something about it: they enlisted a large number of writers—the final total was 82—and took out ads against the war in the March issue of *F&SF* and the June issues of *Galaxy* and *If*. Included in their number were most of the younger New Wave writers such as Harlan Ellison, Barry Malzberg, Norman Spinrad, Robert Silverberg, Philip K. Dick, Terry Carr, and Ursula K. Le Guin, as well as a smattering of old masters like Isaac Asimov, Ray Bradbury, and Fritz Leiber.

Word got out—the rumor is that it was leaked by Fred Pohl, Merril's ex-husband—and the pro-war faction also ran ads in all three magazines. (Pohl had them on facing pages in his two magazines.) Included in the ads were Robert A. Heinlein, Poul Anderson, John W. Campbell Jr. (the only then-current editor to appear on either list), Fredric Brown, Hal Clement, Larry Niven, Jack Vance, and Jack Williamson. The pro-war ads contained only 72 names, leading the anti-war faction to claim that they had "won."

Pohl was editing both *Galaxy* and *If*, and he offered to donate the ad revenues to the person who came up with the best "solution" to the Vietnam War. It was won by Mack Reynolds, but Pohl never published his "solution"; runners-up were Hubert Humphrey, Lyndon Johnson, and Richard Nixon.

Saving the Lensman

E. E. "Doc" Smith was clearly the most famous and most popular writer of the late 1920s and most of the 1930s as well. He broke new ground with the Skylark series, but it was the four Lensman books upon which his fame and adoration rests. (Yes, four; the first two in the six-book series were afterthoughts, *Triplanetary* being expanded and rewritten to become the chronological first in the series, *First Lensman* written last of all to fill a gap between *Triplanetary* and the four Kimball Kinnison books.)

Doc introduced Kimball Kinnison, the Gray Lensman, to the world in 1937, with *Galactic Patrol*, which ran in *Astounding* from September 1937 to February 1938—just about the time a young John Campbell was beginning his lifelong tenure as editor and preparing to reshape the field. This was followed in a few years by *The Gray Lensman* and then *Second Stage Lensman*.

But while Doc was slowly completing the saga of the Kinnison clan, Campbell was bringing Robert A. Heinlein, Isaac Asimov, Theodore Sturgeon, and A. E. van Vogt into the field, and finding room for Fritz Leiber, Clifford D. Simak, and L. Sprague de Camp.

Doc was many things as a writer, but graceful wasn't one of them, and subtle wasn't another. It didn't matter when he was competing against the likes of Nat Schachner and Ray Cummings and Stanton A. Coblentz—but against Campbell's stable he seemed like a dinosaur, thousands of evolutionary eons behind where Campbell had pushed, pulled and dragged the field.

So when he delivered the climactic volume of the Lensman saga, *Children of the Lens*, Campbell didn't want to run it. It just didn't belong in a magazine that had published "Nightfall" and "Sixth Column" and "Slan" years earlier.

One fan had the courage to seek Campbell out and disagree. He's the one who told me this story, and Campbell later kind of sort of grudgingly agreed that it was pretty much the truth. Ed Wood (the fan, not the movie director), who'd been active in fandom for a few years, and would be active for another 50, cornered Campbell and explained that he owed it to Doc, who had given him the original Lensman story when *Astounding* badly needed it, to buy *Children of the Lens*. Moreover, he owed it to the field, for we were not then a book field, and if Doc's novel didn't run in *Astounding*, there was an excellent chance that it would never see the light of day. Campbell finally agreed. The novel appeared without the customary fanfare accorded to a new Doc Smith book, and was the only Lensman novel to receive just a single cover, though it ran for six issues beginning in November of 1947.

So for those of you who are Lensman fans—and tens of thousands of people still are, more than half a century later—you owe two debts of gratitude, one to Doc for writing it, and another to a motivated fan, Ed Wood, for making sure you got to find out how it all ended for Kimball Kinnison and his offspring.

How *Unknown* Was Born

Ask 20 experts (or fans; there's not much difference) which was the greatest science fiction magazine of all time, and you'll get some votes for the 1940s *Astounding*, the 1950s *Galaxy*, the 1960s *New Worlds*, the 1970s *F&SF*, and the 1990s *Asimov's*.

Now ask that same group to name the greatest fantasy magazine, and the odds are that at least 19 will answer *Unknown*. It was that good, that unique, and remains that dominant in the minds of the readers.

How did it begin?

There are two versions.

The first is that John Campbell wanted to start a fantasy magazine, he convinced Street & Smith to publish it, he called it *Unknown*, and it ran 43 issues until the wartime paper shortage killed it off.

The other version, which has been repeated in dozens of venues, is that Campbell was sitting at his desk at *Astounding*, reading submissions, and he came to a novel, *Sinister Barrier*, by Eric Frank Russell. It was too good to turn down, but it didn't fit into the format he had created for *Astounding*, and hence there was nothing to do but create a brand-new magazine, *Unknown*, which could run stories like *Sinister Barrier* and Fritz Leiber's Gray Mouser stories, and Theodore Sturgeon's "Yesterday Was Monday" and Robert A. Heinlein's *Magic, Inc.*, and *that's* how *Unknown* came into being. A number of histories of the field have reported that *this* was the start of *Unknown*.

Which version is true?

The first one, of course—but the second one is so fascinating and evocative that I suspect it'll never die, and if we all keep repeating it enough, why, in another 60 years or so, it'll be History. (See my novel *The Outpost* to discover how these things work.)

Walter Who?

It all began with a radio show hosted by a mysterious male character known only as the Shadow. The show was owned by Street & Smith, the huge magazine publisher, and when it became increasingly obvious that the Shadow was far more popular than the show, they decided they'd better do something to copyright and trademark him before it was too late—so they decided to publish a one-shot pulp magazine about a crimefighter known as the Shadow.

To write the story, they hired magician and sometime pulp author Walter Gibson, and, for whatever initial reason, they decided to have him write it as "Maxwell Grant."

The rest is history. That first issue of *The Shadow* sold out in record time. Street & Smith immediately ordered more novels from Gibson—who was getting $500.00 a novel, not bad pay in the depths of the depression—and in mere months *The Shadow* was selling more than a million copies an issue.

So Street & Smith decided the next step was to go semi-monthly. They called Gibson into their offices and asked if he was capable of turning out a Shadow novel every 15 days. Gibson said he could do it, but since it was no secret that *The Shadow* had, almost overnight, become the best-selling pulp magazine in America, he wanted a piece of this bonanza. He wasn't going to be greedy or hold them up for some phenomenal sum. He'd write two novels a month, never miss a deadline, and keep the quality as high as it had been—but in exchange, he wanted a raise to $750.00 a novel.

His loving, doting publishers immediately metamorphosed into businessmen and said No.

Gibson thought he had them over a barrel. You give me $750.00 a novel, he said, or I'll leave and take my audience with me.

Leave if you want, said Street & Smith, but next week there will be a new Maxwell Grant writing *The Shadow* for us, and who will know the difference?

It took Gibson ten seconds to realize that far from having Street & Smith over a barrel, they had him *inside* the barrel. He went back home and continued to write Shadow novels for $500.00 a shot.

This ploy worked so well that when Street & Smith began publishing *Doc Savage*, which was primarily written by Lester Dent, all the novels were credited to "Kenneth Robeson."

Rivals saw the beauty in this—Street & Smith didn't exactly have a monopoly on publishing's notion of fair play and morality—and thus *The Spider* novels, written mostly by Norvell Page, bore the pseudonym of "Grant Stockbridge."

"Kenneth Robeson," Doc Savage's author, was so popular that "he" also became the author of *The Avenger* pulp series.

And so on. Soon all the other "hero pulps"—pulps with a continuing hero and cast of characters, such as the above-mentioned—were written under house names, so that no author could either hold up the publishers for a living wage or leave and force the magazine to close down.

There was only one exception.

Edmond Hamilton wrote most of the 22 *Captain Future* novels under his own name.

The reason?

He was the only established science fiction writer working for Better Publications, Cap's publisher, and his employers freely admitted that no one else in the house knew the first damned thing about writing that crazy Buck Rogers stuff.

The Mystery of Edson McCann

One day Horace Gold, the editor/publisher of *Galaxy*, got the notion of having a contest for the best novel by an unknown writer. He offered a prize of $7,000—more than the average American made in a year back then—and was immediately whelmed over by hundreds of booklength manuscripts, 99% of them dreadful and the other 1% even worse. (Ask anyone who has ever read a slush pile. This was nothing unusual or unexpected—at least, not by anyone except Horace.)

Horace had already bought *Gravy Planet* (later to become *The Space Merchants*, which eventually outsold, worldwide, just about every other science fiction novel ever written except perhaps for *Dune*.) When he couldn't find an even mildly acceptable novel among the entries, he approached Fred Pohl and Cyril Kornbluth and said he'd like *Gravy Planet* to be the winner. The stipulation, though, was that it had to appear under a pseudonym, since the contest had to be won by an unknown.

Pohl and Kornbluth talked it over, decided they could get $7,000 from normal serial and book rights, and opted to keep their names on it, which disqualified it from the contest.

Now Gold was getting desperate. The deadline was almost upon him, and he still hadn't found a single publishable novel among all the entries. So he turned to Pohl again.

Pohl and his Milford neighbor, Lester del Rey (a whole passel of science fiction writers lived in Milford, Pennsylvania back in the 1950s) had decided to collaborate on a novel about the future of the insurance industry, called *Preferred Risk*. Gold begged them to use a pseudonym and let it be the contest winner. Lester was less concerned with receiving credit for his work than Kornbluth was—or perhaps he was more concerned with a quick profit. At any rate, he agreed, and Pohl went along with him.

They divided up the pen name. Pohl chose "Edson" for a first name, and del Rey came up with "McCann". They invented a whole life for him (for the magazine's bio of the contest winner), in which he was a nuclear physicist working on such a top secret hush-hush project that *Galaxy* couldn't divulge any of the details of his life.

And so it was that *Preferred Risk*, commissioned from two top professionals by Horace Gold, won the $7,000 prize for the Best Novel By An Unknown.

And why did they choose "Edson McCann"?

Well, if you break it down to its initials, it's "E. McC"—or E equals MC squared.

The No-Budget Magazines

Hugo Gernsback is considered the Father of Science Fiction. That title is more than a little at odds with the facts, since Mary Shelley, Jules Verne and H.G. Wells were writing it long before Hugo came along—but Hugo named the field and was the first publisher to bring out a magazine devoted entirely to "scientifiction" (*Amazing Stories* in 1926).

Parenthetically, he also guaranteed that we would be inundated with bad science fiction for years to come…because by creating a market for science fiction, he gave it a place where it no longer had to compete with the best of the other categories. Science fiction writers no longer had to fight for spots in a magazine against Dashiell Hammett and James T. Cain and Frank Gruber and Max Brand; now they competed with Ray Cummings and Nat Schachner and Ross Rocklynne. The first—and for years only—science fiction magazine in the world was edited by Hugo Gernsback, an immigrant whose knowledge of the English language was minimal, and whose knowledge of story construction was nil. He felt science fiction's sole purpose was to interest adolescent boys in becoming scientists, and that was pretty much the way he edited.

The way he published was even worse. He liked to buy stories, but he hated to pay for them. Finally Donald A. Wollheim took him to court for the $10.00 he was owed. Neither Gernsback nor Wollheim ever forgot it.

Now move the clock ahead a few years, to about 1940. Wollheim had helped form the Futurians, that incredibly talented group of youngsters that would someday dominate the field. Among its members were Cyril Kornbluth, Damon Knight, Judith Merril, Frederik Pohl, Isaac Asimov, Robert A.W. Lowndes, James Blish, and Wollheim himself (and indeed, in a year or two they'd be editing just about every magazine in the field except for John Campbell's *Astounding*).

Anyway, while Pohl edited *Astonishing* and *Super Science* on a pitifully small budget, Wollheim picked up two of his own to edit: *Cosmos* and *Stirring Science*. Their pages abounded in stories by Futurians Kornbluth, Pohl, Lowndes, and Knight, with illos by the finest Futurian artist, Hannes Bok. Those magazines put many of the Futurians on the map.

And do you know *why* Wollheim used Futurians almost exclusively?

Because his budget was Zero—not small, not minimal, but zero—and only his fellow Futurians would work for free for the man who once sued Hugo Gernsback for $10 that was owed on a story.

Horace Gold Goes Out to Play

Horace Gold returned home from World War II a disabled veteran…but his disability took a most peculiar form: agoraphobia. He was literally afraid to leave the comfort and security of his New York apartment.

It didn't stop him from selling investors on the idea of *Galaxy* magazine. And it didn't stop him from editing it, and turning it into (in my opinion) the only serious rival the *Astounding* of the late 1930s and early 1940s had for the title of Best Science Fiction Magazine of All Time.

He turned part of his apartment into an office. He worked at home, he ate at home, he slept at home, he wrote at home, he edited at home. Any writer who wanted a face-to-face with Horace visited him at home. He hosted a regular Friday night poker game that included his stable of writers: Bob Sheckley, Phil Klass (William Tenn), Fred Pohl, and Algis Budrys. Lester del Rey occasionally sat in, as did rival editor (of *F&SF*) Tony Boucher.

And because they were his friends, and they thought they were doing him a favor, this coterie of card-players and writers was constantly urging Horace to go outside, to breathe in the fresh air (well, Manhattan's approximation of it, anyway), to just take a walk around the neighborhood so that he would know there were no secret dangers lurking beyond the doors of his apartment. They urged, and they cajoled, and they implored, and finally the big day came.

Horace Gold left his apartment for the first time in years—

—and was promptly hit by a taxi.

(There is a second version of this story, in which he actually spent a few evenings wandering around Manhattan, and then got into a crash while riding home in a taxi. Either way, the result was the same. He stopped eating, stopped editing, and was eventually institutionalized.)

Conclusion: the science fiction (and related) magazines have a long and fascinating history. My fondest hope is that if they talk about *Galaxy's Edge* twenty or thirty years from now, it will *only* be to say that we ran some pretty good stories.

Okay, now you know a bit about the magazines. Next issue I'll tell you about some of the writers and editors who make up this colorful field.

Robert J. Sawyer is the winner of the Hugo, the Nebula, Canada's Aurora, Spain's UPC, and Japan's Seiun Sho Awards. His most recent novel is *Red Planet Blues*.

THE SHOULDERS OF GIANTS

by Robert J. Sawyer

It seemed like only yesterday when I'd died, but, of course, it was almost certainly centuries ago. I wish the computer would just *tell* me, dammitall, but it was doubtless waiting until its sensors said I was sufficiently stable and alert. The irony was that my pulse was surely racing out of concern, forestalling it speaking to me. If this was an emergency, it should inform me, and if it wasn't, it should let me relax.

Finally, the machine did speak in its crisp, feminine voice. "Hello, Toby. Welcome back to the world of the living."

"Where—" I'd thought I'd spoken the word, but no sound had come out. I tried again. "Where are we?"

"Exactly where we should be: decelerating toward Soror."

I felt myself calming down. "How is Ling?"

"She's reviving, as well."

"The others?"

"All forty-eight cryogenics chambers are functioning properly," said the computer. "Everybody is apparently fine."

That was good to hear, but it wasn't surprising. We had four extra cryochambers; if one of the occupied ones had failed, Ling and I would have been awoken earlier to transfer the person within it into a spare. "What's the date?"

"16 June 3296."

I'd expected an answer like that, but it still took me back a bit. Twelve hundred years had elapsed since the blood had been siphoned out of my body and oxygenated antifreeze had been pumped in to replace it. We'd spent the first of those years accelerating, and presumably the last one decelerating, and the rest—

—the rest was spent coasting at our maximum velocity, 3,000 km/s, one percent of the speed of light.

My father had been from Glasgow; my mother, from Los Angeles. They had both enjoyed the quip that the difference between an American and a European was that to an American, a hundred years was a long time, and to a European, a hundred miles is a big journey.

But both would agree that twelve hundred years and 11.9 light-years were equally staggering values. And now, here we were, decelerating in toward Tau Ceti, the closest sunlike star to Earth that wasn't part of a multiple-star system. Of course, because of that, this star had been frequently examined by Earth's Search for Extraterrestrial Intelligence. But nothing had ever been detected; nary a peep.

I was feeling better minute by minute. My own blood, stored in bottles, had been returned to my body and was now coursing through my arteries, my veins, reanimating me.

We were going to make it.

Tau Ceti happened to be oriented with its north pole facing toward Sol; that meant that the technique developed late in the twentieth century to detect planetary systems based on subtle blueshifts and redshifts of a star tugged now closer, now farther away, was useless with it. Any wobble in Tau Ceti's movements would be perpendicular, as seen from Earth, producing no Doppler effect. But eventually Earth-orbiting telescopes had been developed that were sensitive enough to detect the wobble visually, and—

It had been front-page news around the world: the first solar system seen by telescopes. Not inferred from stellar wobbles or spectral shifts, but actually *seen*. At least four planets could be made out orbiting Tau Ceti, and one of them—

There had been formulas for decades, first popularized in the RAND Corporation's study *Habitable Planets for Man*. Every science-fiction writer and astrobiologist worth his or her salt had used them to determine the *life zones*—the distances from target stars at which planets with Earthlike surface temperatures might exist, a Goldilocks band, neither too hot nor too cold.

And the second of the four planets that could be seen around Tau Ceti was smack-dab in the middle of that star's life zone. The planet was watched carefully for an entire year—one of its years, that is, a

Are you a writer?

period of 193 Earth days. Two wonderful facts became apparent. First, the planet's orbit was damn near circular—meaning it would likely have stable temperatures all the time; the gravitational influence of the fourth planet, a Jovian giant orbiting at a distance of half a billion kilometers from Tau Ceti, probably was responsible for that.

And, second, the planet varied in brightness substantially over the course of its twenty-nine-hour-and-seventeen-minute day. The reason was easy to deduce: most of one hemisphere was covered with land, which reflected back little of Tau Ceti's yellow light, while the other hemisphere, with a much higher albedo, was likely covered by a vast ocean, no doubt, given the planet's fortuitous orbital radius, of liquid water—an extraterrestrial Pacific.

Of course, at a distance of 11.9 light-years, it was quite possible that Tau Ceti had other planets, too, small or too dark to be seen. And so referring to the Earthlike globe as Tau Ceti II would have been problematic; if an additional world or worlds were eventually found orbiting closer in, the system's planetary numbering would end up as confusing as the scheme used to designate Saturn's rings.

Clearly a name was called for, and Giancarlo Di-Maio, the astronomer who had discovered the half-land, half-water world, gave it one: Soror, the Latin word for sister. And, indeed, Soror appeared, at least as far as could be told from Earth, to be a sister to humanity's home world.

Soon we would know for sure just how perfect a sister it was. And speaking of sisters, well—okay, Ling Woo wasn't my biological sister, but we'd worked together and trained together for four years before launch, and I'd come to think of her as a sister, despite the press constantly referring to us as the new Adam and Eve. Of course, we'd help to populate the new world, but not together; my wife, Helena, was one of the forty-eight others still frozen solid. Ling wasn't involved yet with any of the other colonists, but, well, she was gorgeous and brilliant, and of the two dozen men in cryosleep, twenty-one were unattached.

Ling and I were co-captains of the *Pioneer Spirit.* Her cryocoffin was like mine, and unlike all the others: it was designed for repeated use. She and I could be revived multiple times during the voyage,

to deal with emergencies. The rest of the crew, in coffins that had cost only $700,000 a piece instead of the six million each of ours was worth, could only be revived once, when our ship reached its final destination.

"You're all set," said the computer. "You can get up now."

The thick glass cover over my coffin slid aside, and I used the padded handles to hoist myself out of its black porcelain frame. For most of the journey, the ship had been coasting in zero gravity, but now that it was decelerating, there was a gentle push downward. Still, it was nowhere near a full g, and I was grateful for that. It would be a day or two before I would be truly steady on my feet.

My module was shielded from the others by a partition, which I'd covered with photos of people I'd left behind: my parents, Helena's parents, my real sister, her two sons. My clothes had waited patiently for me for twelve hundred years; I rather suspected they were now hopelessly out of style. But I got dressed—I'd been naked in the cryochamber, of course—and at last I stepped out from behind the partition, just in time to see Ling emerging from behind the wall that shielded her cryocoffin.

"'Morning," I said, trying to sound blasé.

Ling, wearing a blue and gray jumpsuit, smiled broadly. "Good morning."

We moved into the center of the room, and hugged, friends delighted to have shared an adventure together. Then we immediately headed out toward the bridge, half-walking, half-floating, in the reduced gravity.

"How'd you sleep?" asked Ling.

It wasn't a frivolous question. Prior to our mission, the longest anyone had spent in cryofreeze was five years, on a voyage to Saturn; the *Pioneer Spirit* was Earth's first starship.

"Fine," I said. "You?"

"Okay," replied Ling. But then she stopped moving, and briefly touched my forearm. "Did you—did you dream?"

Brain activity slowed to a virtual halt in cryofreeze, but several members of the crew of *Cronus*—the Saturn mission—had claimed to have had brief dreams, lasting perhaps two or three subjective minutes, spread over five years. Over the span that the

Are you a writer who wants to learn from the best?

Pioneer Spirit had been traveling, there would have been time for many hours of dreaming.

I shook my head. "No. What about you?"

Ling nodded. "Yes. I dreamt about the strait of Gibraltar. Ever been there?"

"No."

"It's Spain's southernmost boundary, of course. You can see across the strait from Europe to northern Africa, and there were Neandertal settlements on the Spanish side." Ling's Ph.D. was in anthropology. "But they never made it across the strait. They could clearly see that there was more land—another continent!—only thirteen kilometers away. A strong swimmer can make it, and with any sort of raft or boat, it was eminently doable. But Neandertals never journeyed to the other side; as far as we can tell, they never even tried."

"And you dreamt—?"

"I dreamt I was part of a Neandertal community there, a teenage girl, I guess. And I was trying to convince the others that we should go across the strait, go see the new land. But I couldn't; they weren't interested. There was plenty of food and shelter where we were. Finally, I headed out on my own, trying to swim it. The water was cold and the waves were high, and half the time I couldn't get any air to breathe, but I swam and I swam, and then…"

"Yes?"

She shrugged a little. "And then I woke up."

I smiled at her. "Well, this time we're going to make it. We're going to make it for sure."

We came to the bridge door, which opened automatically to admit us, although it squeaked something fierce while doing so; its lubricants must have dried up over the last twelve centuries. The room was rectangular with a double row of angled consoles facing a large screen, which currently was off.

"Distance to Soror?" I asked into the air.

The computer's voice replied. "1.2 million kilometers."

I nodded. About three times the distance between Earth and its moon. "Screen on, view ahead."

"Overrides are in place," said the computer.

Ling smiled at me. "You're jumping the gun, partner."

I was embarrassed. The *Pioneer Spirit* was decelerating toward Soror; the ship's fusion exhaust was facing in the direction of travel. The optical scanners would be burned out by the glare if their shutters were opened. "Computer, turn off the fusion motors."

"Powering down," said the artificial voice.

"Visual as soon as you're able," I said.

The gravity bled away as the ship's engines stopped firing. Ling held on to one of the handles attached to the top of the console nearest her; I was still a little groggy from the suspended animation, and just floated freely in the room. After about two minutes, the screen came on. Tau Ceti was in the exact center, a baseball-sized yellow disk. And the four planets were clearly visible, ranging from pea-sized to as big as a grape.

"Magnify on Soror," I said.

One of the peas became a billiard ball, although Tau Ceti grew hardly at all.

"More," said Ling.

The planet grew to softball size. It was showing as a wide crescent, perhaps a third of the disk illuminated from this angle. And—thankfully, fantastically—Soror was everything we'd dreamed it would be: a giant polished marble, with swirls of white cloud, and a vast, blue ocean, and—

Part of a continent was visible, emerging out of the darkness. And it was green, apparently covered with vegetation.

We hugged again, squeezing each other tightly. No one had been sure when we'd left Earth; Soror could have been barren. The *Pioneer Spirit* was ready regardless: in its cargo holds was everything we needed to survive even on an airless world. But we'd hoped and prayed that Soror would be, well—just like this: a true sister, another Earth, another home.

"It's beautiful, isn't it?" said Ling.

I felt my eyes tearing. It *was* beautiful, breathtaking, stunning. The vast ocean, the cottony clouds, the verdant land, and—

"Oh, my God," I said, softly. "Oh, my God."

"What?" said Ling.

"Don't you see?" I asked. "Look!"

Ling narrowed her eyes and moved closer to the screen. "What?"

"On the dark side," I said.

She looked again. "Oh…" she said. There were faint lights sprinkled across the darkness; hard to see, but definitely there. "Could it be volcanism?" asked Ling. Maybe Soror wasn't so perfect after all.

"Computer," I said, "spectral analysis of the light sources on the planet's dark side."

"Predominantly incandescent lighting, color temperature 5600 kelvin."

I exhaled and looked at Ling. They weren't volcanoes. They were cities.

Soror, the world we'd spent twelve centuries traveling to, the world we'd intended to colonize, the world that had been dead silent when examined by radio telescopes, was already inhabited.

The *Pioneer Spirit* was a colonization ship; it wasn't intended as a diplomatic vessel. When it had left Earth, it had seemed important to get at least some humans off the mother world. Two small-scale nuclear wars—Nuke I and Nuke II, as the media had dubbed them—had already been fought, one in southern Asia, the other in South America. It appeared to be only a matter of time before Nuke III, and that one might be the big one.

SETI had detected nothing from Tau Ceti, at least not by 2051. But Earth itself had only been broadcasting for a century and a half at that point; Tau Ceti might have had a thriving civilization then that hadn't yet started using radio. But now it was twelve hundred years later. Who knew how advanced the Tau Cetians might be?

I looked at Ling, then back at the screen. "What should we do?"

Ling tilted her head to one side. "I'm not sure. On the one hand, I'd love to meet them, whoever they are. But…"

"But they might not want to meet us," I said. "They might think we're invaders, and—"

"And we've got forty-eight other colonists to think about," said Ling. "For all we know, we're the last surviving humans."

I frowned. "Well, that's easy enough to determine. Computer, swing the radio telescope toward Sol system. See if you can pick anything up that might be artificial."

"Just a sec," said the female voice. A few moments later, a cacophony filled the room: static and snatches of voices and bits of music and sequences of tones, overlapping and jumbled, fading in and out. I heard what sounded like English—although strangely inflected—and maybe Arabic and Mandarin and…

"We're not the last survivors," I said, smiling. "There's still life on Earth—or, at least, there was 11.9 years ago, when those signals started out."

Ling exhaled. "I'm glad we didn't blow ourselves up," she said. "Now, I guess we should find out what we're dealing with at Tau Ceti. Computer, swing the dish to face Soror, and again scan for artificial signals."

"Doing so." There was silence for most of a minute, then a blast of static, and a few bars of music, and clicks and bleeps, and voices, speaking in Mandarin and English and—

"No," said Ling. "I said face the dish the *other* way. I want to hear what's coming from Soror."

The computer actually sounded miffed. "The dish *is* facing toward Soror," it said.

I looked at Ling, realization dawning. At the time we'd left Earth, we'd been so worried that humanity was about to snuff itself out, we hadn't really stopped to consider what would happen if that didn't occur. But with twelve hundred years, faster spaceships would doubtless have been developed. While the colonists aboard the *Pioneer Spirit* had slept, some dreaming at an indolent pace, other ships had zipped past them, arriving at Tau Ceti decades, if not centuries, earlier—long enough ago that they'd already built human cities on Soror.

"Damn it," I said. "God damn it." I shook my head, staring at the screen. The tortoise was supposed to win, not the hare.

"What do we do now?" asked Ling.

I sighed. "I suppose we should contact them."

"We—ah, we might be from the wrong side."

I grinned. "Well, we can't *both* be from the wrong side. Besides, you heard the radio: Mandarin *and* English. Anyway, I can't imagine that anyone cares about a war more than a thousand years in the past, and—"

"Excuse me," said the ship's computer. "Incoming audio message."

I looked at Ling. She frowned, surprised. "Put it on," I said.

"*Pioneer Spirit*, welcome! This is Jod Bokket, manager of the Derluntin space station, in orbit around Soror. Is there anyone awake on board?" It was a man's voice, with an accent unlike anything I'd ever heard before.

Ling looked at me, to see if I was going to object, then she spoke up. "Computer, send a reply." The computer bleeped to signal that the channel was open. "This is Dr. Ling Woo, co-captain of the *Pioneer Spirit*. Two of us have revived; there are forty-eight more still in cryofreeze."

"Well, look," said Bokket's voice, "it'll be days at the rate you're going before you get here. How about if we send a ship to bring you two to Derluntin? We can have someone there to pick you up in about an hour."

"They really like to rub it in, don't they?" I grumbled.

"What was that?" said Bokket. "We couldn't quite make it out."

Ling and I consulted with facial expressions, then agreed. "Sure," said Ling. "We'll be waiting."

"Not for long," said Bokket, and the speaker went dead.

Bokket himself came to collect us. His spherical ship was tiny compared with ours, but it seemed to have about the same amount of habitable interior space; would the ignominies ever cease? Docking adapters had changed a lot in a thousand years, and he wasn't able to get an airtight seal, so we had to transfer over to his ship in space suits. Once aboard, I was pleased to see we were still floating freely; it would have been *too* much if they'd had artificial gravity.

Bokket seemed a nice fellow—about my age, early thirties. Of course, maybe people looked youthful forever now; who knew how old he might actually be? I couldn't really identify his ethnicity, either; he seemed to be rather a blend of traits. But he certainly was taken with Ling—his eyes popped out when she took off her helmet, revealing her heart-shaped face and long, black hair.

"Hello," he said, smiling broadly.

Ling smiled back. "Hello. I'm Ling Woo, and this is Toby MacGregor, my co-captain."

"Greetings," I said, sticking out my hand.

Bokket looked at it, clearly not knowing precisely what to do. He extended his hand in a mirroring of my gesture, but didn't touch me. I closed the gap and clasped his hand. He seemed surprised, but pleased.

"We'll take you back to the station first," he said. "Forgive us, but, well—you can't go down to the

planet's surface yet; you'll have to be quarantined. We've eliminated a lot of diseases, of course, since your time, and so we don't vaccinate for them anymore. I'm willing to take the risk, but…"

I nodded. "That's fine."

He tipped his head slightly, as if he were preoccupied for a moment, then: "I've told the ship to take us back to Derluntin station. It's in a polar orbit, about 200 kilometers above Soror; you'll get some beautiful views of the planet, anyway." He was grinning from ear to ear. "It's wonderful to meet you people," he said. "Like a page out of history."

"If you knew about us," I asked, after we'd settled in for the journey to the station, "why didn't you pick us up earlier?"

Bokket cleared his throat. "We didn't know about you."

"But you called us by name: *Pioneer Spirit*."

"Well, it *is* painted in letters three meters high across your hull. Our asteroid-watch system detected you. A lot of information from your time has been lost—I guess there was a lot of political upheaval then, no?—but we knew Earth had experimented with sleeper ships in the twenty-first century."

We were getting close to the space station; it was a giant ring, spinning to simulate gravity. It might have taken us over a thousand years to do it, but humanity was finally building space stations the way God had always intended them to be.

And floating next to the space station was a beautiful spaceship, with a spindle-shaped silver hull and two sets of mutually perpendicular emerald-green delta wings. "It's gorgeous," I said.

Bokket nodded.

"How does it land, though? Tail-down?"

"It doesn't land; it's a starship."

"Yes, but—"

"We use shuttles to go between it and the ground."

"But if it can't land," asked Ling, "why is it streamlined? Just for esthetics?"

Bokket laughed, but it was a polite laugh. "It's streamlined because it needs to be. There's substantial length-contraction when flying at just below the speed of light; that means that the interstellar medium seems much denser. Although there's only one baryon per cubic centimeter, they form what seems to be an appreciable atmosphere if you're going fast enough."

"And your ships are *that* fast?" asked Ling.

Bokket smiled. "Yes. They're that fast."

Ling shook her head. "We were crazy," she said. "Crazy to undertake our journey." She looked briefly at Bokket, but couldn't meet his eyes. She turned her gaze down toward the floor. "You must think we're incredibly foolish."

Bokket's eyes widened. He seemed at a loss for what to say. He looked at me, spreading his arms, as if appealing to me for support. But I just exhaled, letting air—and disappointment—vent from my body.

"You're wrong," said Bokket, at last. "You couldn't be more wrong. We *honor* you." He paused, waiting for Ling to look up again. She did, her eyebrows lifted questioningly. "If we have come farther than you," said Bokket, "or have gone faster than you, it's because we had your work to build on. Humans are here now because it's *easy* for us to be here, because you and others blazed the trails." He looked at me, then at Ling. "If we see farther," he said, "it's because we stand on the shoulders of giants."

Later that day, Ling, Bokket, and I were walking along the gently curving floor of Derluntin station. We were confined to a limited part of one section; they'd let us down to the planet's surface in another ten days, Bokket had said.

"There's nothing for us here," said Ling, hands in her pockets. "We're freaks, anachronisms. Like somebody from the T'ang Dynasty showing up in our world."

"Soror is wealthy," said Bokket. "We can certainly support you and your passengers."

"They are *not* passengers," I snapped. "They are colonists. They are explorers."

Bokket nodded. "I'm sorry. You're right, of course. But look—we really are delighted that you're here. I've been keeping the media away; the quarantine lets me do that. But they will go absolutely dingo when you come down to the planet. It's like having Neil Armstrong or Tamiko Hiroshige show up at your door."

"Tamiko who?" asked Ling.

"Sorry. After your time. She was the first person to disembark at Alpha Centauri."

"The first," I repeated; I guess I wasn't doing a good job of hiding my bitterness. "That's the honor—that's the achievement. Being the first. Nobody remembers the name of the second person on the moon."

"Edwin Eugene Aldrin, Jr.," said Bokket. "Known as 'Buzz.'"

"Fine, okay," I said. "*You* remember, but most people don't."

"I didn't remember it; I accessed it." He tapped his temple. "Direct link to the planetary web; everybody has one."

Ling exhaled; the gulf was vast. "Regardless," she said, "we are not pioneers; we're just also-rans. We may have set out before you did, but you got here before us."

"Well, my ancestors did," said Bokket. "I'm sixth-generation Sororian."

"*Sixth* generation?" I said. "How long has the colony been here?"

"We're not a colony anymore; we're an independent world. But the ship that got here first left Earth in 2107. Of course, my ancestors didn't immigrate until much later."

"Twenty-one-oh-seven," I repeated. That was only fifty-six years after the launch of the *Pioneer Spirit*. I'd been thirty-one when our ship had started its journey; if I'd stayed behind, I might very well have lived to see the real pioneers depart. What had we been thinking, leaving Earth? Had we been running, escaping, getting out, fleeing before the bombs fell? Were we pioneers, or cowards?

No. No, those were crazy thoughts. We'd left for the same reason that *Homo sapiens sapiens* had crossed the Strait of Gibraltar. It was what we did as a species. It was why we'd triumphed, and the Neandertals had failed. We *needed* to see what was on the other side, what was over the next hill, what was orbiting other stars. It was what had given us dominion over the home planet; it was what was going to make us kings of infinite space.

I turned to Ling. "We can't stay here," I said.

She seemed to mull this over for a bit, then nodded. She looked at Bokket. "We don't want parades," she said. "We don't want statues." She lifted her eyebrows, as if acknowledging the magnitude of what she was asking for. "We want a new ship, a faster ship." She looked at me, and I bobbed my head in agreement. She pointed out the window. "A *streamlined* ship."

"What would you do with it?" asked Bokket. "Where would you go?"

She glanced at me, then looked back at Bokket. "Andromeda."

"Andromeda? You mean the Andromeda *galaxy*? But that's—" a fractional pause, no doubt while his web link provided the data "—2.2 *million* light-years away."

"Exactly."

"But…but it would take over two million years to get there."

"Only from Earth's—excuse me, from Soror's—point of view," said Ling. "We could do it in less subjective time than we've already been traveling, and, of course, we'd spend all that time in cryogenic freeze."

"None of our ships have cryogenic chambers," Bokket said. "There's no need for them."

"We could transfer the chambers from the *Pioneer Spirit*."

Bokket shook his head. "It would be a one-way trip; you'd never come back."

"That's not true," I said. "Unlike most galaxies, Andromeda is actually moving toward the Milky Way, not away from it. Eventually, the two galaxies will merge, bringing us home."

"That's billions of years in the future."

"Thinking small hasn't done us any good so far," said Ling.

Bokket frowned. "I said before that we can afford to support you and your shipmates here on Soror, and that's true. But starships are expensive. We can't just give you one."

"It's got to be cheaper than supporting all of us."

"No, it's not."

"You said you honored us. You said you stand on our shoulders. If that's true, then repay the favor. Give us an opportunity to stand on *your* shoulders. Let us have a new ship."

Bokket sighed; it was clear he felt we really didn't understand how difficult Ling's request would be to fulfill. "I'll do what I can," he said.

♈

Ling and I spent that evening talking, while blue-and-green Soror spun majestically beneath us. It was our job to jointly make the right decision, not just for ourselves but for the four dozen other members of the *Pioneer Spirit*'s complement that had entrusted their fate to us. Would they have wanted to be revived here?

No. No, of course not. They'd left Earth to found a colony; there was no reason to think they would have changed their minds, whatever they might be dreaming. Nobody had an emotional attachment to the idea of Tau Ceti; it just had seemed a logical target star.

"We could ask for passage back to Earth," I said.

"You don't want that," said Ling. "And neither, I'm sure, would any of the others."

"No, you're right," I said. "They'd want us to go on."

Ling nodded. "I think so."

"Andromeda?" I said, smiling. "Where did that come from?"

She shrugged. "First thing that popped into my head."

"Andromeda," I repeated, tasting the word some more. I remembered how thrilled I was, at sixteen, out in the California desert, to see that little oval smudge below Cassiopeia for the first time. Another galaxy, another island universe—and half again as big as our own. "Why not?" I fell silent but, after a while, said, "Bokket seems to like you."

Ling smiled. "I like him."

"Go for it," I said.

"What?" She sounded surprised.

"Go for it, if you like him. I may have to be alone until Helena is revived at our final destination, but you don't have to be. Even if they do give us a new ship, it'll surely be a few weeks before they can transfer the cryochambers."

Ling rolled her eyes. "*Men*," she said, but I knew the idea appealed to her.

Bokket was right: the Sororian media seemed quite enamored with Ling and me, and not just because of our exotic appearance—my white skin and blue eyes; her dark skin and epicanthic folds; our two strange accents, both so different from the way people of the thirty-third century spoke. They also seemed to be fascinated by, well, by the pioneer spirit.

When the quarantine was over, we did go down to the planet. The temperature was perhaps a little cooler than I'd have liked, and the air a bit moister—but humans adapt, of course. The architecture in Soror's capital city of Pax was surprisingly ornate, with lots of domed roofs and intricate carvings. The term "capital city" was an anachronism, though; government was completely decentralized, with all major decisions done by plebiscite—including the decision about whether or not to give us another ship.

Bokket, Ling, and I were in the central square of Pax, along with Kari Deetal, Soror's president, waiting for the results of the vote to be announced. Media representatives from all over the Tau Ceti system were present, as well as one from Earth, whose stories were always read 11.9 years after he filed them. Also on hand were perhaps a thousand spectators.

"My friends," said Deetal, to the crowd, spreading her arms, "you have all voted, and now let us share in the results." She tipped her head slightly, and a moment later people in the crowd started clapping and cheering.

Ling and I turned to Bokket, who was beaming. "What is it?" said Ling. "What decision did they make?"

Bokket looked surprised. "Oh, sorry. I forgot you don't have web implants. You're going to get your ship."

Ling closed her eyes and breathed a sigh of relief. My heart was pounding.

President Deetal gestured toward us. "Dr. MacGregor, Dr. Woo—would you say a few words?"

We glanced at each other then stood up. "Thank you," I said looking out at everyone.

Ling nodded in agreement. "Thank you very much."

A reporter called out a question. "What are you going to call your new ship?"

Ling frowned; I pursed my lips. And then I said, "What else? The *Pioneer Spirit II*."

The crowd erupted again.

Finally, the fateful day came. Our official boarding of our new starship—the one that would be covered by all the media—wouldn't happen for another four hours, but Ling and I were nonetheless heading toward the airlock that joined the ship to the station's outer rim. She wanted to look things over once more, and I wanted to spend a little time just sitting next to Helena's cryochamber, communing with her.

And, as we walked, Bokket came running along the curving floor toward us.

"Ling," he said, catching his breath. "Toby."

I nodded a greeting. Ling looked slightly uncomfortable; she and Bokket had grown close during the last few weeks, but they'd also had their time alone last night to say their goodbyes. I don't think she'd expected to see him again before we left.

"I'm sorry to bother you two," he said. "I know you're both busy, but…" He seemed quite nervous.

"Yes?" I said.

He looked at me, then at Ling. "Do you have room for another passenger?"

Ling smiled. "We don't have passengers. We're colonists."

"Sorry," said Bokket, smiling back at her. "Do you have room for another colonist?"

"Well, there *are* four spare cryochambers, but…" She looked at me.

"Why not?" I said, shrugging.

"It's going to be hard work, you know," said Ling, turning back to Bokket. "Wherever we end up, it's going to be rough."

Bokket nodded. "I know. And I want to be part of it."

Ling knew she didn't have to be coy around me. "That would be wonderful," she said. "But—but why?"

Bokket reached out tentatively, and found Ling's hand. He squeezed it gently, and she squeezed back. "You're one reason," he said.

"Got a thing for older women, eh?" said Ling. I smiled at that.

Bokket laughed. "I guess."

"You said I was one reason," said Ling.

He nodded. "The other reason is—well, it's this: I don't want to stand on the shoulders of giants." He paused, then lifted his own shoulders a little, as if acknowledging that he was giving voice to the sort of thought rarely spoken aloud. "I want to *be* a giant."

They continued to hold hands as we walked down the space station's long corridor, heading toward the sleek and graceful ship that would take us to our new home.

Copyright © 2000 by Robert J. Sawyer

Kij Johnson won Nebulas in 2010, 2011 and 2012, as well as the 2012 Hugo. Her collection, *At the Mouth of the River of Bees,* came out in late 2012.

SCHRÖDINGER'S CATHOUSE

by Kij Johnson

Bob is driving down Coney Island Avenue in the rain. His dust-blue Corolla veers a little as he struggles with a small box wrapped in brown paper with no return address. He was going to take it home from the post office and open it there but he got curious at a stoplight and now, even though the light's changed and he's splashing toward Brighton Beach in medium traffic, he's still picking at the tape that holds the top shut. A bus pulls in front of him just as the tape peels free and the box opens.

Bob looks around. The room in which he has suddenly found himself is large. The walls are covered with vividly flocked paper, fuchsia and crimson in huge swirls that look a little like fractals. He blinks: no, the pattern is dark blue with silver streaks like the lines of electrons made in a cloud chamber. The bar in front of him is polished walnut, ornately carved with what might be figures and might only be abstract designs. No, it's chrome, cold and smooth under his fingers. Wait a second, he thinks, and he remembers driving his Corolla down Coney Island Avenue in the rain. The box. Bob blinks again: the walls are red and fuchsia again.

There are people in the room. He sees them reflected in the mirror behind the bar. They drape over wing chairs that are covered in a violent red velvet, or they walk across the layered Oriental rugs in poses of languor. They all wear suggestive clothes or things that might pass for clothes: A lilac corset with lemon-yellow stockings and combat boots. A motorcycle jacket over a cropped polo shirt with a popped collar. A red chain harness over a crisp lace-edged white camisole and pantaloons that appear not to have a crotch. A man's red union suit with black Mary Janes. There is something unsettling about them all but Bob isn't sure what it is.

"Well?" The dark bartender slaps a glass onto the walnut bar in front of Bob.

"What?" he says, startled. The bar used to be—something else, he thinks. The man snorts impatiently.

The people reflected in the mirror—what sex are they? Bob turns to look. It's very hard to tell. The men—the ones dressed somewhat like men, anyway—are rather small and fine-boned, and the women—or the ones dressed in corsets and such—seem fairly large. They lounge on what are now aqua leather couches, move across what is now pale gray carpet.

"What can I get you?" The bartender doesn't sound the least curious.

Bob licks his lips, which are suddenly dry, and turns around. The man now has a blond moustache that curls up at the tips. His skin is very pale.

"Didn't you used to be darker?" Bob asks.

The man snorts. "What're you drinking?"

"Gin and—I don't even know *where* I'm drinking."

Now clean-shaven and dark-skinned, the bartender walks away. "But my drink—" Bob starts.

The bartender picks up another glass.

Bob looks down and there is a glass of oily clear fluid on the bar, which is now chrome dully reflecting the blue-and-silver wallpaper. Bob squeezes his eyes shut.

"I know, it's strange." The voice in Bob's ear is calm and slightly amused. A cool hand touches his wrist. "The first visit is very unsettling. You have to figure out what you know and then you'll feel better."

"I don't know what you mean," Bob says, eyes still closed.

"There's always a bar." The voice sounds as though it's cataloguing. "There is always a mirror. The seating is always in the same places. It changes, though, which can be upsetting if you're sitting on it. The beds upstairs—they stay. Well, of course they would. We are a whorehouse. Members of the staff change a bit, but after a few visits you'll be able to recognize most of us most of the time. It's not so bad. Open your eyes."

"Where am I?" Bob asks.

"La Boîte." The voice sounds amused. "C'mon."

Bob slits one eye at his drink. The bar is walnut again but his drink is still clear. He picks it up, lifts it to his mouth. The gin is sharp and spicy, ice-cold.

He gasps a little and opens his other eye. A mirror: yes. The people are still reflected in it. Or Bob thinks so; they could be different people. The aqua couches with the blue walls; when he blinks, yes, red armchairs again with the flocked wallpaper. Next to the cash register on the bar is a card with the Visa and MasterCard icons on it and in handwriting beneath them: CASH OR CHARGE ONLY—NO CHECKS! The cash register doesn't change, he notes.

"Feel better?"

Bob does feel better. He takes another drink—still gin, still ice-cold, still a little like open-heart massage—and eyes his reflection. Still Bob. He turns to the person who's been speaking to him.

She—if it is a she—is a redhead, with a smooth flat haircut that stops at her strong jaw line. She's wearing a fur coat, apparently with nothing else. Bob gets glimpses of peach-colored skin and downy blond hairs where the coat falls away from her thigh. In her left ear she wears a single earring, a crystal like a chandelier's drop. Her? *Hot*, he thinks, *if it's a woman.*

"I'm Jacky," she says and holds out her hand. It seems big for a woman's hand but maybe a little small for a man.

"Bob," Bob says. "Um, where exactly am I? You said but I didn't quite…."

"La Boîte." She picks up a stemmed glass filled with something pink. "'The Box.' Ha ha, right? One of the Boss's little jokes."

"The Boss?"

"Mr. Schrödinger." Jacky tilts her head to one side so that her earring hangs away from her face. It's in her right ear now.

Bob clenches his eyes shut again. "Jesus Christ."

Jacky's voice continues. "It's your first time, poor thing. No one's explained any of this, have they?"

"Just go away. You're all some sort of dream."

There is a sound that might be a fingernail pushing an ice cube around a lowball glass. "Well, you know about the cat, don't you? Everyone does. She's around but we can't let her into the bar because of health regulations. So," she says, and she sounds like she's spelling something out to a slow child. "This. Is. The. Box."

Bob maneuvers the glass he still holds to his lips and drains it. Still gin. He glances sidelong at Jacky. Earring in the left ear. Was that where it was last time? The gin is making itself felt. "This is like limbo?"

Jacky shrugs and the fur slips fetchingly, briefly exposing a smooth shoulder, broad but still well within range for a woman. "It's a lot more like a whorehouse. I'm thirsty."

Bob leans across the bar and taps the bartender on the shoulder.

Jacky sips something pink from her full glass.

"Jesus, how do you guys *do* that?" Bob asks. "It was empty a second ago."

Jacky smirks. "It both was and was not empty. It partook of both states at once." She holds up her hand as Bob opens his mouth. "I don't understand it either, so don't ask me. Look at your glass. Empty or full?"

Bob looks down. "Empt—No, it's—" he stops.

"Don't think too much. Take a sip."

Bob sips. Gin. He gulps. When his eyes have stopped watering, he says, "This is all pretty confusing."

"That's okay. Are you interested in going upstairs?"

His cock hardens when he thinks of it. But the broad shoulders, the big hands—"Uh, no thanks."

She pouts. "Are you sure? If you would prefer someone else, perhaps we can—"

"No," Bob says and swallows hard. "No, I like you fine, I like you best of everyone here, you're very, uh, attractive. But I think my type is more, well, feminine." The earring has changed places once more, he's positive of it this time. That long neck…He's getting hard again and hopes she won't notice.

But she slides her hand down his belly, cupping his cock through his jeans in her broad fingers. The pressure makes his heart skip a beat. "I thought you preferred me?"

It's getting difficult to think. "Well, what are you?"

Jacky laughs something that would be a giggle if Bob were a little more sure of her gender, and drops her fur from her shoulders. Her skin is smooth and she is moderately muscled, with small nipples half-erect in the air. Jacky has soft ash-blonde pubic hair, with a small trail of fur leading down from her navel. What Jacky *doesn't* have is sexual characteristics: no penis, no breasts, no labia. She's—Bob's not certain of that she again—too muscled to look comfortably feminine, too smooth to be really male. "I might be either. It changes."

Bob can feel himself shriveling, looking at her. "How can you do this?"

"I can be whatever I want here," Jacky says. "How often can you say you have that choice? Back out there, would you fuck a man?"

"No," he admits. "*Would* I be fucking a man?"

"Maybe. What's inside the box? Me. And I could be a pussy, or I could be a pistol." She leans forward until her face is inches from Bob's. Her breath is warm against his lips, "Either way, I'll be the best fuck you've ever had."

"All—" Bob stops and clears his throat. "Can we go upstairs now?"

Jacky leads him up a broad flight of stairs lavishly ornamented with statuary depicting fauns and satyrs being ravished by nymphs—or is it the other way around? Bob's looking at Jacky, cannot wait to pull aside that coat and do whatever it is they're about to do. Jacky keeps moving up the stairs, pulling him along by the fur that he is trying to pull off Jacky.

He pulls Jacky close at the door to a room, kissing hard, Jacky's body pressed against him, the flatness of chest and silky skin stretched over hard muscle, a hand sliding under his belt flat-palmed against his belly, moving down until his rigid cock throbs. Bob fumbles the door open and they cascade into a room that might be red or might be honey-colored. They pull apart for a second. Jacky drops the fur coat. At the sight of the body Bob hesitates again.

"What's wrong?" Jacky says, moving to stand chest to chest with him. Jacky is just his height.

"I just wish I knew what you are, that's all."

Jacky laughs once, a low bark. "Except you never do know. You only think you do."

The bus accelerates until Bob can see around it. The box from the post office lies in his lap, its flaps folded closed. Rain's smearing the windshield. Bob adjusts the timer and turns on the headlights before he remembers the whorehouse. The bar that kept changing, Jacky and that strange conversation, and the room—So which was she—he?

Bob's most of the way to Brighton Beach before he figures it out. The Box is closed, after all.

Copyright © 1993 by Kij Johnson

Nick DiChario is a multiple Hugo nominee, a Campbell nominee, and a World Fantasy Award nominee. He is the author of two novels.

CREATOR OF THE COSMOS JOB INTERVIEW TODAY

by Nick DiChario

He entered a sun-white room. The furniture was lean and silvery, the walls made of satin steel. A faint smell of clean, crystalline air tickled his nose. An alien—tall, pale, slick, lean, bipedal, female—came in and seated herself at the desk. She did not speak, but adjusted her long white robe and stared at him with her three vermillion eyes.

He walked over and sat opposite her as if it was expected of him, although he had no idea how he could have known such a thing. He glanced at himself in the glazed steel panels behind the alien's desk. He had a bushy scrub of black hair. He wore jeans and a T-shirt and sandals, the strap on his left sandal hung unfastened, and his knapsack lay tattered at his feet. He didn't recognize himself, although he thought he looked like a human.

"Can you tell me why you're here?" asked the alien. Her voice held the tight, musical crispness of a violin.

"No," he said. Truthfully. But then he thought about it. "Wait. I was walking along the street outside and saw the sign in front of the building: Creator of the Cosmos Job Interview Today. Come Inside."

"So you thought you would just sashay in and have an interview, is that it?"

He shrugged. "I guess so. Something like that. When I saw the sign, I thought, for some reason, the message was meant for me."

"Is that right?"

"Yes."

Her wide, flat ears moved slightly, like palm fronds in the wind. "You say that as if you're pretty sure of yourself. Are you?"

He scratched at his curly bush of hair. "Now I get it. This is all part of the job interview, right?"

She sniffed through a single, flat nostril on the side of her left cheek, feigning boredom. "If you say so. Do you say so?"

"Sure," he said. "I say so."

"Okay, so, according to you, the sign was put out there specifically for you, and this line of questioning is all part of the job interview. Tell me why I should care. What makes you Creator of the Cosmos material?"

The woman's tone was casual but challenging. She leaned forward and placed her elbows on the desk. Her two arms were as long as her body, which gave her the somewhat imposing look of a giant mantis.

He sat back and crossed his legs, picked at the hole in the knee of his jeans, started to say something, glanced around, stood up, walked slowly from here to there and back again with his hands clasped behind his back. Thinking. Trying to remember. As he walked, he could hear the faintest snick of gears, the moto-robo-electronic zizzing of invisible mechanics in the room around him. Where was he? Who was he? *Why* was he? He had no idea.

"Where's the door?" he asked.

"What door?"

"I'm sure I came in through a door. Didn't I?"

"You say that as if it's important there is a door."

"Yes. It's important. Very important. I need to go in and out of it, don't I?"

"Why?"

"I don't know. But it seems important." He walked a bit more, the floor illuminating his soft footfalls, lighting his steps from underneath. He wasn't sure if his feet were telling the floor where to light, or if the floor was telling his feet where to walk. It was an odd sensation. "Wait. Something's coming to me. A memory. I'm meant to go in and out. I'm *meant* to do it, aren't I?"

"*Meant*? Are you sure that's the right word?"

"No. Not one hundred percent."

"Okay, let's start with something a little simpler, then, shall we? Do you know where you came from?"

"No, I don't."

"Do you know where you're going?"

"No, I'm sorry, I don't."

The alien's expression seemed indifferent, but she sat up straight, as if her body had taken an interest. "Excellent. So far you're doing very well. Incredibly well."

"You mean with the interview?" He perched on the edge of the chair. "Hold on. I remember something else. About the questions and answers. This isn't the first time I've interviewed, is it? No, of course not. I come in. I ask questions. And then…I remember what's important…and I go out again, right?"

"Why?" she asked, an anticipatory tremor in her voice. "What is it that's so important that you have to remember? What's the point of the interview? Why do you have to answer questions at all and go in and out of the room?"

"Because…that's the way I am…*designed*… 'designed' is the right word…not *meant*."

The woman's eyes came alive with encouragement. "Yes. Go on."

"Well, something makes me think that for everything to work in the cosmos…all the planets, the galaxies, the universes, the life…this interview has to take place to help me remember…so that I can go out and forget again…and somehow the remembering and forgetting is integral to the life cycle… without me knowing how or why…without anyone knowing how or why…the cosmos are reborn…" That didn't exactly make sense to him, but there it was, he'd said it, and it felt right.

The alien gripped the edge of the desk and pulled herself forward. "Yes? Yes? Go on. You're doing very well. Incredibly well. There is just one question and answer that you have to remember now. Just one. What is it?"

He jumped to his feet as soon as the question popped into his head. "Who is the Creator of the Cosmos?"

"Yes! And the answer?"

"I am the Creator of the Cosmos! Me! Already! Right now! I created everything! It was me! Me!"

"Ahhh," she said. "Ahhh. Rebirth." She released all the tension in her body and slumped back in her chair. "*Ahhhhh.*"

He knew the interview was over now. He bent down and lifted the knapsack, walked toward the wall. A hidden door slid open in front of him right where he knew it would be.

Outside there were two bold suns overhead, red clouds, azure skies, gold mountains, black space. A gust of wind threw back his mop of hair. The music of the world rose up around him. A pterodactyl screeched, sky ships roared, an elephant trumpeted, billions of humans and aliens died while billions more were born, stars burned out and fell from space, and new ones flared to life across an infinite canvas of galaxies.

He closed his eyes and breathed it in. Yes, the Creator breathed it all in, and then breathed it all out again.

The alien rushed over and kneeled before him, pulled the loose strap on his sandal and snugged it in place, lowered herself to her hands and knees and kissed his feet. "Until the morrow," she said.

"Is that how it works?" he asked. "Every day? We have to go through this every single day for the cosmos to work? Is that the way I wanted it? Is that the way I set it up? Why? Why did I do it this way? It makes no sense."

"Exactly," said the woman, waving to him as the door slid shut between them.

"Wait! I have one last question. How long is a day? How long—"

But it was too late. She was gone. How frustrating! He was already beginning to forget.

He turned around to face the cosmos.

Strange, he thought. *Wasn't there a sign here just a moment ago? Something about a job interview?*

Original (First) Publication
Copyright © 2013 by Nick DiChario

Six different stories set in a single neighborhood, each totally independent, but each tangentially touching the others.

"Great writing, vivid scenario, and thoughtful commentary...the stories will linger after the last page is turned."—*Publishers Weekly* [Starred Review]

CAPTIVE DREAMS

MICHAEL FLYNN
AUTHOR OF *EIFELHEIM* & *THE WRECK OF THE RIVER OF STARS*

"Great writing."—*Publishers Weekly* (Starred Review)

"Unique."—*ForeWord Reviews*

"One of the best SF writers of our time."—*New York Times* bestselling author Harry Turtledove

FROM THE HEART'S BASEMENT

by Barry Malzberg

Barry N. Malzberg won the very first Campbell Memorial Award, and is a multiple Hugo and Nebula nominee. He is the author or co-author of more than 90 books.

The Carlin Effect

In a late-life routine on our country's politics, George Carlin was neither encouraging nor optimistic. Lobbies, kickbacks, celebrity television, press conferences, security barriers, manipulative lies. Pseudo-gemeinschaft all the way. "It's a big f—-ing club," Carlin observed. "And you're not in it." (Characteristic of Carlin's integrity, he didn't say "We're not in it." That would have been Just Folks Common Guy Posturing, which is the property of Rush Limbaugh or Sean Hannity.) This made me think of science fiction (all roads lead to Rome) and how profoundly that remark might apply to our own lovable field. It's a big club all right.

And a lot of you are not in it.

Count me—unlike Carlin—in that number. Once I was on the margins of that club myself, mentored early by Harry Harrison, helped no little by my employment at Scott Meredith's Agency, and I was able to use factors like this to get attention paid to my work and even publish a good deal of it…but age withereth, custom stales, and I think of myself as an ex-member. My get-up-and-go just got up and went. My badge was taken, my credentials expired, and if I were to appear at a Science Fiction and Fantasy Writers of America annual Editors' Reception in October I would not know 90% of the writers and editors attending, and reciprocally they would not know me. A shadowy figure, an Edward Wellen or Stanton E. Coblentz of this modern era, I might be able to find a codger or two in a corner and retreat with them into murmurs of Jakobbson's early seventies massacre of manuscripts at *Galaxy* or Horace Gold's even more brutal misprision twenty years before that. We would if our voices became too loud intercept a pitying glance here or there. But re-admission to the club? We would not receive even a pitying stare.

It's a big club all right, and most of you are not in it. I am not in it anymore either if that makes you feel any better, but the history is definitive. Harlan Ellison wrote in the sixties in one of his *Dangerous Visions* story introductions that almost every writer who sells even one story finds that she is almost instantly known and categorized and somehow placed in the lexicon. Tiptree and Cordwainer Smith notwithstanding (and they did not have to contend with the Web, with Google, with Facebook, with YouTube), it was almost impossible to slip into print incognito, without personal detail. Sure the field was a lot smaller almost fifty years ago. But the intimacy, the social network, has merely expanded. The difference now is one of degree rather than kind. The fundamental rules still apply as time goes by. Science fiction—to which that twenty-ton elephantine beast fantasy has become its dominant and controlling companion—is a network of spavined relationships, scraps of shared (and often libelous) history and relationships which obsessively include but are hardly limited to the sexual. That science fiction conventions in the old days were a forest of sexual opportunity was one of the great *foma*, and perceived by many as one of the principal advantages of club membership. (I am an old guy now and can tell you nothing about the current situation, but I am free to carry inference and so are you.)

It is fun being in a big f—-ing club as Newt Gingrich or Sean Hannity could attest, but in relation at least to our outcast field which was founded and reached greatness as a despised outsider literature… well, it can lead to problems. This *is* an outsider literature, transgressive or visionary at its best, sullen and idiosyncratic at its worst, and it was founded upon the emotional isolation of young readers who might have looked to the stars because the schoolyard was a kind of hell. The outsiders and isolates found themselves creating and managing a big fing club, of course, but being part of such a club is not likely to foster or impel the dreams of anger, the

yearning of desire which was instrumentally at the heart of science fiction. (Remember your Bradbury.)

At the Readercon some years ago, I saw X for the first time since the last Readercon (he had been a regular for some years), and asked him how he was doing. Glad to see him, etc. X, a scientist, successful in academia and research, had come to science fiction writing later in life than most of us, he had attended one of the important workshops and almost immediately found himself able to sell short stories to the major markets in quantity. In a few years he had managed to accumulate more than two dozen sales, had his name on magazine covers and so on. "Not sure how I am doing," X said. "Frankly, I don't even know if I should be here."

"The problem is this," he continued, "I am on the verge of becoming part of the inner circle now, hanging out with the pros here, making a name on panels, learning the personal histories, hearing the gossip. The problem, I am afraid, is that I am losing the very isolation which formed me as a writer, which made me want to write. How can I be one of the members here and retain the sense of exclusion, the anger, the loneliness, which were the basis of my ambition to be a writer? I just don't feel comfortable hanging around here anymore. I don't think it is doing me any good as a writer."

Well, many would disagree. Many of us were brought here, encouraged, directed and eventually adopted by the Harry Harrisons of the world we wanted to join. But one has to ask: How much did being part of that big f—-ing club help Walter Miller? How much did it help Phil Klass, who knew everyone and hung out everywhere, and who, in the last forty years of his life (he had fled to academia in the mid-sixties), produced four published short stories? How much did being "Science Fiction's Little Mother" help Judith Merril, who was washed up as a writer before she was forty, and who fled to Canada and community-founding at the age of 45? How much did being a charter, an originating member of the club, help Cyril Kornbluth, whose ambition in the last years before his death (at 35) was to write no more science fiction? What did these people know and when did they know it?

When for that matter did *I* know it? When did I find myself thinking more about my relative position and opportunities in science fiction than I did about writing it? When did so many of us become science fiction's counterpart to the late Harold Brodkey (1930-1996) who told *New York Magazine* that before he began working on his endless novel *The Runaway Soul* (delivered twenty years later than the contract date) he would spend two morning hours on the telephone, "Checking my position in the community."?

All topics for thought and discussion. There will be a short quiz at our next club meeting in the secret anteroom. In the meantime I propose them for consideration. And greet my three or four readers. You are all invited to a Secret Meeting. Write (not tweet) for details. No, I will not give contact information. If you have to ask, you're not a potential member.

"Just a Second" is Lou Berger's second professional sale. We predict that you'll be hearing a lot more from him.

JUST A SECOND

by Lou J. Berger

There are biological bastards, who are forgivable, and then there are bastards like Frederick Thomas.

The bell over the shop door jangled as he walked in. He glanced at his watch, waiting for his eyes to adjust to the dark interior of the store. It was 8:30 in the morning and he didn't want to be late for his 9 o'clock meeting. He didn't want to be early either. This place would be the perfect spot to kill a few minutes.

It was a store he'd passed hundreds of times in the past, never giving it much thought. A sign in the window, facing the street, encouraged customers to "Buy a Second!" Over the course of years, the sign had never changed. He had no idea what it could possibly mean.

A fat orange-and-black cat lay asleep on a red plush pillow set in a low, wicker basket, a shaft of sunlight warming it, dust sparkling and dancing around like gnats. A musty smell filled the air, partially obscured by a teapot bubbling jasmine-scented steam on a low counter.

The store was some sort of a curio shop, Frederick decided, with incense, small statues of dragons clutching faceted crystal balls and candles filling the walls and shelves. A shelf near the back of the store held many dusty books. Some were arranged neatly, others stacked in a haphazard fashion.

"I can help you?" a woman asked, in a strange accent. Hungarian, maybe? Frederick whirled to see her standing at the counter along the back wall. She must have stepped through the beaded curtain hanging in the doorway to the back. Heavy mascara rimmed her eyes and hoops dangled from her ears. She wore a brightly colored dress yet her fingernails were long and painted black. Her skin was ghostly pale. He smiled. How cliché.

"I noticed the sign in the window…" he began. She smiled and extended a claw-shaped hand.

"I see. My name Iselda."

He took her hand, holding just the fingers. It was small, with delicate bones, and her long nails lay in his palm like talons. Her skin felt hot and dry, like a paper bag left too long in the sun. He retrieved his hand and casually brushed it against his slacks.

"Many people see sign and keep going, never wondering what it means." Iselda's lips twisted in a sly grin. She appeared pleased that he'd asked about it.

The cat stood in its basket, stretched, and turned around twice before settling again.

"Many years ago, my mother learned to harness rhythm of time. She created potion to give person extra second, whenever needed. If you control heartbeat of time, you control everything. The first vial is one hundred dollars."

She waited.

"Well?" A smile teased her mouth but her eyes were cold, obsidian marbles.

"I don't understand," Frederick said, frowning. "You mean to tell me that you are selling a magic potion? What century do you think this is?" He laughed easily and she joined him, but it sounded dutiful.

"You mock what you don't know." Her voice sounded tired, as if she had told this story countless times. "But many people, even *smart* ones, come in to buy potions."

Frederick looked around the shop again and then checked his watch. His meeting. There was still time, but not much.

"So how does it work?" he asked.

She shrugged. "You drink it, you get extra second." Her tone implied he was a simpleton. She leaned forward and the artificial smile fell from her lips. "Is not rocket science, is magic potion."

He shrugged and reached into his pocket, opened his wallet and dropped a hundred-dollar bill on the counter top. It didn't seem to detract from the pile remaining in his wallet. Besides, he'd flunked science anyway. "Okay, sold."

She reached beneath the counter and produced a vial of clear liquid, which she then handed him. He opened it. It smelled like water. He looked at her

with a question in his eyes and she made a "hurry up" gesture with her hands.

He closed his eyes, tilted back his head, and drained the vial. It tasted like water, too.

"Well, that's that, I guess," he said, squinting at the empty vial in the light. "Expensive water, right?" He searched her face to see if the whole thing had been a joke.

She shook her head and moved toward the beaded curtain. "See you soon," she said.

Frederick, who had turned to head out the door, stopped and looked back. "What makes you think I'll come back?"

She peered at him coyly through the beaded curtain. "Oh, you will." She raised a bony finger. "Of this, I have no doubts."

Later, in the office, Frederick was pleased with how his day was shaping up. Having made his meeting with moments to spare, he had worked filling client orders on the phone. He'd opened, for a particularly wealthy customer, a position on an enormous block of shares scant moments before the stock's quarterly earnings report hit the news. He leaned back in his chair and grinned at the computer monitor as the stock's value leaped higher. He'd just made another killing for a satisfied customer by getting the order in quickly. Just like that. He snapped his fingers.

Jenny, the new receptionist, peeked around the corner, a tendril of brunette hair falling in front of her right eye. "You need me, Mr. Thomas?"

Frederick made to wave her away, then changed his mind. "Jenny, come inside and sit down. Close the door."

She pulled the door behind her and walked to the chair in front of his desk, uncertain on her heels, skirt tight around her knees. She sat gingerly, her back ramrod straight, and looked him right in the eyes. Blue. Her eyes were so blue. "Yes, Mr. Thomas?"

Frederick leaned back in his chair. He knew it was wrong, but he'd not allowed himself any fun lately. He'd been too busy climbing the commission and bonus ladder. He removed his glasses and pinched the bridge of his nose. "Jenny, if we are going to work together, why not call me Fred?"

"Yes, Mr. Thom…er, Fred." Her lilting voice hesitated, and Frederick stole a glance in her direction.

There was a pretty little frown line over her nose. He wanted to reach across the desk and wipe it away with his thumb. It was the only blemish on her perfect little doll face.

"Thank you. Now, I want to go over the quarterly commission reports tonight but I'm completely swamped. Do you have plans tonight?"

She bit the corner of her lower lip and, after a moment, shook her head.

"Good. Then it's settled. I'll pick you up out front of the building at six. Thanks, Jenny, that will be all."

She rose slowly and walked to the door, put her hand on the knob. She turned and looked at him and drew in a breath, as if to say something.

Frederick frowned. "That will be *all*, Jenny," he said, ice creeping into his voice.

She nodded and left, pulling the door closed behind her.

The next morning, when he awoke, the first thing he noticed was that his mouth tasted foul. He grimaced and rolled over to sit up on the edge of the bed. Rubbing his face, he marveled at how the hangover seemed to make even his hair hurt. He went into the bathroom and splashed water on his face. With water dripping from his chin, he peered into the mirror and brushed his lanky brown hair with his fingers, pulling it from over his forehead. He shook his head and winked at his reflection. "You sly dog," he muttered, then threw two pills down his throat, chasing them with tap water.

Walking back to the bed, he froze. In the dim pre-dawn light he could see a series of long curves distorting the sheets. He drew in a deep breath of regret. He raised his hand and brought it down with a large smack on the highest curve. Jenny's bleary face burst from the sheets, her eyes unfocused.

"Wha...?" she said, her little kitten voice sounding confused. She dragged the hair out of her eyes with long fingernails, snagging it briefly in her fingertips. She shook them free with annoyance. "What time is it?"

Frederick sat on the edge of the bed, a smile playing on his lips. "I didn't say you could sleep over, Jenny," he said, his voice reasonable. "What were you thinking?"

She frowned, that little line appearing on her forehead again. It had lost its appeal overnight.

"I don't know, Fred. I figured..." she waved her hand at the bed, implying a great deal of assumptions in a simple sweep of her arm.

"Well, you figured incorrectly. Now get up, get dressed and go home. This was a mistake."

Her mouth opened in slow shock and then she closed it with a click, set her jaw and tore the covers from her body. She stood and stalked across the carpet to the chair, where she grabbed her dress and held it over her head, dropping it over her shoulders. She tugged the waist down, twisting it until it was lined up properly and then stepped into her heels. She made for the door and then stopped, turning to face him. Her hair looked like a mare's nest, wild and in disarray.

"So what was this? Just a quick roll in the hay?"

Frederick shrugged and climbed under the sheets. "Whatever you want to call it is fine with me, Jenny. I call it unprofessional...on your part." He closed his eyes and smiled when she slammed the door. He waited a full minute, then lifted his phone and dialed. When he heard the beep, he cleared his throat and spoke.

"Yes, Marge? It's Frederick Thomas. I know it's early in the morning so I just wanted to leave you a quick message. It's about Jenny. She got drunk last night and followed me to my apartment, banging on the door and making a scene. Nothing happened, but I wouldn't be surprised if she tried to make trouble. Can you just let her go? Give her a month's severance; maybe that will shut her up. Thanks, Marge. I know I owe you one for this. Can you send me a new girl?" He hung up and snagged a cigarette from the nightstand, lighting it and drawing the smoke deep. He smiled in the dark. Maybe the next one would be a blonde.

Over the next few days, he noticed how his trades would settle almost instantly, confirmation replies showing up shortly after he pressed his "enter" key rather than after a typical delay.

Additionally, his commute seemed to shorten. At stop signs he would turn his head to face oncoming traffic and notice an approaching "wolf pack" of cars. In the past, more often than not, the pack was too close for him to jump in front and avoid the wait. Since the visit to the shop, however, he always seemed to have enough room to accelerate from a full stop and continue on his way before the cars could reach him. Also, he seemed to be sliding through intersections under more yellow lights. His drive to work was about ten minutes shorter on average than before the potion.

Two weeks or so later, Frederick grew convinced that his orders were closing faster. He stopped by Brian's office and stood in front of the desk.

"Hold on," Brian mouthed, finger raised, phone on his shoulder, head tilted to the side. Frederick waited.

Brian spoke a few words and then hung up. He looked at Frederick. "What's up?"

"Not much…did we upgrade the ordering system?"

Brian frowned. "Why, is something wrong? I told that creep in IT to hold off on installing any upgrades until the weekend." He reached for the phone, but Frederick held up a hand.

"No, that's not necessary. Let me ask a different question. Are your orders closing a bit more quickly lately?"

Brian snorted and clicked his keyboard, frowning at the screen.

"Nope, these are typical closing speeds over the last thousand transactions. Specifically, a six-and-a-quarter-second average over the past three hundred orders."

"Thanks," called Frederick, heading back to his own office. "I appreciate your checking!"

Sitting back at his desk, he gazed at the statistics glowing on his own monitor. Five-and-a-tenth seconds, on average, over his last thousand orders. The numbers glowed, serene and unassailable.

The days flew by. Although normally impossible to get IPO shares due to massive demand, he filled every order immediately. He didn't wait for anything. It was luck, pure and simple, he thought. Wasn't it?

He stopped and pondered. His drive to work was shorter because he kept getting lucky at traffic lights and at stop signs. His trades executed faster and he spent less time filling orders and more time talking to happy customers. As a result, his sales had increased, creating a nice spike in his commissions. A very nice spike. Twenty-five grand more commissions this quarter than last quarter. Twenty-five

thousand dollars. Well, he thought. That made his next decision easy.

The next morning, the jangling bell in the shop brought Iselda from behind the curtain again. The same cat lay sleeping in the same shaft of sunlight. Nothing had changed. Frederick smiled at her.

"Back for another?" Her eyes danced with mischief. "I told you you'd return."

"Yup. I don't know how, but your magic potion seems to be working."

He reached into his pocket and pulled out a hundred-dollar bill. Dropping it on the counter, he smiled expectantly.

Iselda gazed at the money and moved her eyes up to his. "I'm sorry. Is more for the second potion."

"What do you mean?" Frederick frowned. He didn't like being played for a fool. Warmth built under his collar.

"The first potion cost a hundred dollars, and is worth it, no?"

Frederick thought. He was reluctant to let her know how much he wanted a second one, given how valuable the first one had been. She could charge him twice as much and he'd still pay.

"Well," she spread her hands. "That is the way of things. The next second is worth much more than first because magic is…" She leaned forward and spoke very slowly. "…compounded."

She fumbled under the counter and brought up another vial, which she held balanced on her palm, holding it just out of reach.

"Now costs a thousand dollars." Her voice was stone.

He opened his mouth, and then shut it tight. Twenty-five thousand up, what was a simple thousand? Better not to argue. He reached into his wallet again and threw nine more bills down on the counter.

She handed him the vial and scooped up the money, her long nails clicking like beetles on the glass surface as her hands gathered up the bills. He drained the vial in one gulp, tossed the empty vial to clatter on the glass, whirled and left the store.

The next few months were pure magic. He broke office sales records and hit his annual quota by July. His commission percentage, accelerated as he broke through level after level, hit stratospheric heights for the first time ever. Every stoplight turned to green as his brand-new Lexus approached. When his co-workers asked for his secret, he shrugged. "Timing," he'd say, then wink. He'd laugh at their confused faces, then walk back to his office.

His boss summoned him to a conference room one afternoon and Frederick closed the door, noting the two men in suits already there.

"What's up, Walt?" he asked.

"Sit down." Walt pointed at a chair.

Frederick sat.

"These guys are with the Securities and Exchange Commission. They wanted to talk to you a bit."

Frederick leaned back in his chair and loosened his tie. Two hours later, he shook the men's hands, grinned, shot Walt with his forefinger, and strolled out of the office. They wouldn't have believed him anyway. The clear advantage he was enjoying was, they'd decided, unusual but rational luck.

On a muggy August Wednesday, he entered Iselda's shop again. The cat was gone from its typical cushion, and some time passed before Iselda emerged. Nobody else was in the store. Frederick wondered, idly, how they stayed in business.

"How much…" he began.

She held up her hand, stopping him. Her face was unusually pale and worry lines etched the corners of her eyes.

"No more potion," she said. Her voice was flat, and he could see worry…and something else in her eyes. Perhaps fear.

He paused. His mind raced through dozens of possible arguments, but asked a question instead. "Why not?"

She looked at him. "Is not safe. One potion, maybe two, they are nothing, they don't mean much. But three," she paused and then her voice grew firm. "Is too much."

What was she talking about?

"I have cash, and it doesn't look like you should be turning down the sale." He looked around the empty store and raised his eyebrows. He pulled out a wad of bills.

"How much?" he said again and began to count the bills.

She hesitated, glanced at the pile of bills in his hand and shuddered. She closed her eyes and bowed her head, long black hair cascading like twin curtains alongside her face.

"Ten thousand," she whispered.

He snapped the bills off one at a time, raining them down like autumn leaves on the glass counter, creating a small pile.

She reached behind the counter and produced another vial. "Please, don't," she said, gripping the vial in her bony fingers.

He snatched the vial from her hand, opened it, lifted it in mock salute, and drained it. He threw the bottle against the floor, shattering it. The door slammed so hard upon his exit that the bell fell to the floor, its jangling silenced by a thick rug.

He spied her for the first time at a restaurant a month later.

The third vial had really seemed to transform his luck. Not only had he not seen a red light since his latest visit to Iselda, it also appeared as if there were fewer people in the world. He snorted to himself. That was silly, he knew, but it certainly felt that way. If he arrived late to a dinner engagement, a car would pull away from the parking spot nearest the door just as he drove up. If a traffic jam formed on the highway, his lane would speed through without interruption, no matter which lane he happened to be in. It was as if the world was cleverly staged to accommodate him. Only for him. He patted his lips with his napkin, looking at the remains of his sandwich on the plate.

He dropped a bill on the table and got up. Out of the corner of his eye he saw a woman looking at him but, by the time he turned his head, she had whirled around and was walking away. He liked her shoulders, the sway of her hips, the easy physicality she projected without effort. Unlike Jenny, this one seemed to be a mature woman, not just a girl. The strong neck, the posture, these attributes added up to a very confident woman. He chuckled to himself.

Girls like Jenny weren't enough for him anymore, not for a guy on his way up. He needed a power partner, somebody who would be his intellectual equal. A peer. Somebody strong-willed enough to stand up to his personality. He followed her casually. As he stepped from the restaurant onto the sidewalk, she turned the corner a half-block away.

He jogged to the end of the block, tie flapping, and looked down the alley, but she was just disappearing from view around the next corner. He sniffed the air, thinking he could smell a faint odor of jasmine, but it quickly wafted away. He shrugged and went home.

He saw her again a week later, during a speech he was giving to a local volunteer group. They had asked him in to give a short talk on the life of a successful stockbroker. The guy who invited him implied that they were considering him for inclusion. Right. As if he'd join their little social club. The food was free, so why not?

As he was wrapping up his talk with a wry anecdote about a wealthy customer who could never be satisfied, she walked by the open door of the hotel conference room, glanced in and paused for just a moment. He looked up, a fraction of a second too late to see her face, and she was gone. He knew it was her again. Her posture, her shoulders. There was no doubt.

He excused himself, made apologies and hurried to the door. Looking to his left, he saw just the end of her skirt and her leg as she turned a corner. He sprinted down the hallway, not caring who was watching, and stopped at the corner. She was gone. But, again, there was a faint smell of jasmine in the air. He inhaled deeply, as if by memorizing her scent he'd learn something about her.

He glimpsed her, again and again, through the following weeks, just out of reach, never seeing her face, and always being just a moment too late to actually catch up to her. The downtown crowds of people would thin and part, offering a glance at her strong, alabaster neck, her well-defined shoulders, a nicely turned calf, before they would reform and swallow her again. Given the luck he'd experienced recently, with everything going his way, his inability to meet her in person was growing intolerable. He vowed to find her, no matter the cost.

So, on a Saturday morning, he drove downtown and entered the store again. Iselda was there, but the cat was still missing from the basket. She came to the counter, her face wrinkled in disdain.

"Listen, Iselda," he began, a note of apology in his voice.

She held up her hand to stop him, her pale skin glowing. "No, you are not welcome here anymore. I cannot sell you another potion. You have already…"

Frederick bowed his head. "Listen, I'm sorry for the way I left things last time. I came across a bit too strong and I want to apologize." He gave her his best boyish grin and, as he had expected, a look of doubt crept into her eyes. He allowed some warmth to enter his smile and pushed his advantage. "Look, I should have listened to you. Three was too much."

She nodded, glad he understood. "Is bad to tempt fate, is all I meant to tell you," she finished, her voice weak. She smiled at him and he thought, for a moment, that she looked very vulnerable. He leaned forward to seal the deal.

"I was meaning to ask you. There's this certain woman I keep seeing, but I keep missing her. I want to introduce myself, but I can't seem to catch her. Do you think, just maybe, that I might get a fourth…" He stopped. Her face had gone, if possible, even more pale.

"Who is this woman? Describe her to me!"

Frederick licked his lips. "Well, she's very athletic, and she has long dark hair and she's always just… barely…out of reach."

Iselda nodded, her mouth set in a firm line. "Is bad news, this woman. You must stay far away. Do not approach her."

"No," he shook his head. "I need to meet her. She's been on my mind and I can't stand not knowing who she is. Just for a moment," he pleaded. "Let me have a fourth potion and I'll never come back again. I don't care what the price is!"

She shook her head in reply and crossed her arms. No amount of wheedling worked and he left the store angry and frustrated. He paused on the sidewalk and looked back inside, through the window. Thinking that he'd moved out of sight, Iselda opened the drawer and held a vial up to the light, shaking her head. She put the vial back and closed the drawer. Frederick checked the posted store hours and walked back to his car.

That night, Frederick parked on the curb in front of the store. He killed the engine and sat in the car, listening to the engine tick in the cool night air. Pulling on a pair of gloves and opening the car door, Frederick stepped to the sidewalk. In his right hand, he held a prybar. Three long strides took him to the store's front door and, a moment later, he slipped the prybar between the door and its jamb, exerted force, and, with the sound of crunching wood, popped open the door. Frederick held his breath, listening for alarms, but nothing sounded.

He stepped inside, picking his way around shelves by the moonlight streaming in through the front windows. The cat was back in the basket and it lifted its head, gazing at him with baleful yellow eyes. It stood and hissed, once, and the fur along its spine fluffed. Frederick stepped behind the counter, opened the drawer and removed the vial. He was back in the car and driving away, breathing quickly, within moments. On the palm of his leather glove, the glass vial caught and reflected the streetlights on the drive home.

Once home, Frederick sat in his room, on his bed, and gazed at the vial. He slowly opened the stopper. Inside, the potion still resembled water but, this time, the strong scent of jasmine poured out. He wrinkled his nose but drank the liquid anyway. It still tasted like water. He grew dizzy and lay back on the bed, falling unconscious.

Upon waking the next morning, Frederick noticed that the smell of jasmine had grown even stronger. The drive to work was uneventful, as smooth and efficient as he'd ever seen, and the day fairly flew by. He was very pleased with himself. At lunch, he sat outside, on the sidewalk of an outdoor café, at a small table. He watched the crowds until he saw her approaching. Her hair swung in front of her face, hiding it. He gulped down the last of his water and dropped a bill on the table.

Vaulting the low rail separating the diners from the sidewalk, he fell in behind her, noticing how her heels clicked on the pavement. He let his gaze travel slowly along her strong neck, to the alabaster skin of her arms, to the radiant waterfall of raven hair spilling across her shoulders. He admired her calves as they flexed, the way her heels made her legs look, how they made her hips sway.

He followed her into an alley and, quickly, moved closer. He touched her shoulder.

"Miss," he said, keeping his voice li[gh]... have a word with you? I've been wanting you."

She turned around. He gasped and took an [un]conscious step back. He'd assumed that her lithe, powerful body, attractive as it was, had a face to match. It didn't. Her gaunt, hollow face was heavily lined, and her eyes were inky pools of blackness.

"*You* have been trying to introduce yourself to *me*?" she chuckled, her voice a deep contralto. "That's not how it normally works. I'm so very pleased to meet you anyway, Frederick."

A cold chill gripped his heart. How did she know his name? He stepped back again. Her face disgusted him, with lined gray skin and cold, dead eyes. She looked a million years old. She gazed at him and pointed a thin, crooked finger.

"You met Iselda?" Her mouth pursed and she licked her lips. "She works for me. The potion shop is my little honey trap to find…diversions. It gets *so* lonely through the centuries." She stepped forward and traced a fingernail up his tie, then pressed it against the knot at his throat. "Fortunately, you came along at just the right time. I've been missing a man's touch." She squeezed his bicep and shuddered with delight. "You'll do, oh, yes you will!"

Frederick recoiled in disgust. "Now, wait a moment. I have no idea what you are talking about!"

"If you don't know now, you will soon," she said with a predatory smile.

"You *own* the potion shop?"

"You were warned against manipulating the fabric of Time. But you knew better, didn't you? So used to getting your way in things, you felt you *deserved* whatever you desired." She smiled, exposing ghastly teeth. Frederick gasped. When she spoke again, her voice was mocking. "Most people spend their lives running away from me, but, *you*…you actually chased me down. Well here I am, Frederick. I'm all yours. Have me." She spread her arms wide, inviting.

He shook his head. "No, there's been some sort of mistake. I have a meeting. Look, it was nice to meet you but I have to go."

"Look around you, Frederick!" Her sharp voice froze him in place. She waved her bony arms. "You see how alone we are? This was *your* doing! You bought the potion, you drank it willingly." She held

ur times! I didn't have to lure you
l her dark hair with long finger-
ve been decades, Frederick," she
l's voice. "Decades. But you came
our own!" She clapped her hands
iis stomach churn. "And now, my
you are all mine!"

Frederick grimaced and turned to go.

With incredible speed, she grabbed his jacket lapels. Drawing him close, her ice-cold hands burned through his clothing and numbed his chest. She pulled his face down to hers and kissed him. She clamped her lips hard against his mouth and inhaled, pulling his breath into her body.

He grew numb and felt his knees buckle as his strength left him. He thought, "Just a second…"— but there wasn't any more time.

Original (First) Publication
Copyright © 2013 by Lou J. Berger

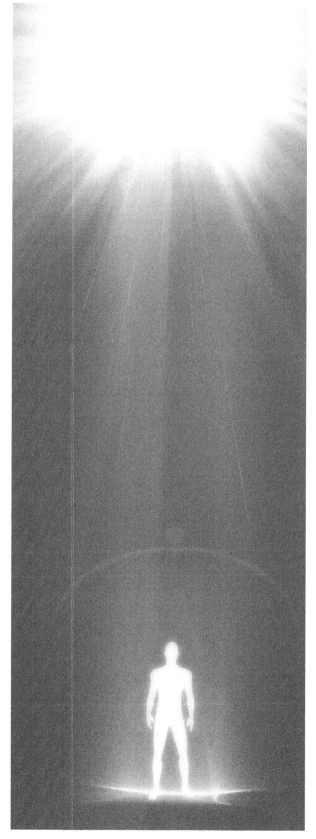

Jack McDevitt is a Nebula winner (and seventeen-time Nebula nominee) as well as a Hugo nominee. His most recent book is *The Cassandra Project* in collaboration with Mike Resnick.

ACT OF GOD

by Jack McDevitt

I'm sorry about showing up on such short notice, Phil. I'd planned to go straight to the hotel when the flight got in. But I needed to talk to somebody.

Thanks, yes, I will take one. Straight, if you don't mind.

You already know Abe's dead. And no, it wasn't the quake. Not really. Look, I know how this sounds, but if you want the truth, I think God killed him.

Do I *look* hysterical? Well, maybe a little bit. But I've been through a lot. And I know I didn't say anything about it earlier but that's because I signed a secrecy agreement. *Don't tell anybody.* That's what it said, and I've worked out there for two years and until this moment never mentioned to a soul what we were doing.

And yes, I really think God took him off. I know exactly how that sounds, but nothing else explains the facts. The thing that scares me is that I'm not sure it's over. I might be on the hit list too. I mean, I never thought of it as being sacrilegious. I've never been that religious to start with. Didn't used to be. I am now.

Did you ever meet Abe? No? I thought I'd introduced you at a party a few years ago. Well, it doesn't matter.

Yes, I know you must have been worried when you heard about the quake, and I'm sorry, I should have called. I was just too badly shaken. It happened during the night. He lived there, at the lab. Had a house in town but he actually stayed most nights at the lab. Had a wing set up for himself on the eastern side. When it happened it took the whole place down. Woke me up, woke everybody up, I guess. I was about two miles away. But it was just a bump in the night. I didn't even realize it *was* an earthquake until the police called. Then I went right out to the lab. Phil, it was as if the hill had opened up and just swallowed everything. They found Abe's body in the morning.

What was the sacrilege? It's not funny, Phil. I'll try to explain it to you but your physics isn't very good so I'm not sure where to start.

You know the appointment to work with Abe was the opportunity of a lifetime. A guarantee for the future. My ship had come in.

But when I first got out there it looked like a small operation. Not the sort of thing I'd expected to see. There were only three of us, me, Abe, and Mac Cardwell, an electrical engineer. Mac died in an airplane crash about a week before the quake. He had a pilot's license, and he was flying alone. No one else was involved. Just him. The FAA said it looked as if lightning had hit the plane.

All right, smile if you want to. But Cardwell built the system that made it all possible. And I know I'm getting ahead of things here so let me see if I can explain it. Abe was a cosmologist. Special interest in the big bang. Special interest in how to generate a big bang.

I'd known that before I went out there. You know how it can be done, right? Actually *make* a big bang. No, I'm not kidding. Look, it's not really that hard. Theoretically. All you have to do is pack a few kilograms of ordinary matter into a sufficiently small space, *really* small, considerably smaller than an atomic nucleus. Then, when you release the pressure that constrains it, the thing explodes.

No, I don't mean a nuke. I mean a big bang. A *real* one. The thing expands into a new universe. Anyhow, what I'm trying to tell you is that he *did* it. More than that, he did it *thirty* years ago. And no, I know you didn't hear an explosion. Phil, I'm serious.

Look, when it happens, the blast expands into a different set of dimensions, so it has no effect whatever on the people next door. But it *can* happen. It *did* happen.

And *nobody* knew about it. He kept it quiet.

I *know* you can't pack much matter into a space the size of a nucleus. You don't have to. The initial package is only a kind of cosmic seed. It contains the trigger and a set of instructions. Once it erupts, the process feeds off itself. It creates whatever it needs.

The forces begin to operate, and the physical constants take hold. Time begins. *Its* time.

I'd wondered what he was doing in Crestview, Colorado, but he told me he went out there because it was remote, and that made it a reasonably safe place to work. People weren't going to be popping in, asking questions. When I got there, he sat me down and invited me to sign the agreement, stipulating that I'd say nothing whatever, without his express permission, about the work at the lab. He'd known me pretty well and I suddenly realized why I'd gotten the appointment over several hundred people who were better qualified. He could trust me to keep my mouth shut.

At first I thought the lab was involved in defense work of one kind or another. Like Northgate. But this place didn't have the security guards and the triple fences and the dogs. He introduced me to Mac, who was a little guy with a beard that desperately needed a barber, and to Sylvia Michaels. Sylvia was a tall, stately woman, dark hair, dark eyes, a hell of a package, I'm sure, when she was younger. She was the project's angel.

I should add that Sylvia's also dead. Ran her car into a tree two days after the quake. Cops thought she was overcome with grief and wasn't paying attention to what she was doing. Single vehicle accident. Like Mac, she was alone.

Is that an angel like in show business? Yes. Exactly. Her family owned a group of Rocky Mountain resorts. She was enthusiastic about Abe's ideas, so she financed the operation. She provided the cash, Mac designed the equipment, and Abe did the miracles. Well, maybe an unfortunate choice of words there.

Why didn't he apply for government funding? Phil, the government doesn't like stem cells, clones, and particle accelerators. You think they're going to underwrite a *big bang*?

Yes, of course I'm serious. Do I look as if I'd kid around? About something like this?

Why didn't I say something? Get it stopped? Phil, you're not listening. It was a going concern long before I got there.

And yes, it's a real universe. Just like this one. He kept it in the building. More or less. It's hard to explain. It extended out through that separate set of dimensions I told you about. There *are* more than

three. It doesn't matter whether you can visualize them or not. They're there. Listen, maybe I should go.

Well, okay. No, I'm not upset. I just need you to hear me out. I'm sorry, I don't know how to explain it any better than that. Phil, we could *see* it. Mac had built a device that allowed us to observe and even, within limitations, to guide events. They called it the *cylinder* and you could look in and see star clouds and galaxies and jets of light. Everything spinning and drifting, supernovas blinking on and off like Christmas lights. Some of the galaxies had a glare like a furnace at their centers. It was incredible.

I know it's hard to believe. Take my word for it. And I don't know when he planned to announce it. Whenever I asked him, he always said *when the time is ripe*. He was afraid that, if anyone found out, he'd be shut down.

I'm sorry to hear you say that. There was never any danger to *anybody*. It was something you could do in your garage and the neighbors would never notice. Well, you could do it if you had Mac working alongside you.

Phil, I wish you could have seen it. The cosm— his term, not mine—was already eight billion years old, relative. What was happening was that time was passing a lot faster in the cosm than it was in Crestview. As I say, it had been up and running for thirty years by then.

You looked into that machine and saw all that and it humbled you. You know what I mean? Sure, it was Abe who figured out how to make it happen, but the magic was in the process. How was it possible that we live in a place where you could pack up a few grams of earth and come away with a living universe?

And it *was* living. We zeroed in on some of the worlds. They were *green*. And there were animals. But nothing that seemed intelligent. Lots of predators, though. Predators you wouldn't believe, Phil. It was why he'd brought *me* in. What were the conditions necessary to permit the development of intelligent life? Nobody had ever put the question in quite those terms before, and I wasn't sure I knew the answer.

No, we couldn't see any of this stuff in real time. We had to take pictures and then slow everything down by a factor of about a zillion. But it worked. We could tell what was going on.

We picked out about sixty worlds, all overrun with carnivores, some of them that would have gobbled down a T-rex as an appetizer. Abe had a technique that allowed him to reach in and influence events. Not physically, by which I mean that he couldn't stick a hand in there, but we had some electromagnetic capabilities. I won't try to explain it because I'm not clear on it myself. Even Abe didn't entirely understand it. It's funny, when I look back now I suspect Mac was the real genius.

The task was to find a species with potential and get rid of the local carnivores to give it a chance.

On some of the worlds, we triggered major volcanic eruptions. Threw a lot of muck into the atmosphere and changed the climate. Twice we used undersea earthquakes to send massive waves across the plains where predators were specially numerous. Elsewhere we rained comets down on them. We went back and looked at the results within a few hours after we'd finished, our time. In most cases we'd gotten rid of the targets, and the selected species were doing nicely, thank you very much. Within two days of the experiment we had our first settlements.

I should add that none of the occupants looked even remotely human.

If I'd had my way, we would have left it at that. I suggested to Abe that it was time to announce what he had. Report the results. Show it to the world. But he was averse. *Make it public?* he scowled. *Jerry, there's a world full of busybodies out there. There'll be protests, there'll be cries for an investigation, there'll be people with signs. Accusing me of playing God. I'll spend the rest of my life trying to reassure the idiots that there's no moral dimension to what we're doing.*

I thought about that for several minutes and asked him if he was sure there wasn't.

He smiled at me. It was that same grin you got from him when you'd overlooked some obvious detail and he was trying to be magnanimous while simultaneously showing you what a halfwit you are. "Jerry," he said, "what have we done other than to provide life for thousands of generations of intelligent creatures? If anything, we should be commended."

Eons passed. Tens of thousands of subjective years, and the settlements went nowhere. We knew they were fighting; we could see the results. Burned out villages, heaps of corpses. Nothing as organized as a war, of course. Just local massacres. But no sign of a city. Not anywhere.

Maybe they weren't as bright as we thought. Local conflicts don't stop the rise of civilization. In fact there's reason to think they're a necessary factor. Anyhow, it was about this time that Mac's plane went down. Abe was hit pretty hard. But he insisted on plunging ahead. I asked whether we would want to replace him, but he said he didn't think it would be necessary. For the time being, we had all the capability we needed.

"We have to intervene," he said.

I waited to hear him explain.

"Language," he added. "We have to solve the language problem."

"What language problem?" I asked.

"We need to be able to talk to them."

The capability already existed to leave a message. No, Phil, we didn't have the means to show up physically and conduct a conversation. But we could deposit something for them to find. If we could master the languages.

"What do you intend to do?" I asked.

He was standing by a window gazing down at Crestview, with its single large street, its lone traffic light, Max's gas station at the edge of town, the Roosevelt School, made from red brick and probably built about 1920. "Tell me, Jerry," he said, "Why can none of these creatures make a city?"

I had no idea.

One of the species had developed a written language. Of sorts. But that was as far as they'd gotten. We'd thought that would be a key, but even after the next few thousand local years, nothing had happened.

"I'll tell you what I think," Abe said. "They haven't acquired the appropriate domestic habits. They need an ethical code. Spouses who are willing to sacrifice for each other. A sense of responsibility to offspring. And to their community."

"And how would you propose to introduce those ideas, Abe?" I should have known what was coming.

TUCKER'S GROVE

KEVIN J. ANDERSON

IN THE HEARTLAND.
BLOOD FLOWS AND
SHADOWS RISE

"We have a fairly decent model to work with," he said. "Let's give them the Commandments."

I don't know if I mentioned it, but he was moderately eccentric. No, that's not quite true. It would be closer to the mark to say that, for a world-class physicist, he was unusual in that he had a wide range of interests. Women were around the lab all the time, although none was ever told what we were working on. As far as I knew. He enjoyed parties, played in the local bridge tournaments. The women loved him. Don't know why. He wasn't exactly good-looking. But he was forever trying to sneak someone out in the morning as I was pulling in.

He was friendly, easy-going, a *sports* fan, for God's sake. You ever know a physicist who gave a damn about the Red Sox? He'd sit there and drink beer and watch games off the dish.

When he mentioned the Commandments, I thought he was joking.

"Not at all," he said. And, after a moment's consideration: "And I think we can keep them pretty much as they are."

"Abe," I said, "what are we talking about? You're not trying to set yourself up as a god?" The question was only half-serious because I thought he might be on to something. He looked past me into some indefinable distance.

"At this stage of their development," he said, "they need something to hold them together. A god would do nicely. Yes, I think we should do precisely that." He smiled at me. "Excellent idea, Jerry." He produced a copy of the King James, flipped pages, made some noises under his breath, and looked up with a quizzical expression. "Maybe we *should* update them a bit."

"How do you mean?"

"'Thou shalt not hold any person to be a slave.'"

I had never thought about that. "Actually, that's not bad," I said.

"'Thou shalt not fail to respect the environment, and its creatures, and its limitations.'"

"Good." It occurred to me that Abe was off to a rousing start. "Maybe, 'Thou shalt not overeat.'"

He frowned and shook his head. "Maybe that last one's a bit much for primitives," he said. He pursed his lips and looked again at the leather-bound Bible.

"I don't see anything here we'll want let's stop with twelve."

"Okay."

"The Twelve Commandments."

"Okay," I said. "Let's try it."

"For Mac," he said. "We'll do it for Mac."

The worlds we'd been working with had all been numbered. He had a system in which the number designated location, age, salient characteristics. But you don't care about that. He decided, though, that the world we had chosen for our experiment should have a *name*. He decided on *Utopia*. Well, I thought, not yet. It had mountain ranges and broad seas and deep forests. But it also had lots of savages. Smart savages, but savages nonetheless.

We already had samples of one of the languages. That first night he showed them to me, and played recordings. It was a musical language, rhythmic, with a lot of vowels and, what do you call them, diphthongs. Reminded me of a Hawaiian chant. But he needed a linguistic genius to make it intelligible.

He called a few people, told them he was conducting an experiment, trying to determine how much data was necessary to break in and translate the text of a previously unknown language. Hinted it had something to do with SETI. The people on the other end were all skeptical of the value of such a project, and he pretended to squirm a bit but he was offering lots of cash and a bonus for the correct solution. So everybody had a big laugh before coming on board.

The winner was a woman at the University of Montreal. Kris Edward. Kris came up with a solution in *five* days. I'd have thought it was impossible. A day later she'd translated the Commandments for him into the new language. Ten minutes after he'd received her transmission, we were driving over to Caswell Monuments in the next town to get the results chiseled onto two stone tablets. Six on each. They looked *good*. I'll give him that. They had dignity. Authority. *Majesty*.

We couldn't actually transport the tablets, the Commandments, physically to Utopia. But we *could* relay their image, and their substance, and reproduce them out of whatever available granite there might be. Abe's intention was to put them on a mountain-

e directed lightning to draw
to find them. It all had to
system, because as I said the
e much too quick for anyone
the least, skeptical. But Abe
that we were on track at last.
e way back with the tablets.
Maybe we should have taken
that as a sign. Anynow, by the time we'd arranged
to get picked up, and got the tire changed, and had
dinner, it had gotten fairly late. Abe was trying to
be casual, but he was anxious to start. "No, Jerry," he
said, "we are not going to wait until morning. Let's
get this parade on the road." So we set the tablets
in the scanner and sent the transmission out. It was
9:46 p.m. on the twelfth. The cylinder flashed amber lamps, and then green, signaling success, it had
worked, the package had arrived at its destination.
Moments later we got more blinkers, confirming
that the storm had blown up to draw the shaman
onto the mountain.

We looked for results a few minutes later. It would
have been time, on the other side, to build the pyra-
mids, conquer the Mediterranean, fight off the Van-
dals, get through the Dark Ages, and move well into
the Renaissance. If it had worked, we could expect
to see glittering cities and ships and maybe even 747s.
What we saw, however, were only the same dead-
end settlements.

We resolved to try again in the morning. Maybe
Moses had missed the tablets. Maybe he'd not been
feeling well. Maybe the whole idea was crazy.

That was the night the quake hit.

That's stable ground up in that part of the world.
It was the first earthquake in Crestview's recorded
history. Moreover, it didn't hit anything else. Not
Charlie's Bar & Grill, which is at the bottom of the
hill on the state road. Not any part of the Adams
Ranch, which occupied the area on the north, not
any part of the town, which is less than a half mile
away. But it completely destroyed the lab.

What's that? Did it destroy the cosm? No, the
cosm was safely disconnected from the state of Colorado. Nothing could touch it, except through the
cylinder. It's still out there somewhere. On its own.

But the whole thing scares me. I mean, Mac was
already dead. And two days later Sylvia drove into
the tree at about sixty.

That's okay, you can smile about it, but I'm not
sleeping very well. What's that? Why would God
pick on us? I don't know. Maybe he didn't like
the idea of someone doing minor league creations.
Maybe he resented our monkeying around with the
Commandments.

Why do you think he didn't say anything to Moses about slavery? What, you've never thought about
it? I wonder if maybe, at the beginning, civilization
needs slaves to get started. Maybe you can't just
jump off the mark with representative democracy.
Maybe we were screwing things up, condemning
sentient beings to thousands of years of unnecessary
savagery. I don't know.

But that's my story. Maybe it's all coincidence.
The quake, the plane crash, Sylvia. I suppose stranger
things have happened. But it's scary, you know what
I mean?

Yeah, you think I'm exaggerating. I know the God
you believe in doesn't track people down and kill
them. But maybe the God you believe in isn't there.
Maybe the God who's actually running things is just
a guy in a laboratory in another reality. Somebody
who's a bit less congenial than Abe. And who has
better equipment.

Well, who knows?

The scotch is good, by the way. Thanks. And listen,
Phil, there's a storm blowing up out there. I don't
like to impose, but I wonder if I could maybe stay
the night?

Copyright © 2004 Cryptic, Inc.

Alex Shvartsman is a writer, translator and game designer, with more than 30 short stories to his credit. He recently edited the anthology *Unidentified Funny Objects.*

REQUIEM FOR A DRUID

by Alex Shvartsman

My job that morning was to banish a demon, but I was determined to finish my cup of coffee first.

I sipped my java in front of Demetrios' warehouse in Sunset Park, enjoying the panoramic view of the Manhattan skyline and the New York harbor. Next to me, Demetrios was shaking like a leaf.

"What in the world are you thinking, Conrad?" Demetrios spoke in his typical rapid-fire fashion. "You're just going to go in there, alone, to face this infernal thing? Without any help or backup from others at the Watch? Without even a priest? This is all kinds of crazy."

"I can handle it." I said, trying to project casual confidence. "You did ask for this to be resolved quickly, and it's not like I haven't dealt with an occasional demon before."

In fact, I've never even seen any demons. I'm not in any way equipped to deal with a supernatural being of that magnitude. That's the bad news. The good news is, I've never heard of a demon showing up in Brooklyn. Even if one arrived, it wouldn't be slumming in Demetrios' warehouse. And if, by some miracle, a major baddie decided to take up residence here, Demetrios wouldn't have survived the encounter long enough to come crying for my help. Something else was going on, but if the guy with a checkbook wanted to believe the job to be extremely dangerous, who was I to dissuade him?

"Quickly, yes," said Demetrios. "You wouldn't believe how far behind this has made us fall with the deliveries. My customers are screaming bloody murder. On top of everything, there's a shipment of Sumatran persimmons that is already beginning to rot. So I hope you really know what you're doing. I don't relish the thought of having to scrape what's left of you off the container walls."

"That's the Demetrios I know and love. Sentimental to the end. Here, hold this." I handed him the empty foam cup and headed for the entrance.

The warehouse was packed with every kind of package and crate imaginable. Huge metal shipping containers clustered in the center, with just enough room left to maneuver them in and out. Around the edges, mountains of smaller parcels occupied every available nook and cranny, arranged in an order apparent only to Demetrios and his staff. There was plenty of room to hide for whatever was haunting the building.

Since I didn't know what sort of trouble to expect, I brought as many weapons, charms, and amulets as I could carry without making my reliance on such tools apparent. I've made a lot more enemies than friends over the years and having any of them learn the truth would be incredibly dangerous.

Far as I know, I'm unique. Only one out of every 30,000 people is born gifted. They can See magic and cast it. I can See perfectly; casting is another story. Not even my superiors at the Watch know about my disability. I suspect they wouldn't keep me around if they ever found out. So I pretend to be a badass wizard and do my job well, giving no one cause to think otherwise. One day I hope to find a cure for my condition. Or, failing that, at least a damn good explanation.

I worked my way through the labyrinth of packages until I heard faint growling sounds emanating from a few aisles over. I pulled out a revolver loaded with silver bullets doused in holy water. Cliché, I know, but in my experience only the most effective solutions get to become clichés in the first place. Weapon drawn, I advanced slowly toward the noise. I turned the corner of a ceiling-high shelving unit stocked with wooden crates and found myself face to face with a Lovecraftian nightmare.

The creature was shaped like a ten-foot-tall bulldog, with several rows of jagged teeth protruding from its oversized mouth. It stared at me with cold fish eyes and emitted a low rumble from deep within its ugly as sin belly. Definitely not a demon. I smiled in relief as I studied the telltale shimmer barely visible around the critter's frame.

"Nice doggie," I told it as I rummaged through the inner pockets of my trench coat. Moving very slowly so as not to spook it, I withdrew a plastic pill bottle filled with orange powder.

"Want a treat?" I said in a soothing voice as I holstered the revolver and struggled momentarily with the childproof cover.

Annoyed with my apparent lack of desire to run away terrified, the critter let out a thunderous roar that, I hoped, Demetrios could hear outside. While it was busy posturing, I took a pair of quick steps forward and flung the contents of the pill bottle at its midsection.

The monstrous visage quivered, gradually losing its shape, and disappeared. At my feet lay a furry little animal that looked like an ugly koala bear, knocked out cold by the sleeping powder. The Sumatran changeling snoring on the ground before me was a harmless creature. Its kind project images of big, scary monsters in order to repel predators, but they're all bark and no bite. Poor thing must've gotten into the persimmon shipment and munched the long journey away, happy in the container full of its favorite snacks. The potent orange mix would keep the changeling dormant until I could get it to a buddy of mine at the Bronx Zoo who cared for a menagerie of supernatural animals.

I checked the rest of the building to make sure there were no more changelings. Also, just to be nosy. Demetrios ran the city's largest shipping company that handled arcane imports and I was always curious to know what he was up to. After a sufficient amount of time spent wandering the aisles I took off my trench coat and wrapped it gently around the changeling. Carrying the bundle under my arm, I exited the warehouse.

"That was one nasty hellspawn." I smiled at Demetrios, who was pacing nervously outside. "See, it even made me break a sweat."

"Is it gone now? Did you banish it?" he demanded.

"It will not be bothering you again," I said with utmost confidence.

Demetrios was thrilled to pay me handsomely for a morning's work, and all it cost me was a vial of sleeping powder. What's more, he would tell anyone who cared to listen about how I went one-on-one with a demon and won. So grows the legend of Conrad Brent.

When I drove off from Demetrios' parking lot, I noticed another car pulling into traffic behind me.

I was being followed by amateurs. The black Lincoln Town Car lingering in my rearview mirror had stalked me along the congested Brooklyn streets without any grace or subtlety. Its driver must have thought he was very clever, always keeping one or two vehicles between us. I made a few turns, just to be sure. The Lincoln stayed with me, conspicuous as a polar bear in the desert.

Sensing my concern, my car's various magical protections began to activate. To say that my car didn't look like much would be an understatement. It was an '84 Oldsmobile with crooked bumpers, a few months overdue for a car wash. On the inside though, it sported more nasty tricks than the Batmobile. It had the best defensive enchantments money could buy, and a few that were literally priceless. All of them woke up as the car prepared itself for a possible confrontation. Some of the arcane shields interfered with the radio, which only served to annoy me further. I pulled over and watched the Lincoln pull into a parking spot a few yards behind me.

I got out of the car, strolled over there, and tapped on the driver side tinted window.

"Hey there, chum. I got news for you: you aren't very good at this trailing thing. So either leave me alone and go back to picking up fares at the airport, or roll down this window and explain what it is you want."

The driver didn't respond. Instead, the passenger door opened and a petite redhead in a business suit climbed out.

"Don't frighten the help, Mr. Brent. He was simply doing his job." There was a healthy amount of amusement in her voice, as though she was delighted by this turn of events. She spoke with a hint of a British accent. Her looks and her voice were almost enough for me to forgive the imposition. Almost.

"Well," I grumbled, "he wasn't doing it very well."

"On the contrary," she said, "I intended for you to see us. I had no doubt that a man of your reputation would notice being followed. What I really wanted was to see how you'd handle it."

She offered me a business card. According to the fancy font her name was Moira O'Leary and she was a security consultant.

"Watching someone react to a perceived threat is very instructive. I like to learn as much as I can about the people I'm going to work with. I'll admit that your rather…direct approach was delightfully unexpected."

"I'm glad I managed to entertain you," I said, "but what makes you think we're going to be working together?"

"Oh, we will." She smiled. "Your boss owes my client a favor or two. I'm sure he'll be in touch with you shortly. He might even say 'pretty please.'"

Not bloody likely. Mose didn't have to say please because no one was foolish enough to question his orders. When he said jump, you jumped, and you didn't dare to ask how high.

"My organization isn't in the habit of owing favors. Your client must be pretty special," I said, fishing for a little more information. Turned out, Ms. Security Consultant wasn't going to make me guess.

"Of course he's special," she said sweetly. "He's Bradley Holcomb."

O'Leary wasn't kidding; people at the offices of the Watch were falling all over themselves to accommodate her real estate magnate boss. I was told to assist him in any way I could, with special emphasis on the fact that these orders came from Mose himself. I called the number on Moira's business card and was promptly summoned to Holcomb Tower.

I don't like venturing into Manhattan. It is the capital of Weird in the New World. Beings of immense power walk the streets beneath its gleaming skyscrapers. Terrible schemes are hatched behind closed doors in offices with prestigious addresses—and I'm not just talking about the Wall Street financiers. Dangerous men, women, and creatures of all kinds congregate there, and they make Brooklyn feel like a sleepy suburb. I try to keep my visits into the Big Apple's rotten core brief and infrequent. But, sometimes, things can't be helped.

I was ushered into a large office furnished with a mismatched collection of items of art and antiquity. They may not have fit together particularly well, but they all shared one common trait: hefty price tags. A supersized mahogany desk was installed in the center of the room. Leaning back in a lambskin office chair was the man himself.

Bradley Holcomb, real estate king of New York, reality TV host, and—at least in his own mind—a curator of the upwardly mobile lifestyle. His name, slapped indiscriminately on everything from condo developments to cologne, was the gilded standard for the bourgeoisie. Even surrounded by the opulence of his office, Holcomb looked less impressive in person than he did on TV. They always do.

"Mr. Brent," he said, studying me intently, "thank you for coming to see me on such short notice. Also, forgive me for staring. All kinds of important people visit my office, but I've never had the pleasure of meeting a wizard before. I imagined you to be…" He paused, looking for the right words to express his disappointment with my being so ordinary, "…older."

"In my experience people rarely live up to their hype," I said. Holcomb either chose to ignore the barb, or it went over his head. He continued to ogle me as though I was some kind of a circus freak.

"What is it I can do for you, Mr. Holcomb?" I prodded.

"I've been working on a fascinating project," he said, snapping out of it. "I acquired a nice plot of land adjacent to Marine Park. Beautiful space. Naturally secluded, yet right off of Belt Parkway, so it's easy to reach. I'm building a high-end theme resort there. Gonna make the place look like ancient Rome."

Holcomb's face lit up and his entire demeanor shifted when he started talking about his hotel. He became almost likable.

"It'll be a perfect combination of classic style and ultra-modern amenities. I'm even building a miniature copy of the Coliseum, with a boxing ring in the center. Holcomb's Rome is going to make theme hotels in Vegas and Atlantic City look like gaudy McMansions in comparison."

I nodded patiently. Holcomb would know a thing or two about gaudy.

"It took forever to get the permits," he said. "But once construction began, strange things started to happen. Floor plans went missing from a locked safe. Every worker on the demolition crew simultaneously came down with terrible headaches. Sabotage of all kinds has been derailing the project."

Holcomb reached for a stress ball on his desk and squeezed it, hard.

"I'm a practical man, not taken to flights of fancy. When it was first suggested to me that my problems were supernatural in origin, I laughed it off. But I'm not laughing any longer. I tripled security, accomplishing exactly nothing. Then a business associate recommended that I hire O'Leary as an arcane consultant. She was the one who filled me in on the crazy stuff going on in the world that we muggles aren't supposed to know about."

"We prefer to call you ungifted," I said.

"Whatever works," said Holcomb. "O'Leary told me about the Watch and helped me get in touch with Mr. Mose. It wasn't all that difficult to persuade him. Money, it seems, can buy magic just like any other service."

Mose must've charged this arrogant fat cat through the nose to make me do house calls like some sort of a plumber. Still, someone was using magic to mess with the ungifted—exactly the kind of thing the Watch was created to guard against. The fact that the victim was Holcomb didn't obviate my obligation to look into the matter.

"All right," I said. "Fetch whatever maps and floor plans for this thing that weren't stolen from your safe and let's take a look."

Perched between Marine Park and the coastline of Deep Creek was one of the last undeveloped areas remaining in the borough of Brooklyn. Thousands of people drove past it every day, commuting via the always-busy Belt Parkway. There was no off-ramp by Marine Park. Drivers could only marvel from afar at the glimpses of primordial wilderness and the scenic view of the Atlantic.

Holcomb would change that. His plans called for building an Exit 10 off Belt Parkway, which would deliver travelers right to his new hotel's front door. For now, I had to drive all the way to the Flatbush Avenue exit, park at the Gateway Marina, and walk.

I spent several unpleasant hours slogging around Holcomb's construction site. Whoever was messing with the project was thorough, devious, and definitely supernatural. Signs of arcane interfer-

ence were everywhere. Tree trunks had runes carved into their bark, enchantments spun like shimmering spider webs hung from the tree branches, and stones covered with glyphs were spread along the sandy beach. An ancient magic was at work, intent on disrupting the construction. It was effective and considerably unpleasant, but never lethal.

This magic was different from the types I'd encountered in the past. I was clueless as to what manner of creature was protecting its territory, but had a pretty good idea of how to flush it out. I set to disarming the trickster traps and clearing the area of supernatural hindrances.

It was slow going. With no magic of my own, I had to rely on various arcane tools. Each action that any other gifted could perform by merely flexing their abilities was taking me minutes of careful tinkering with artifacts that operated on other people's stored power. My feet got wet and the bottom of my trench coat was caked with mud. I cursed as the wild shrubs scraped against my skin. There's a reason I choose to live in an urban environment. I'll take a paved road over a grassy path any day of the week.

"You shouldn't do that."

I was knee-deep in disrupting a particularly elaborate enchantment when a voice caught me by surprise. I spun around to see who managed to sneak up on me. It was a man in his late forties, dressed in an earth-tone windbreaker, tough khaki pants, and hiking boots. He was far better prepared for an excursion to this area than I.

"Don't break it," he said. "Do you have any idea how much effort goes into weaving an enchantment like this one? It'll take us weeks to repair all the damage you've caused today."

"Repair?" I said. "Oh no, no. We can't have that. The Watch takes a dim view of magic being used against the ungifted."

"I know who you are and what you represent, Mr. Brent," said the stranger. "My people have deep respect for the Watch. It is a grave disappointment that you choose to side against us."

"Back up for a moment," I said. "I'm not picking any sides. I don't even know who or what I'm dealing with, and I don't like that one bit. Care to bring me up to speed?"

"My name is Graeme Murray. I sit on the ruling council of the Circle of the Sacred Oak." He saw a blank expression on my face and elaborated: "We're druids, Mr. Brent."

I displayed my encyclopedic and brilliant command of history: "I thought druids were, you know, extinct?"

"There are still a few of us around, carrying on the traditions of our forefathers. Walk with me, Mr. Brent, and I will endeavor to, as you put it, bring you up to speed." The druid headed deeper into the brush. I followed him, the still-active enchantment threads glowing faintly behind us.

"My people ruled the British Isles since the beginning of history," said Murray. "Openly at first, then behind the scenes, after the Romans came. But things were changing. With time, our numbers and influence began to wane. To make matters worse, the ruling council got us mired in a war against the Cabal in the 1700s."

I'd heard about the Cabal before. It was a shady organization of European mystics and sorcerers. They were vastly powerful in the Victorian era and still influential in modern day. The Watch and Cabal had butted heads many a time in the past.

"The Cabal devastated us. Druids were hunted in Britain and Ireland like common criminals. Siobhan Keane, one of the few on the ruling council to oppose the war, gathered her remaining loyalists and set sail for the New World."

We walked toward the far end of the property, near the edge of Marine Park.

"Druids share a bond with the land; most would rather die than abandon their sacred groves. To convince so many to leave the British Isles, to begin life anew elsewhere, was a gargantuan feat. Siobhan Keane wasn't merely a leader—she was our founder, our savior, as important to us as Jesus and Mohammed are to their followers."

We arrived at a small clearing, surrounded by ancient oak trees overgrown with mistletoe.

"This," said Murray "is Siobhan Keane's final resting place. It's the one sacred site for my people in exile, and we'll do whatever we have to in order to prevent anyone—gifted or ungifted—from bulldozing it down."

The two of us stood quietly for a moment and listened as the Atlantic breeze rustled the yellowing leaves in nature's requiem for the queen of the druids.

It took some doing, but I managed to set up a meeting between Holcomb and the druids.

We sat in the conference room of a nondescript hotel by the airport. Holcomb probably didn't feel comfortable inviting a bunch of hostile gifted into his home office. He wouldn't even take my calls, leaving it up to O'Leary to handle the preliminary negotiations. The man was a big fan of delegating, at least according to his reality TV show. To her credit, O'Leary got him to consider the druids' side of things enough to come meet with the ruling council of the Circle of the Sacred Oak.

Six rather ordinary-looking men and women, my new pal Graeme among them, sat around the large oval table broadcasting various degrees of annoyance, frustration and overall bad karma. Holcomb was running late. Really late. The druid leaders didn't appreciate being made to wait. Several of them took to shooting venomous glances my way, as though the real estate mogul's tardiness was somehow my fault. I kept a neutral expression, hating every minute of it.

After what felt like hours, the conference room door finally swung open to admit Moira O'Leary and a dozen grim-looking men. They fanned out in a semi-circle, taking positions against the walls and blocking the entrance. Every one of them was gifted and every one of them was heavily armed. They aimed their weapons at the druids.

"What is the meaning of this?" demanded a councilman. "Where is Holcomb?"

"He won't be coming," O'Leary said. "Mr. Holcomb has left it up to me to deal with this nuisance." She turned her attention to me. "I want to thank you, Conrad, for flushing out the pagan scum. We'll take it from here. You should leave. Now."

The double-dealing, two-faced mercenary had played me. And I was just beginning to like her.

"These people are here to negotiate." I remained seated, so O'Leary and her goons couldn't see me searching through the pockets of my coat. "You

"Entertaining" —*The Denver Post*

"A suspenseful scientific mystery and a good adventure story" —*Science Fiction Chronicle*

FORTRESS
on the
SUN

PAUL COOK
Author of *The Engines of Dawn*

"Cook turns the tension up...well worth reading" —*Locus*

wouldn't want to jeopardize that with some sort of a rash vigilante action."

O'Leary laughed.

"Rash? We've been hunting their kind for centuries. Don't let the nature-loving act fool you. They are terrorists, ruthless killers of women and children. They've waged a guerilla war against the Cabal for several hundred years, and their hands are elbow-deep in blood."

So she was a Cabal agent, and the hate in her voice sounded genuine. I wished I hadn't gotten out of bed that morning.

"Our faction wants no part of your war," said Graeme. "Our ancestors traveled across the ocean so that we could live at peace."

"These people are civilians, Moira. Look at them. They didn't try to hurt Holcomb's workers and they're certainly no threat to the Cabal." I smiled and waved my right hand, palm out. "Come on. You know these aren't the druids you're looking for."

No one even chuckled. So much for diffusing the situation with humor.

"Do keep in mind that these negotiations are guaranteed by the Watch. I'm sure both of us would rather avoid the possibility of friction between our organizations?"

O'Leary was having none of that. "We have no quarrel with your band of do-gooders, so long as you stay out of our way. You're free to go and play at policeman somewhere else. But if you stay, you die with them."

The smart move would've been to take her up on her offer. I had no business interfering in a centuries-old war. Besides, what chance did I have against a dozen gifted? Yet, I couldn't bring myself to walk out and leave six innocent people to their doom. After years of making careful, calculated decisions I surprised myself by abandoning caution and following my gut.

"You really shouldn't have called me a cop," I said, rising from the chair. "It upsets me."

Before anyone could react I drew a pencil-thin turquoise glass vial from one of my pockets and threw it as hard as I could against the wall.

The vial shattered, unleashing a Chinook wind bottled inside. Powerful gusts wreaked havoc in the confines of the room. Hurricane-like currents lift-ed people and chairs from the ground. Intense fog made it impossible to see beyond arm's length. The air had become hot and moist, as though someone had run a long, steamy shower.

The pandemonium around me kept the bad guys busy and gave me a chance to set up a portal. Transportation magic is unreliable and takes at least a dozen heartbeats to activate. What's worse, a portal charm is only good for a single one-way trip and very difficult to replace. I winced as I activated it, but using up a prized possession was better than facing a Cabal army.

Someone managed to open the conference room door and the Chinook swooshed out into the hallway. As the fog began to dissipate, everyone could see a portal the size of a manhole cover floating a few feet above the floor.

"Go!" I shouted at the druids while ripping a golden bracelet off my wrist. The action triggered a force barrier, cutting off the other half of the room. That particular toy was reusable, but it would take four lunar months to recharge. This mess was costing me dearly.

Druids stumbled toward the portal but the Cabal mages got their act together. They unleashed a coordinated attack on the barrier and within seconds it began to collapse. I desperately tried to think of a way to buy us more time but had no trinkets capable of stopping a dozen hostile gifted working in concert.

A druid woman in her early fifties turned around. In a few steps she was at the barrier, touching it lightly with her fingertips. Her entire body began to shimmer as she worked her own magic. Infused with whatever power she lent it, the barrier strengthened despite the continued attack from the other side. She appeared calm, almost serene, but I could see the new wrinkles appear on her face and her hair visibly turning gray as she gave up her life force to maintain the barrier.

The rest of the druids were through the portal now. It was beginning to wobble and would dissipate soon. I took one last look at the woman who did not hesitate for even a moment before choosing to sacrifice herself in order to save her people. A small part of me wanted to stay, to fight and probably die alongside her once the barrier failed, but I knew better. I was no hero. I was just a guy with a few arcane gadgets and lots of bravado.

I hurled myself into the portal, fervently hoping that its erratic magic wouldn't teleport me into a concrete wall.

The portal spat me out in a parking lot. The five druids were just getting their bearings when I arrived. Graeme helped me up.

"Thank you," he said as I brushed dust off my coat. "It seems you've chosen a side after all."

"Couldn't just walk out on you lot. Would've been bad for my reputation."

We watched the portal flicker and finally collapse. No one else would be coming through.

"They got Alice," said one of the druids, tears rolling down his cheeks. "This can't be left unanswered."

"We must gather everyone," said another. "Sound the call. We will march to the Holcomb Tower and bring it down on the treacherous bastard's head."

"Hold on," I said. "Holcomb isn't gifted. He told me that, until a week ago, he didn't even know that our kind existed. I don't buy him as a member of the Cabal."

"You only have his word for that," said Graeme.

"I've watched this guy on TV," I said. "He isn't that good a liar. I bet O'Leary set up the trap by herself and never even told him about you."

"We will rip the truth out of him," growled another druid. Everyone began to speak at once. The druids were primed to take some sort of action, anything to avenge Alice and lash out at their persecutors. Then my phone rang, and O'Leary's number displayed on the caller ID.

"Yeah," I grunted, taking a few steps away from the druids. Bent on their revenge plans, they barely noticed.

"That was very impressive," O'Leary said with that hint of cheerful amusement in her voice I would find endearing had she not just betrayed and then tried to kill me. "I suppose I should have expected no less."

"What do you want?" For once, I wasn't in a mood for banter.

"I assume you're still with the druids," said O'Leary. "I want you to pass along a message. We'll be waiting for them at the tomb of their precious founder. If they don't show by sunset, we'll burn down the trees, demolish the stones, then dig up her grave and spend a fun evening coming up with ways to desecrate the remains."

"That's a big mistake," I told her. "You and your people should leave town, before the Watch stomps on you, hard."

"Nonsense," she said. "Mose will never get the Watch involved. After all, the druids were the ones picking on the ungifted. I'm merely trying to set things right on behalf of Mr. Holcomb. Whatever other disagreements my organization may have with the druids falls well outside of the Watch's purview."

I said nothing, hating the fact that she was right.

"I suspect," she went on, "that Mose won't be too pleased with you for siding with them just now. So why don't you be a good boy and give the tree huggers my message. They won't be able to resist trying to protect their sacred swamp and we'll mop 'em up. Everybody wins. Mose doesn't even have to know about your error in judgment. What do you say?"

"I'll pass the message along," I conceded. "This isn't over."

She started to say something snide, but I ended the call.

I relayed the message to the druids and contemplated my next move. There were less than four hours of daylight remaining.

O'Leary's plan was working perfectly. Compelled to defend what they believed in, the druids showed up in force, like so many lambs to slaughter. Nearly thirty men and women joined their leaders in an effort to protect their sacred ground. They were all gifted—but they were no warriors, and no match for the hardened Cabal mercenaries.

I walked with them, prodding along a prisoner. By my side, disheveled and dragging his Italian loafers through the brown mud, was Bradley Holcomb.

Moira O'Leary and her people waited for us at Siobhan Keane's gravesite. There were nearly three dozen Cabal fighters this time, weapons and magic at the ready. They parted to let our procession approach.

"I've got your boss," I told O'Leary once we reached the clearing. I shoved Holcomb back into the arms of several druids. "If any fighting takes place here, I'll make sure he's among the first to die. So, why don't we talk things out instead?"

"You're a fool," said O'Leary. "And a desperate fool, at that. I heard that you abducted Holcomb from his office in broad daylight. Talk about abusing the ungifted! And for what? Did you really think that saving his skin would get me to back off? Now that we've lured out the druids, Holcomb is useless to me."

Bradley Holcomb straightened up, stepped forward and looked down his nose at O'Leary.

"You were right, Mr. Brent," he said. "It appears my arcane security consultant never had my best interests at heart after all."

"Moira," Holcomb said with as much aplomb and dignity as he could muster under the circumstances. "You're fired!"

That was all we needed to hear. Holcomb stepped back into the relative safety of the cluster of druids and four of my fellow members of the Watch dropped their concealment spell. I would take any two of them against all the Cabal goons present. Together they were an overwhelming force that should make any sensible gifted think twice.

Cabal agent Moira O'Leary wasn't the sensible type.

O'Leary signaled her men to attack. The tranquil burial site turned into a war zone. Fireballs, curses and bullets flew as both sides unleashed everything they had at each other.

Terrie Winter of Queens wielded an enchanted staff so powerful you could physically feel the presence of its magic. She moved gracefully, jabbing at enemies and dodging their attacks in fluid, ballet-like motion.

Father Mancini from Staten Island held a large silver cross with sharpened edges in one hand and a .44 Magnum revolver in another. He had no trouble reconciling his arcane ability with his faith, and Lord help any gifted sinner who got in his way. The good priest stood his ground, striking down any Cabal fighters within reach while quoting scripture.

Gord from the Bronx stood seven feet tall, courtesy of the giant blood somewhere deep in his family's Romany past. He carried a sawed-off shotgun that could blast through any obstacle, physical or magic. Gord fired off a few shots, and then took sev-

eral large strides that placed him in the midst of the enemy. He used his shotgun as a club, tossing men around like rag dolls.

Manhattan's John Smith stood empty-handed and smiled nastily at his enemies, his own magic far more powerful than any mere weapon. Elegant in a three-piece Armani suit and a white silk scarf tied around his neck which contrasted smartly against his ebony skin, John cast spell after spell, conjuring ephemeral horrors. They materialized in the air, swooping from above to maul the Cabal mages with their ghostly fangs and claws.

I used whatever protective charms and devices I had to keep Holcomb and myself out of harm's way, but my supplies were running out fast, and Cabal mages were about to corner us. Suddenly, a ten-foot monster appeared before them, gnashing its teeth and growling loud enough to be heard over the sounds of the fighting. Cabal goons took a good look at it and decided that they were needed elsewhere on the battlefield.

I would have to recapture the Sumatran changeling after this was over.

Unable to defend against the far superior talents of the Watch, those Cabal fighters who could still move broke ranks and fled. I watched O'Leary and a handful of her people escape through a portal similar to the one I used earlier. After being routed so thoroughly, I didn't expect to be seeing her again anytime soon.

"Guess this means you owe each of us one, for a change," said Father Mancini afterward.

"That," added Terrie Winter, "and you're the one who has to explain this mess to Mose. He won't be pleased about being kept out of the loop. I think I'll go ahead and skip that meeting entirely."

Reporting to Mose wasn't something I looked forward to. This was definitely one of those scenarios where asking forgiveness was easier than asking permission. The big man wouldn't have approved—and my theory about Moira becoming fair game for the Watch once Holcomb severed his connection with her was tenuous at best. Still, everything worked out, and Mose wasn't the type to punish success.

I walked over to Graeme and the rest of the council. Holcomb was talking at them faster than a used car salesman.

"It's gonna be great," he said. "Just picture it: Holcomb's Stonehenge! We'll build a replica of those standing stones instead of the Coliseum. Make the hotel druid-themed. We'll leave this shrine alone, and fence it off from the tourists. Your people can come and go whenever they please, and no one will be the wiser."

Holcomb was actually making sense. The druids must've thought so too; they were listening intently to what the real estate mogul had to say. After all, who would suspect one of Holcomb's resorts to be anything more than it appeared? Besides, Holcomb's legal ownership of the site would help secure the Watch's protection in case the Cabal ever decided to take another run at the druids.

I left them to talk business. Holcomb might not have been gifted, but he was sure good at his job. The man was about to convince an ancient order to let him build a theme resort around their sacred site. And if that sort of salesmanship doesn't take a bit of magic, I don't know what does.

Original (First) Publication
Copyright © 2013 by Alex Shvartsman

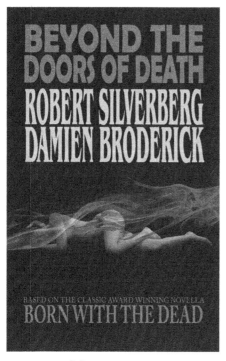

May 31, 2013
Trade Paperback, Kindle Nook, More
Pre-order on Amazon.com

Steven Leigh, who also writes under the pen name of S. L. Farrell, is the author of more than 25 novels published by such major houses as Ace, Avon, DAW, Harper Voyager, Bantam, and Roc.

THE BRIGHT SEAS OF VENUS

by Stephen Leigh

I hate you.

Mine is a hatred that is complete and without any reservation. That's all you really need to know. Yes, I know, "hate" is an overused word that is too generic to have much meaning, and no *real* writer would use it, but I could dump out the thesaurus and find other, more specific words that you may substitute, if you wish: abhor, loathe, detest, despise, execrate, abominate, am repulsed by, feel revulsion for…Choose one if you prefer, but the bottom line's the same.

I hate you.

You know it, too, because you feel the same way toward me. We're locked in mutual antipathy, mutual enmity (there's that thesaurus again; I know how much you love word games). If I were standing right in front of you right now, you'd be nodding your head, thinking "Oh, it's *you*. Yeah, I know exactly what you mean, you asshole."

But right now I imagine you're actually blinking a bit in confusion. You're looking back at the title and the byline and wondering what the hell's going on. Where's the promised "Bright Seas of Venus"? Did the magazine get screwed up somehow?

You stupid idiot. I *know* you. I know you don't buy print magazines anymore. Everything you read is online. E-text. Downloaded. You read on your laptop, on your phone, on your tablet. You prefer phosphor dots on a screen, not ink on actual paper. And the e-world, well, as you know (or you will recall once you figure out who's actually writing this, because it's sure not that "Stephen Leigh" hack), the online world is my area of expertise. It wasn't particularly easy, mind you, but it also wasn't impossible. All I had to do was watch you—no, don't bother looking over your shoulder; I'm not there now—and figure out when you were going to download this particular magazine, and run my little program. *Poof!* There goes "The Bright Seas of Venus"—which, by the way, is an incredibly mediocre story without any redeeming literary value; I have to believe that the editor bought it only because this Leigh guy is a friend of his—and that eminently forgettable but sadly much longer story is replaced with this one. *My* story. Which, incidentally, you're the only one reading, as everyone else who is looking at this issue gets to read the tedious "The Bright Seas of Venus." At least that's what happened assuming the program worked as planned. I can't imagine any of the readers who are stuck with the original story are enjoying themselves as much as I am. For a single good reason.

I fucking hate you.

Oh, you're having a few thoughts *now*, aren't you? You're going over all the people you know who might just have the technical expertise to do what I just mentioned. You're running down the list of names, and you're frowning because you don't think any of them actually *hate* you. They might not *like* you, but *hate*…?

C'mon, give me some credit. I'm much more subtle than that. You remember the time when we were all together at the holiday party, and you made that nasty crack about me and the way I look? Everyone's eyes widened a little, because the comment went way over the line into intentional cruelty (not that you noticed; you thought you were being extraordinarily witty), but did I allow myself to show my anger? Did I snarl and tell you just what a goddamn jerk you were being? Did I tell you how you have no goddamn clue what I am and what someone like me is capable of?

No, I didn't. Instead, I swallowed all the bile. I waved my hand in your direction and laughed it off, which allowed everyone else to laugh also. Then you proceeded to further reveal your bigotry, close-mindedness, and general asshollery for the rest of the night. Remember how, one by one, everyone drifted away from you and stopped making eye contact while you were walking around the room trying to force your way into conversations? Here's why:

It seems most everyone who gets close enough to you ends up with a universal dislike of you as a human being. But me…I straight-out hate you.

I suppose the final straw was the time you saw me with that fantasy and horror anthology. You pointed at the book and laughed your hideous laugh so that everyone else turned to see what was so funny. "What a bunch of stupid crap," you said. "Science fiction, fantasy…Shit like that is made for readers who aren't intellectually capable of processing or appreciating genuine literature. It's cotton candy; pure empty calories and when you try to find substance in it, it just melts away. The entire genre's nothing but escapist garbage for those who are stuck in their adolescence. How can anyone with any intelligence believe any of that stuff? Vampires, zombies, and, monsters—oh my!" You nearly sing the words. "None of it's *real*."

"Maybe not, but I still enjoy reading it," I answered, lifting up the book as I gave you a last opportunity to step back from your comments, to realize how insulting and pretentious you were acting. Giving you the opportunity to apologize.

You laughed again. "Well, I'd expect *you* would," you answered.

Once more, you demonstrated that despite your judgments and mockery, you don't know me. Not at all.

Oh, I shrugged and went on without another remark, but I smiled inside. You see, by then I already knew the truth about you. I'd already hacked into your accounts. I knew the type of reading you preferred yourself—after all, you'd ordered the same book I was then holding (though in e-book form) just a week before. I knew that as much as you protested how wonderful "real" literature was, it also wasn't what you chose to read yourself.

I knew that everything about you was a useless, pretentious, arrogant lie.

I hate you…but you know that already at this point. I suppose there's no reason to keep repeating it.

By now, you're undoubtedly wondering why I keep going on about how I feel about you and where I'm going with this. Fine. Let's end the tale. In fact, I think you already have a premonition of how things turn out.

You're already starting to feel it, aren't you? It's subtle at first, almost unnoticeable: the feeling that someone's staring at you from shadows behind you, their gaze burrowing into your shoulder blades. Then the sense intensifies. You hear a creaking—what *was* that? A stealthy footstep? Your mouth has gone dry and you can't gather enough spit to swallow. You want to laugh your horrible, mocking laugh again, but you can't quite manage it.

Now comes a quick prickling rush along your spine that makes you want to shiver, a feeling so intense that you're afraid to even turn around to dispel the notion. You can nearly imagine hands reaching out for you: terrible, clawed, deformed things ready to rend and tear, to lay you open to the white bones as your blood sprays. You've read those stories, right? Then the smell hits you: a whiff of sulphur and rot and decay that slides past you like a cold, dead breath. But you keep reading these words, because now you're shaking and afraid that if you stop, you'll find out that your growing unease isn't entirely caused by the words you're reading.

You hear the beginnings of my sinister, amused chuckle, and you *know*…

Fantasy—at least the dark, horrific, and nasty kind—is all too real.

And it hates you.

Robert T. Jeschonek is a prolific author of short stories and articles, and has four novels to his credit, including the recent National Literature Award winner *My Favorite Band Does Not Exist.*

THE SPINACH CAN'S SON

by Robert T. Jeschonek

I am the can of spinach in a sailor man's hand. He squeezes, expecting me to burst open and launch a blob of green power into his gaping maw.

But I do not burst. He gets no mouthful of spinach, no surge of energy pumping up his arms to three times their size. That's not how it works on this side of the tracks, my friend.

You're not in the funny pages anymore.

Potpie the Sailor tries again with both hands, straining for all he's worth. "C'mon, ya ratfinsk!" He squints up at the threat looming before him, the whole reason he needs his spinach. "We've gotsk to drive this *she-hag* off me boat!"

What threat could be awful enough to strike fear in the sailor man's heart? Is it Bobo the comic-strip bully, back for another knock-down, drag-out?

Not even close.

The figure standing before Potpie and me isn't a drawing at all. There's nothing pen-and-ink about her. "Sir!" She's a three-dimensional woman in what looks like a spacesuit out of a 1950s movie—silver metallic tights and a bubble helmet. Her black hair is arranged in tight waves beneath the glass. "Please, calm down! I just want to ask you some questions." She pulls a photo out of a pouch on the belt slung diagonally over her hips. "Have you seen this man?"

"Never seen 'im before in me lifesk!" Potpie squeezes me harder than ever. I try my best to help, pushing from within, for one simple reason.

I recognize the man in the picture, with his dark brown hair and square-jawed features. I know him like I know my own self, in fact.

Because he *is* myself. Myself in another life.

And I know her, too. Her name is Molly. She's my wife.

And I know why she's after me.

"Take another look, please," she says. "It's urgent that I find him."

Potpie shifts the corncob pipe from one side of his mouth to the other without ever touching it. "I ain't seen him, she-hag!" He shakes a fist at her. "Now putsk 'em up!"

Molly takes a step toward him. "You're sure you haven't seen him?"

Potpie scrambles backward, knocking over a stack of spinach crates. Crying out, he puts me to the only use he can think of—hurling me right at her.

Molly ducks, and I go sailing over her head. It's not a clean getaway, though; the bracelet on her wrist starts beeping as I pass.

Here in the Underfunnies, I'm an anomaly, a deformity in the panel geography—the panelography—and her equipment has detected me.

Good thing a true Panelnaut like me can swim the currents here like a dolphin through water. Focusing my energies, I dive deep into the sea of words and images, hunting a good place to resurface.

Found it. I cross the borders in full flight and land with a shock that takes my breath away.

This time, I am the brick in the hand of a mouse.

I bounce lightly in his grip as he jounces along through a strange landscape, surrounded by abstract objects straight out of a surrealist painting. He gives off a thick smell of stinky cheese and whistles a jaunty tune from his pointy gray snout.

I know him well—Ixnay the Mouse. Once again, I've gravitated toward my favorite stomping grounds, the panelography of the early 20th century. In this case, the *Hazy Kat* strip.

Or should I say, the *Underfunnies* version of that strip. The reverse of it, the flip side where things don't work the way they should. The negative space that accrues in the collective unconscious of the readership around these tiny, panel-bound stories. The land of things unsaid and hopes unrealized.

For each time Potpie the sailor pops open a can, gobbles the spinach, and beats up the bully, we know in our hearts there must be times when the can doesn't open. That's just the way life works. And our expectations create this flip-side place that until recently no one knew about.

I am a Panelnaut, an explorer of this place. Though "fugitive" might be a better word for what I've become.

"Boy," says Ixnay. "Have I got one cooked up for that idiot cat this time." He hops up on what looks like a warped sundial and calls out into the hot wind. "Oh, Haaazyyy!"

Without delay, the creature known as Hazy Kat comes bounding over the horizon. She's wearing a polka-dot scarf and matching tutu. "Comink, mine treasur-ed pession flour!"

"Make it snappy, willya?" hollers Ixnay. "Yer burnin' daylight here!"

Hazy flops to a stop in front of us and gapes with a love-struck goofy grin. "Dost Rumeo have a heart-wiltin' sonnet plucked out to make his Joliet swoon'st?"

"Ohh, yeah." Ixnay turns me over in his grip. "Ya ever hear of *iambrick pentameter*?"

Hazy claps her paws together and giggles. "But-ter 'course, o bard o' the mousehole! Hit me with that iambrick pentagrammer to yer li'l ol' heart's continent!"

"You asked for it." Ixnay hauls me back, ready to throw. "Be sure to notice the rhythmic counterpoint of strike and release. Or should I say the *opposite*?"

At that exact moment, Molly flashes to life between us and Hazy. The second she materializes, her bracelet starts beeping.

She points her wrist in my direction and nods. "I know you're here, Everett. You've figured out how to assume local forms, haven't you?" Watching the bracelet, she walks toward us. "You're inside the mouse, aren't you?"

Before Ixnay can say a word, Molly suddenly snaps backward. As she drops to the dusty ground, I see Hazy has her paws on her.

"You stays awake from my little Ixnay mouses!" Hazy flaps her paws like pancakes at Molly's helmet. "He is my preshiss poet and certifiable booblekins! Don't try steelin' his heart, you hussy!"

"Everett!" Molly shoves the cat away and scrambles to her feet. "I've come to talk to you! You sent me a message through the comic strips—our prearranged emergency signal! Don't pretend you didn't!"

She's right, I can't, because I sent it. But the signal wasn't a cry for help—it was bait. All part of the secret I've been keeping.

"I'm serious, Everett." Molly takes another step toward us. "I'll do what it takes to get through to you."

Ixnay just watches, juggling me from hand to hand. "Whoever this dame is, I gotta admit, I like her style."

Hazy, never much good in a fight, weakly bats at Molly's calves. "'Ev'ritt,' you say? Is that some other word for 'mouses'?"

"Shut up, cat!" says Molly. "Everett, listen…"

Ixnay's little mouse heart thumps like a big bass drum. It pushes out his chest in the shape of a cartoon heart as it throbs. "I think I'm in love!"

Naturally, this makes him raise me into throwing position again.

Molly sees the danger but doesn't stop talking. "It's time to come home, Everett. You can't keep running away." She spreads her arms wide. "We both miss him, Everett. But you can't make things right on your own."

I want to tell her how wrong she is, but I don't get the chance. Ixnay whips me at her glass-helmeted head before I can get the words out.

"Sech fe'rce percision!" says Hazy Kat. "His peshion must be deeper than I yimagined!"

As I blast toward her helmet, I focus my strength on changing course. Ixnay's throw is off, which helps; in the Underfunnies, things don't work the way they normally do, including his brick-pitching aim.

So I fly wide and hurtle on past, soaring through the ochre skies…casting my mind toward another refuge. I've gotten so good, I find one instantly, and I set my sights.

But I wait another moment to dive. Because the truth is, I'm not trying to lose her at all.

Her bracelet has alerted her to my presence in the brick, and she charges after me, calling my name. Calling another name, too.

"Henry's gone, Everett!" That's what she says just before I dive. "I miss him, too! But we need to move on without him!"

She's wrong. Dead wrong. And I'm going to prove it.

When I'm sure she's got a lock on me, I throw myself into the panelography. I ride the swirling currents of the Underfunnies, swooping away from the bizarre realm of Hazy Kat.

As I travel, I think of Henry. I think of our son. I remember how miraculous he was, how full of life and personality from the day he was born. I remember his bright blue eyes fixing on me with pure love and expectation. The way his lips moved as he repeated the things I said, as if he were memorizing each and every word.

He was the greatest thing to ever happen to me, to us. A dream come true—a dream I'd never known I had until he arrived.

A dream that ended the day he died.

I remember the sound of screeching tires, the screams of Molly as she ran. But never a sound from Henry. Not even a last gasp of breath when I got to his side in the street. Only silence from him.

And only blame between Molly and me. Blame become hatred, hatred become rage. I threw myself into my work, pioneering the exploration of the richest vein of the Underfunnies, born of the comic strips of the early 20th century. Anything to lose myself in the black and white of simple line work, the discoveries of Subtextual Space. Anything to forget Henry and stay away from Molly.

And then, one day, I got The Idea. And I knew it would work. It *will* work, if only I can get her to where she needs to be.

Suddenly, the flow of my thoughts is interrupted as I pop free into a fresh setting. I feel the tingle of something sparking on my body—the crackle of a tiny flame burning at one end of me.

This time, I am a lit stick of dynamite in the hand of a child.

"Zo!" says the little boy, a chubby creature with thick hair as black as his old-fashioned waistcoat. "Vhat do you say, Fritzie? Vill der Admiral like zis special *bratwurst* ve have for his dinner?" He holds me up and grins.

"Oh, ja," says his brother, also chubby but with blond hair and white coat. "I zink maybe he von't haff zo many *chores* for us tomorrow, Helmut!"

We're in a kitchen, surrounded by the smell of cooking sauerkraut. The boy's Auntie toils away on the other side of the room, stirring a bubbling pot. Her work is never done, taking care of the mischievous and ungrateful Schnitzeljammer Brats.

"Time to serve der first course!" Blond Fritz grabs a plate and holds it out.

Helmut drops me on the plate with a devilish smile. "Vhat a lovely presentation! Der Admiral ist sure to ask for *seconds*!"

"Ja!" Fritz laughs. "*Thirty* seconds till she *blows*!"

With that, they march me out through the swinging door to the dining room. The Admiral awaits them, sitting at the table in his seaman's cap and scrub-brush mustache.

"Dinner iss served!" Fritz plunks the plate in front of him.

"*Bomb Appétit!*" says Helmut, and then he catches himself. "I mean *Bon Appétit!*"

The Admiral doesn't seem to notice there's dynamite on his plate instead of bratwurst. He raises his fork and knife, ready to dig in…

But before his utensils make contact, his cap leaps off his head and flops down over me. Cut off from the air, my fuse fizzles and stops burning with just an inch to go.

Then, I hear her voice—Molly's voice, speaking from the substance of the cap. "You're not the *only* one who knows how to manipulate the supertexture of the Underfunnies!"

I'm surprised. Following me into the panelography is one thing; possessing resident iconography is quite another.

Apparently, my wife did her homework before she got here.

"Now *listen* to me," she says. "I want you to come *home* with me, Everett. You've been in here too *long*."

For the first time since she found me, I answer her. "You don't know what you're talking about."

"Oh yes, I do," she says. "Don't you think I tried to hide from the world, too? Don't you think I wanted to run away and never come back—never remember what happened to Henry? Don't you think I loved him, too?"

Her words settle around me like comic strip snow. Should I remind her, again, that I was trimming hedges in the back yard when it happened, and she was the one who was supposed to be watching him when he wandered into traffic? That she was the one who turned her back to talk to a neighbor when she should have had her eyes glued to Henry at all times?

Only if rubbing salt in the wound is my goal. "Leave me alone," I tell her. "Go back to reality."

"I'm not leaving without you. That's final." Just as she says it, she's lifted away, leaving me uncovered on the plate.

Fritz makes a grab, but I dive out of the realm of the Schnitzeljammer Brats before his pudgy hand can touch me. I've got to keep moving, keep running, keep drawing her along in my wake.

Until it's too late to stop what I've got planned.

It wouldn't be enough to tell her the story straight up, to tell her The Idea I've set in motion. I can't take the chance she won't believe it's possible, that she won't cooperate.

Not to mention that it breaks every tenet of the Panelnaut protocols. Protocols that I helped create.

Diving through the foamy black-and-white tides toward my next destination, I remember the early days of exploration. I wasn't the first to discover the Underfunnies, but I found the first doorway and made the first trip inside.

It was so thrilling back then, such a novelty—plying the byways of this vast psychic substrata. Jumping into manifestations of comic strips from various eras, existing side-by-side with beloved characters as well as obscure ones. Before long, I discovered I hadn't accessed the primary reality of those strips, but a flip-side echo where nothing works the way it should—a negative space where expectations can't be trusted. The place where Potpie's spinach can won't burst on cue, where Ixnay the mouse can't toss a brick on target, where the Schnitzeljammer Brats' dynamite sticks won't stay lit.

Did I understand the full implications back then? Hell, no. The best I thought we Panelnauts could do was influence the collective unconscious—plant messages that guide humanity toward a state of peace and harmony. We wrote protocols forbidding extreme intervention, anything that disrupted the essential integrity of the panelography.

And now I'm throwing them all away. The ultimate disruption is in motion; every moment brings it closer to final fruition.

And I'm the one who engineered it. I'm the one who knows how close we are to the grand finale.

Very close, now. It's time to pick up the pace.

I need to move her along quickly, not give her time to think or catch her breath. I need to flash like a skipping stone from world to world to world until we reach the last one.

The one I've prepared.

So I fling myself out of the current and surface in another place. This time, I'm a cigar in the mouth of Moo Mullet, rascally gambler and ne'er-do-well. Seconds later, I hear Molly's voice coming from the black derby hat on Moo's little brother, Kozy.

"Please, Everett," says the derby hat. "No more running."

"Say! What gives?" Moo snatches the hat from Kozy's head and gives it a smack with the back of his hand. "Now I gotta take *lip* from a *lid*?"

"We can get through this together," says Molly, "if you'll just come home."

"That topper's positively *brimmin'* with yap, ain't it?" says Kozy.

"Leave me alone!" I shout, just as I dive out of the scene.

"Now my *cigar's* runnin' at the mouth?" I hear Moo say as I leave. "What's next? My *racin' form* tellin' me which *horse* to bet?"

Once again, the currents bear me onward. I'm closer still to our final destination and the consummation of all my efforts.

Leaping from the flow, I become a club in the hands of Allie Hoop the caveman. Molly becomes the collar around the neck of his pet dinosaur, Finny.

"Please give me a chance!" The sound of her voice makes Finny grunt and run into a tree.

"What the heck?" says Allie. "How come you sound like a *girl* all of a sudden, Finny?"

I leap away without a word, and she follows.

Next, I become the fireman's hat on Smokin' Stovepipe, and Molly's the bell on his kooky one-man fire truck. I linger there for less time than it takes Smokin' to utter his catchphrase, "Fwoooo."

We're closer now, almost there. I speed up even more.

At our next stop, I'm the clodhopper boots on Li'l Asner the hillbilly. Molly's the pipe in his old Maw's mouth.

Then, I'm the giant sandwich in Ragwood Rumstead's hands, and she's the polka-dotted bow tie at his throat.

Another hop, and I'm the TV wristwatch on Rick Tracer's arm. She's his lemon yellow trench coat.

Then, I'm the bald head on Daddy Bigbucks, and she's Orphan Agnes' curly orange hair.

"Please stop!" says Molly, giving Agnes quite a start. "Just stop running!"

"Bleepin' blizzards!" yelps Orphan Agnes.

In spite of Molly's pleas, I leap again just the same. Because finally, we've reached the end. My whole purpose in leading her on this chase through the Underfunnies.

I swoop through the currents and burst free at our last stop. This time, I appear as myself, not disguised as some comic strip prop. She does the same, returning to her familiar form in the silver spacesuit and bubble helmet.

Finally. Here we are. In a child's darkened bedroom.

"What is this?" She stares at the black-haired boy on the bed between us. "Who is this?"

"His name is Little Nino," I tell her. "And he's a dreamer."

Even as I say it, Little Nino stirs and sits up in bed. He rubs his eyes, and then he looks at me, and smiles.

"Oh!" he says. "You are here!"

Grinning, I tousle his hair. "Just like we talked about, Nino. Are you ready?"

He smiles and nods.

"What's happening here?" Molly scowls. "What are you talking about, Everett?"

"Little Nino's been having a crazy dream," I tell her. "Haven't you, Nino?"

"Why yes, I have." Little Nino crawls down off the bed and pads across the room in his fuzzy white footie pajamas. "I have been dreaming about the music in my closet."

As we watch, he opens the door of his closet. Beams of rainbow light stream out around him.

At the same time, a sweet piping song skirls forth—the sound of flutes and chimes and strings weaving in delicate harmony.

Little Nino smiles back at us. "Do you hear it?"

"Yes, we do," I tell him. "Let's have a closer listen, shall we?"

"That will be fine." Without hesitation, Little Nino shuffles through the closet doorway, disappearing into the rainbow light.

"Come on." I take Molly's elbow. "I want to show you something."

She frowns at me. "That song. I know it, don't I?"

I just shrug and pull her toward the closet.

As soon as we cross the threshold, the doorway disappears behind us. Suddenly, we're standing on a beach at night, facing a bonfire that burns in rainbow colors.

At first, we're alone there with Little Nino. "I remember what comes next," he says. "Would you like to see the rest of the dream?"

"Yes, we would." I let go of Molly's elbow and take her hand. "We would like that very much."

Little Nino waves his arms, and figures descend from above, floating down one at a time from the starry sky. They are comic strip women, all of them, descending like wingless angels to land lightly on the wet sand around the rainbow bonfire.

There's Potpie's girlfriend, Olives…Ragwood's wife, Blonder…Li'l Asner's gal Dandelion Meg… Rick Tracer's true love Bess Bluehart…Allie Hoop's cavegirl Moolah…and so many more. Every woman you can think of from the funny pages, every one of them from the sublimely beautiful to the utterly ridiculous. Dozens of them, hundreds of them.

This is it. This is what I've been working for; this is why I summoned Molly.

Because this is where the impossible can happen. Here in a child's dream in a flip-side place where things don't happen the way they should.

Only here could I do what had to be done.

Hand in hand, Molly and I walk to the fire. We stand before the women, their faces and forms flickering in the dancing rainbow light.

"Oh!" Suddenly, Little Nino runs forward and gazes into the flames. "There is something inside!" Without hesitation, he plunges his arms into the fire.

When he pulls them back out again, unburned, there's a bundle in his hands. Something wrapped in a comic strip blanket, all black ink and wooly crosshatched texture.

Grinning, Little Nino turns and offers the bundle to Molly. "Please take this," he says. "It is for you."

"From all of us," says Olives in her nasally voice. "Every last one of us."

That's exactly what it took—the combined power of several hundred female icons projected together. Merged with my own hopes and memories in one supreme act of will.

Not sex, but creation nonetheless. The ultimate surrogate motherhood.

Molly peels back the blanket, and a tiny face looks out at her. The face of a comic strip baby boy, eyes big and dark and shining.

This, then, is my secret son, a child conceived in the panelography. A child of pure hope and imagination—an homage to the son we lost.

And perhaps much more than that.

"Think of Henry," I tell her. "Remember everything you can about him. Every detail."

She looks at me with tears rolling down her face. "But that won't…this isn't…"

"Trust me." I lift the helmet from her head and kiss her wet cheek. "Think of Henry."

She casts her eyes up at me with a look of anguished disbelief. I brush the dark hair back behind her ears and shake my head.

"I can't do it myself," I say. "I need you. Your half of the memories. Your half of who he is." I kiss her cheek again. "Please try."

I watch as she cradles the squirming bundle in her arms. As she closes her eyes and frowns, reaching deep to dredge up those memories.

The comic strip women huddle close, caught up in the moment. I can practically see the pen-and-ink waves of hope ripple out from their exaggerated forms.

Maybe it's the force of their collective willpower. Maybe it's the power of the dream we're in, a dream within a dreamlike realm where human disbelief is suspended. Where comic-strip life works in reverse, so harsh human reality can change direction, too.

Or maybe it's just her memories and love for him. *Our* memories and love pouring into a vessel of India ink. Pulling him back from the vanishing point—pulling all three of us back.

Whatever the reason, a new strip debuts tonight, a full-color single-panel above the fold in the Sunday pull-out section. Here's how we kick off the run:

A mob of famous comic strip women stands around a rainbow bonfire. At panel center, classic child character Little Nino stands on tiptoe, gazing at a swaddled babe in the arms of a woman in a skintight silver spacesuit.

Little Nino says, "Oh my! Look at his eyes! They're not black anymore!"

The woman in the spacesuit weeps with joy. The square-jawed man beside her bends down to kiss the infant's forehead.

We can see, in the firelight, that the baby's eyes are the brightest blue that the four-color printing process will allow.

The caption at the bottom of the panel reads as follows: "Welcome back, Henry!"

James Patrick Kelly is a multiple Hugo winner (including one for this story), a Nebula winner, and a frequent Hugo, Nebula, and Sturgeon nominee. His most recent book is *Digital Rapture*, co-edited with John Kessel.

THINK LIKE A DINOSAUR

by James Patrick Kelly

To the reader of "Think Like A Dinosaur"

I owe this story, which had the cover of the June 1995 *Asimov's*, to John Kessel and Tom Godwin. In the early nineties, my friend John Kessel incited a dustup about Godwin's seminal sf story, "The Cold Equations." He questioned the rigor of the science in a story that had long been at the center of the hard sf canon, and took a rather dim view of its socio-political subtext. A lively discussion ensued in the pages of the *New York Review of Science Fiction*. My contribution to the debate was to be a short-short shocker with a working title of "The Cold Equation." But in the course of researching the story, I had the good fortune to read Kip Thorne's wonderful *Black Holes and Time Warps: Einstein's Outrageous Legacy*. By the time I was done with Thorne's book, I had far more material than I could have possibly crammed into a couple-of-thousand-word short story. The piece grew in size and complexity until I was ready to bring it to the Cambridge Science Fiction Workshop, where it got a fiery reception. I remember that we took a break after we were "done" with the critique of my manuscript and people were still arguing about the morality of what Michael Burr had done when we reassembled to begin the next story. I knew then that I had written something that would get under people's skins.

I am not ashamed to admit that another influence on this story was St*r Tr*k. I have always been disturbed by its transporter technology. Maybe after you read this, you will be, too. But I was not fully conscious of a much more important influence until Barry Malzberg wrote me to ask if I had intended to borrow from Algis Budrys' *Rogue Moon*. I had only a vague memory of reading this fine novel. When I went to my bookshelf, I found a paperback copy that had been printed in 1960 but that bore the imprint of a used bookstore in Nashua, New Hampshire. I lived in Nashua from 1975 to 1980 and presumably read it then, internalized its ideas and forgot all about the source material. In fact, until I got Barry's letter, I was rather proud of having come up with a glitzy new sf gizmo all on my own!

This is without doubt my most famous story, and it may well be that the lead of my obit will read something like "This was the guy who wrote 'Think Like A Dinosaur.'"

I am very cool with that.

Jim

jim@jimkelly.net

***

Think Like A Dinosaur

Kamala Shastri came back to this world as she had left it—naked. She tottered out of the assembler, trying to balance in Tuulen Station's delicate gravity. I caught her and bundled her into a robe with one motion, then eased her onto the float. Three years on another planet had transformed Kamala. She was leaner, more muscular. Her fingernails were now a couple of centimeters long and there were four parallel scars incised on her left cheek, perhaps some Gendian's idea of beautification. But what struck me most was the darting strangeness in her eyes. This place, so familiar to me, seemed almost to shock her. It was as if she doubted the walls and was skeptical of air. She had learned to think like an alien.

"Welcome back." The float's whisper rose to a *whoosh* as I walked it down the hallway.

She swallowed hard and I thought she might cry. Three years ago, she would have. Lots of migrators are devastated when they come out of the assembler; it's because there is no transition. A few seconds ago Kamala was on Gend, fourth planet of the star we call Epsilon Leo, and now she was here in lunar orbit. She was almost home; her life's great adventure was over.

"Matthew?" she said.

"Michael." I couldn't help but be pleased that she remembered me. After all, she had changed my life.

I've guided maybe three comings *and* goings—since study the dinos. Kamala S tum scan I've ever pirate care; I suspect this is a allow themselves. I kno as she was three years a self. When the dinos sent h 50,391.72 grams and her red cell coun lion per mm³. She could play the *nagasvaram*, a kin of bamboo flute. Her father came from Thana, near Bombay, and her favorite flavor of chewyfrute was watermelon and she'd had five lovers and when she was eleven she had wanted to be a gymnast but instead she had become a biomaterials engineer who at age twenty-nine had volunteered to go to the stars to learn how to grow artificial eyes. It took her two years to go through migrator training; she knew she could have backed out at any time, right up until the moment Silloin translated her into a superluminal signal. It was explained to her many times, what it meant to balance the equation.

I first met her on June 22, 2069. She shuttled over from Lunex's L1 port and came through our airlock at promptly 10:15, a small, roundish woman with black hair parted in the middle and drawn tight against her skull. They had darkened her skin against Epsilon Leo's UV; it was the deep blue-black of twilight. She was wearing a striped clingy and velcro slippers to help her get around for the short time she'd be navigating our .2 micrograv.

"Welcome to Tuulen Station." I smiled and offered my hand. "My name is Michael." We shook. "I'm supposed to be a sapientologist but I also moonlight as the local guide."

"Guide?" She nodded distractedly. "Okay." She peered past me, as if expecting someone else.

"Oh, don't worry," I said, "the dinos are in their cages."

Her eyes got wide as she let her hand slip from mine. "You call the Hanen dinos?"

"Why not?" I laughed. "They call us babies. The weeps, among other things."

She shook her head in amazement. People who've never met a dino tended to romanticize them: the wise and noble reptiles who had mastered superluminal physics and introduced Earth to the wonders

vilization. I doubt Kamala had ever
play poker or gobble down a screaming
d she had never argued with Linna, who
sn't convinced that humans were psychologi-
ready to go to the stars.

Have you eaten?" I gestured down the corridor
toward the reception rooms.

"Yes…I mean, no." She didn't move. "I am not
hungry."

"Let me guess. You're too nervous to eat. You're
too nervous to talk, even. You wish I'd just shut up,
pop you into the marble, and beam you out. Let's
just get this part the hell over with, eh?"

"I don't mind the conversation, actually."

"There you go. Well, Kamala, it is my solemn duty
to advise you that there are no peanut butter and
jelly sandwiches on Gend. And no chicken vindaloo.
What's my name again?"

"Michael?"

"See, you're not *that* nervous. Not one taco, or a
single slice of eggplant pizza. This is your last chance
to eat like a human."

"Okay." She did not actually smile—she was
too busy being brave—but a corner of her mouth
twitched. "Actually, I would not mind a cup of tea."

"Now, tea they've got." She let me guide her toward
reception room D; her slippers *snicked* at the velcro
carpet. "Of course, they brew it from lawn clippings."

"The Gendians don't keep lawns. They live
underground."

"Refresh my memory." I kept my hand on her
shoulder; beneath the clingy, her muscles were rigid.
"Are they the ferrets or the things with the orange
bumps?"

"They look nothing like ferrets."

We popped through the door bubble into reception D, a compact rectangular space with a scatter
of low, unthreatening furniture. There was a kitchen
station at one end, a closet with a vacuum toilet at
the other. The ceiling was blue sky; the long wall
showed a live view of the Charles River and the
Boston skyline, baking in the late June sun. Kamala
had just finished her doctorate at MIT.

I opaqued the door. She perched on the edge of a
couch like a wren, ready to flit away.

While I was making her tea, my fingernail screen
flashed. I answered it and a tiny Silloin came up in

discreet mode. She didn't look at me; she was too
busy watching arrays in the control room. =A problem,= her voice buzzed in my earstone, =most neg-
ligible, really. But we will have to void the last two
from today's schedule. Save them at Lunex until first
shift tomorrow. Can this one be kept for an hour?=

"Sure," I said. "Kamala, would you like to meet a
Hanen?" I transferred Silloin to a dino-sized window
on the wall. "Silloin, this is Kamala Shastri. Silloin is
the one who actually runs things. I'm just the doorman."

Silloin looked through the window with her near
eye, then swung around and peered at Kamala with
her other. She was short for a dino, just over a meter
tall, but she had an enormous head that teetered on
her neck like a watermelon balancing on a grapefruit.
She must have just oiled herself because her silver
scales shone. =Kamala, you will accept my happi-
est intentions for you?= She raised her left hand,
spreading the skinny digits to expose dark crescents
of vestigial webbing.

"Of course, I…"

=And you will permit us to render you this
translation?=

She straightened. "Yes."

=Have you questions?=

I'm sure she had several hundred, but at this point
was probably too scared to ask. While she hesitated,
I broke in. "Which came first, the lizard or the egg?"

Silloin ignored me. =It will be excellent for you to
begin when?=

"She's just having a little tea." I said, handing her
the cup. "I'll bring her along when she's done. Say
an hour?"

Kamala squirmed on couch. "No, really, it will not
take me…"

Silloin showed us her teeth, several of which were
as long as piano keys. =That would be most appropriate, Michael.= She closed; a gull flew through the
space where her window had been.

"Why did you do that?" Kamala's voice was sharp.

"Because it says here that you have to wait your turn.
You're not the only migrator we're sending this morning." This was a lie, of course; we had had to cut the
schedule because Jodi Latchaw, the other sapientologist assigned to Tuulen, was at the University of Hip-
parchus presenting our paper on the Hanen concept
of identity. "Don't worry, I'll make the time fly."

For a moment, we looked at each other. I could have laid down an hour's worth of patter; I'd done that often enough. Or I could have drawn her out on why she was going: no doubt she had a blind grandma or second cousin just waiting for her to bring home those artificial eyes, not to mention potential spin-offs which could well end tuberculosis, famine and premature ejaculation, *blah, blah, blah*. Or I could have just left her alone in the room to read the wall. The trick was guessing how spooked she really was.

"Tell me a secret," I said.

"What?"

"A secret, you know, something no one else knows."

She stared as if I'd just fallen off Mars.

"Look, in a little while you're going some place that's what…three hundred and ten light years away? You're scheduled to stay for three years. By the time you come back, I could easily be rich, famous and elsewhere; we'll probably never see each other again. So what have you got to lose? I promise not to tell."

She leaned back on the couch, and settled the cup in her lap. "This is another test, right? After everything they have put me through, they still have not decided whether to send me."

"Oh no, in a couple of hours you'll be cracking nuts with ferrets in some dark Gendian burrow. This is just me, talking."

"You are crazy."

"Actually, I believe the technical term is logomaniac. It's from the Greek: *logos* meaning word, *mania* meaning two bits short of a byte. I just love to chat is all. Tell you what, I'll go first. If my secret isn't juicy enough, you don't have to tell me anything."

Her eyes were slits as she sipped her tea. I was fairly sure that whatever she was worrying about at the moment, it wasn't being swallowed by the big blue marble.

"I was brought up Catholic," I said, settling onto a chair in front of her. "I'm not anymore, but that's not the secret. My parents sent me to Mary, Mother of God High School; we called it Moogoo. It was run by a couple of old priests, Father Thomas and his wife, Mother Jennifer. Father Tom taught physics, which I got a "D" in, mostly because he talked like he had walnuts in his mouth. Mother Jennifer

taught theology and had all the warmth of a marble pew; her nickname was Mama Moogoo.

"One night, just two weeks before my graduation, Father Tom and Mama Moogoo went out in their Chevy Minimus for ice cream. On the way home, Mama Moogoo pushed a yellow light and got broadsided by an ambulance. Like I said, she was old, a hundred and twenty something; they should've lifted her license back in the '50s. She was killed instantly. Father Tom died in the hospital.

"Of course, we were all supposed to feel sorry for them and I guess I did a little, but I never really liked either of them and I resented the way their deaths had screwed things up for my class. So I was more annoyed than sorry, but then I also had this edge of guilt for being so uncharitable. Maybe you'd have to grow up Catholic to understand that. Anyway, the day after it happened they called an assembly in the gym and we were all there squirming on the bleachers and the cardinal himself telepresented a sermon. He kept trying to comfort us, like it had been our *parents* that had died. When I made a joke about it to the kid next to me, I got caught and spent the last week of my senior year with an in-school suspension."

Kamala had finished her tea. She slid the empty cup into one of the holders built into the table. "Want some more?" I said.

She stirred restlessly. "Why are you telling me this?"

"It's part of the secret." I leaned forward in my chair. "See, my family lived down the street from Holy Spirit Cemetery and in order to get to the carryvan line on McKinley Ave., I had to cut through. Now this happened a couple of days after I got in trouble at the assembly. It was around midnight and I was coming home from a graduation party where I had taken a couple of pokes of insight, so I was feeling sly as a philosopher-king. As I walked through the cemetery, I stumbled across two dirt mounds right next to each other. At first I thought they were flower beds, then I saw the wooden crosses. Fresh graves: here lies Father Tom and Mama Moogoo. There wasn't much to the crosses: they were basically just stakes with crosspieces painted white and hammered into the ground. The names were hand-printed on them. The way I figured it, they were there to mark the graves until the stones got delivered. I didn't need any insight to recognize a once-in-a-

Sail to Success

A SERIES OF SEMINARS/WORKSHOPS FOR THE SERIOUS WRITER

onboard a luxury cruiseliner visiting the Bahamas, 12/2/2013– 12/6/2013

www.SailSuccess.com

Intensive Instruction

Personal critique (in-class) of portions of your manuscript & query letter

Limited Class Size (22 students per class)

All-Inclusive Cost (Includes Cruise / Food / Entertainment)

Award-Winning / Industry-Leading Faculty

Eleanor Wood

Head of the Spectrum Literary Agency, a premier New-York-based literary agency representing SF and Fantasy authors (established 1976). Representations include Lois McMaster Bujold and the estate of Robert A. Heinlein.

Jack Skillingstead

Author and teacher who has lectured at the Taos Toolbox and has had a number of stories published in *Asimov's Science Fiction* and other venues.

Rebecca Moesta

Award-winning *New York Times* bestselling author, specializing in young adult literature. Writers of the Future judge.

Eric Flint

New York Times bestselling author and the creator of the 1632 universe.

Toni Weisskopf

Publisher. Head of Baen Books. One of the most influential people in the genre today. Was executive editor at Baen until Jim Baen's death in 2006, after which she took over as publisher.

Mike Resnick

First on Locus list of all-time award winners (short fiction), living or dead. Author of Hugo-nominated *The Business of Publishing*. Guest of Honor at the 2012 Worldcon (Chicon 7) and a Writers of the Future judge.

Nancy Kress

The "Queen" of novellas. Multiple major writing and teaching awards. Has taught at the University of Leipzig, Clarion Writers Workshop (University of California) and the Taos Toolbox. Author of ground-breaking novella *Beggars in Spain* (Hugo/Nebula).

Kevin J. Anderson

50 bestsellers and more than 23 million copies of books in print. Judge in the Writers of the Future contest. Co-writer of the Dune prequels.

DISCOUNTS FOR EARLY SIGN-UP.

LIMITED SPACE DUE TO RESTRICTED CLASS SIZE

Get Details & Sign Up at **www.SailSuccess.com**

lifetime opportunity. If I switched them, what were the chances anyone was going to notice? It was no problem sliding them out of their holes. I smoothed the dirt with my hands and then ran like hell."

Until that moment, she'd seemed bemused by my story and slightly condescending toward me. Now there was a glint of alarm in her eyes. "That was a terrible thing to do," she said.

"Absolutely," I said, "although the dinos think that the whole idea of planting bodies in graveyards and marking them with carved rocks is weepy. They say there is no identity in dead meat, so why get so sentimental about it? Linna keeps asking how come we don't put markers over our shit. But that's not the secret. See, it'd been a warmish night in the middle of June, only as I ran, the air turned cold. Freezing, I could see my breath. And my shoes got heavier and heavier, like they had turned to stone. As I got closer to the back gate, it felt like I was fighting a strong wind, except my clothes weren't flapping. I slowed to a walk. I know I could have pushed through, but my heart was thumping and then I heard this whispery seashell noise and I panicked. So the secret is I'm a coward. I switched the crosses back and I never went near that cemetery again. As a matter of fact," I nodded at the walls of reception D on Tuulen Station, "when I grew up, I got about as far away from it as I could."

She stared as I settled back in my chair. "True story," I said and raised my right hand. She seemed so astonished that I started laughing. A smile bloomed on her dark face and suddenly she was giggling too. It was a soft, liquid sound, like a brook bubbling over smooth stones; it made me laugh even harder. Her lips were full and her teeth were very white.

"Your turn," I said, finally.

"Oh, no, I could not." She waved me off. "I don't have anything so good…" She paused, then frowned. "You have told that before?"

"Once," I said. "To the Hanen, during the psych screening for this job. Only I didn't tell them the last part. I know how dinos think, so I ended it when I switched the crosses. The rest is baby stuff." I waggled a finger at her. "Don't forget, you promised to keep my secret."

"Did I?"

"Tell me about when you were young. Where did you grow up?"

"Toronto." She glanced at me, appraisingly. "There *was* something, but not funny. Sad."

I nodded encouragement and changed the wall to Toronto's skyline dominated by the CN Tower, Toronto-Dominion Centre, Commerce Court and the King's Needle.

She twisted to take in the view and spoke over her shoulder. "When I was ten we moved to an apartment, right downtown on Bloor Street so my mother could be close to work." She pointed at the wall and turned back to face me. "She is an accountant, my father wrote wallpaper for Imagineering. It was a huge building; it seemed as if we were always getting into the elevator with ten neighbors we never knew we had. I was coming home from school one day when an old woman stopped me in the lobby. 'Little girl,' she said, 'how would you like to earn ten dollars?' My parents had warned me not to talk to strangers but she obviously was a resident. Besides, she had an ancient pair of exolegs strapped on, so I knew I could outrun her if I needed to. She asked me to go to the store for her, handed me a grocery list and a cash card, and said I should bring everything up to her apartment, 10W. I should have been more suspicious because all the downtown groceries deliver but, as I soon found out, all she really wanted was someone to talk to her. And she was willing to pay for it, usually five or ten dollars, depending on how long I stayed. Soon I was stopping by almost every day after school. I think my parents would have made me stop if they had known; they were very strict. They would not have liked me taking her money. But neither of them got home until after six, so it was my secret to keep."

"Who was she?" I said. "What did you talk about?"

"Her name was Margaret Ase. She was ninety-seven years old and I think she had been some kind of counselor. Her husband and her daughter had both died and she was alone. I didn't find out much about her; she made me do most of the talking. She asked me about my friends and what I was learning in school and my family. Things like that…."

Her voice trailed off as my fingernail started to flash. I answered it.

=Michael, I am pleased to call you to here.= Silloin buzzed in my ear. She was almost twenty minutes ahead of schedule.

"See, I told you we'd make the time fly." I stood; Kamala's eyes got very wide. "I'm ready if you are."

I offered her my hand. She took it and let me help her up. She wavered for a moment and I sensed just how fragile her resolve was. I put my hand around her waist and steered her into the corridor. In the micrograv of Tuulen Station, she already felt as insubstantial as a memory. "So tell me, what happened that was so sad?"

At first I thought she hadn't heard. She shuffled along, said nothing.

"Hey, don't keep me in suspense here, Kamala," I said. "You have to finish the story."

"No," she said. "I don't think I do."

I didn't take this personally. My only real interest in the conversation had been to distract her. If she refused to be distracted, that was her choice. Some migrators kept talking right up to the moment they slid into the big blue marble, but lots of them went quiet just before. They turned inward. Maybe in her mind she was already on Gend, blinking in the hard white light.

We arrived at the scan center, the largest space on Tuulen Station. Immediately in front of us was the marble, containment for the quantum nondemolition sensor array—QNSA for the acronymically inclined. It was the milky blue of glacial ice and big as two elephants. The upper hemisphere was raised and the scanning table protruded like a shiny gray tongue. Kamala approached the marble and touched her reflection, which writhed across its polished surface. To the right were a padded bench, the fogger, and a toilet. I looked left, through the control room window. Silloin stood watching us, her impossible head cocked to one side.

=She is docile?= She buzzed in my earstone.

I held up crossed fingers.

=Welcome, Kamala Shastri.= Silloin's voice came over the speakers with a soothing hush. =You are ready to open your translation?=

Kamala bowed to the window. "This is where I take my clothes off?"

=If you would be so convenient.=

She brushed past me to the bench. Apparently I had ceased to exist; this was between her and the dino now. She undressed quickly, folding her clingy into a neat bundle, tucking her slippers beneath the bench. Out of the corner of my eye, I could see tiny feet, heavy thighs, and the beautiful, dark smooth skin of her back. She stepped into the fogger and closed the door.

"Ready," she called.

From the control room, Silloin closed circuits which filled the fogger with a dense cloud of nano-lenses. The nano stuck to Kamala and deployed, coating the surface of her body. As she breathed them, they passed from her lungs into her bloodstream. She only coughed twice; she had been well trained. When the eight minutes were up, Silloin cleared the air in the fogger and she emerged. Still ignoring me, she again faced the control room.

=Now you must arrange yourself on the scanning table,= said Silloin, =and enable Michael to fix you.=

She crossed to the marble without hesitation, climbed the gantry beside it, eased onto the table and laid back.

I followed her up. "Sure you won't tell me the rest of the secret?"

She stared at the ceiling, unblinking.

"Okay then." I took the canister and a sparker out of my hip pouch. "This is going to happen just like you've practiced it." I used the canister to respray the bottoms of her feet with nano. I watched her belly rise and fall, rise and fall. She was deep into her breathing exercise. "Remember, no skipping rope or whistling while you're in the scanner."

She did not answer. "Deep breath now," I said, and touched a sparker to her big toe. There was a brief crackle as the nano on her skin wove into a net and stiffened, locking her in place. "Bark at the ferrets for me." I picked up my equipment, climbed down the gantry, and wheeled it back to the wall.

With a low whine, the big blue marble retracted its tongue. I watched the upper hemisphere close, swallowing Kamala Shastri, then joined Silloin in the control room.

I'm not of the school who think the dinos stink, another reason I got assigned to study them up close. Parikkal, for example, has no smell at all that I can tell. Normally Silloin had the faint but not unpleasant smell of stale wine. When she was under stress, however, her scent became vinegary and biting. It must have been a wild morning for her. Breathing through my mouth, I settled onto the stool at my station.

EDITED BY MIKE RESNICK

BUG-EYED MONSTERS & BIMBOS

A HILARIOUS COLLECTION OF PARODIES BY SOME OF THE GREATEST WRITERS OF SCIENCE FICTION

Isaac Asimov

Arthur C. Clarke

Poul Anderson

She was working quickly, now that the marble was sealed. Even with all their training, migrators tend to get claustrophobic fast. After all, they're lying in the dark, in nanobondage, waiting to be translated. Waiting. The simulator at the Singapore training center makes a noise while it's emulating a scan. Most compare it to a light rain pattering against the marble; for some, it's low-volume radio static. As long as they hear the patter, the migrators think they're safe. We reproduce it for them while they're in our marble, even through scanning takes about three seconds and is utterly silent. From my vantage I could see that the sagittal, axial, and coronal windows had stopped blinking, indicating full data capture. Silloin was skirring busily to herself; her comm didn't bother to interpret. Wasn't saying anything baby Michael needed to know, obviously. Her head bobbed as she monitored the enormous spread of readouts; her claws clicked against touch screens that glowed orange and yellow.

At my station, there was only a migration status screen—and a white button.

I wasn't lying when I said I was just the doorman. My field is sapientology, not quantum physics. Whatever went wrong with Kamala's migration that morning, there was nothing I could have done. The dinos tell me that the quantum nondemolition sensor array is able to circumvent Heisenberg's Uncertainty Principle by measuring spacetime's most crogglingly small quantities without collapsing the wave/particle duality. How small? They say that no one can ever "see" anything that's only 1.62×10^{-33} centimeters long, because at that size, space and time come apart. Time ceases to exist and space becomes a random probabilistic foam, sort of like quantum spit. We humans call this the Planck-Wheeler length. There's a Planck-Wheeler time, too: 10^{-45} of a second. If something happens and something else happens and the two events are separated by an interval of a mere 10^{-45} of a second, it is impossible to say which came first. It was all dino to me—and that's just the scanning. The Hanen use different tech to create artificial wormholes, hold them open with electromagnetic vacuum fluctuations, pass the superluminal signal through and then assemble the migrator from elementary particles at the destination.

On my status screen I could see that the signal which mapped Kamala Shastri had already been compressed and burst through the wormhole. All that we had to wait for was for Gend to confirm acquisition. Once they officially told us that they had her, it would be my job to balance the equation.

Pitter-patter, pitter-pat.

Some Hanen technologies are so powerful that they can alter reality itself. Wormholes could be used by some time-traveling fanatic to corrupt history; the scanner/assembler could be used to create a billion Silloins—or Michael Burrs. Pristine reality, unpolluted by such anomalies, has what the dinos call harmony. Before any sapients get to join the galactic club, they must prove total commitment to preserving harmony.

Since I had come to Tuulen to study the dinos, I had pressed the white button maybe three hundred times. It was what I had to do in order to keep my assignment. Pressing it sent a killing pulse of ionizing radiation through the cerebral cortex of the migrator's duplicated, and therefore unnecessary, body. No brain, no pain; death followed within seconds. Yes, the first few times I'd balanced the equation had been traumatic. It was still…unpleasant. But this was the price of a ticket to the stars. If certain unusual people like Kamala Shastri had decided that price was reasonable, it was their choice, not mine.

=This is not a happy result, Michael.= Silloin spoke to me for the first time since I'd entered the control room. =Discrepancies are unfolding.= On my status screen I watched as the error-checking routines started turning up hits.

"Is the problem here?" I felt a knot twist suddenly inside me. "Or there?" If our original scan checked out, then all Silloin would have to do is send it to Gend again.

There was a long, infuriating silence. Silloin concentrated on part of her board as if it showed her firstborn hatchling chipping out of its egg. The respirator between her shoulders had ballooned to twice its normal size. My screen showed that Kamala had been in the marble for four minutes plus.

=It may be fortunate to recalibrate the scanner and begin over.=

"*Shit.*" I slammed my hand against the wall, felt the pain tingle to my elbow. "I thought you had it fixed." When error-checking turned up problems, the solution was almost always to retransmit. "You're sure, Silloin? Because this one was right on the edge when I tucked her in."

Silloin gave me a dismissive sneeze and slapped at the error readouts with her bony little hand, as if to knock them back to normal. Like Linna and the other dinos, she had little patience with what she regarded as our weepy fears of migration. However, unlike Linna, she was convinced that someday, after we had used Hanen technologies long enough, we would learn to think like dinos. Maybe she's right. Maybe when we've been squirting through wormholes for hundreds of years, we'll cheerfully discard our redundant bodies. When the dinos and other sapients migrate, the redundants zap themselves—very harmonious. They tried it with humans but it didn't always work. That's why I'm here. =The need is most clear. It will prolong about thirty minutes,= she said.

Kamala had been alone in the dark for almost six minutes, longer than any migrator I'd ever guided. "Let me hear what's going on in the marble."

The control room filled with the sound of Kamala screaming. It didn't sound human to me—more like the shriek of tires skidding toward a crash.

"We've got to get her out of there," I said.

=That is baby thinking, Michael.=

"So she's a baby, damn it." I knew that bringing migrators out of the marble was big trouble. I could have asked Silloin to turn the speakers off and sat there while Kamala suffered. It was my decision.

"Don't open the marble until I get the gantry in place." I ran for the door. "And keep the sound effects going."

At the first crack of light, she howled. The upper hemisphere seemed to lift in slow motion; inside the marble she bucked against the nano. Just when I was sure it was impossible that she could scream any louder, she did. We had accomplished something extraordinary, Silloin and I; we had stripped the brave biomaterials engineer away completely, leaving in her place a terrified animal.

"Kamala, it's me. Michael."

Her frantic screams cohered into words. "Stop… don't…oh my god, someone help!" If I could have, I would've jumped into the marble to release her, but

the sensor array is fragile and I wasn't going to risk causing any more problems with it. We both had to wait until the upper hemisphere swung fully open and the scanning table offered poor Kamala to me.

"It's okay. Nothing's going to happen, all right? We're bringing you out, that's all. Everything's all right."

When I released her with the sparker, she flew at me. We pitched back and almost toppled down the steps. Her grip was so tight I couldn't breathe.

"Don't *kill* me, don't, *please*, don't."

I rolled on top of her. "Kamala!" I wriggled one arm free and used it to pry myself from her. I scrabbled sideways to the top step. She lurched clumsily in the microgravity and swung at me; her fingernails raked across the back of my hand, leaving bloody welts. "Kamala, stop!" It was all I could do not to strike back at her. I retreated down the steps.

"You bastard. What are you assholes trying to do to me?" She drew several deep shuddering breaths and began to sob.

"The scan got corrupted somehow. Silloin is working on it."

=The difficulty is obscure,= said Silloin from the control room.

"But that's not your problem." I backed toward the bench.

"They lied," she mumbled and seemed to fold in upon herself as if she were just skin, no flesh or bones. "They said I wouldn't feel anything and here… do you know what it's like…it's…."

I fumbled for her clingy. "Look, here are your clothes. Why don't you get dressed? We'll get you out of here."

"You bastard," she repeated, but her voice was empty.

She let me coax her down off the gantry. I counted nubs on the wall while she fumbled back into her clingy. They were the size of the old dimes my grandfather used to hoard and they glowed with a soft golden bioluminescence. I was up to forty-seven before she was dressed and ready to return to reception D.

Where before she had perched expectantly at the edge of the couch, now she slumped back against it. "So what now?" she said.

"I don't know." I went to the kitchen station and took the carafe from the distiller. "What now, Silloin?" I poured water over the back of my hand to wash the blood off. It stung. My earstone was silent. "I guess we wait," I said finally.

"For what?"

"For her to fix...."

"I'm not going back in there."

I decided to let that pass. It was probably too soon to argue with her about it, although once Silloin recalibrated the scanner, she'd have very little time to change her mind. "You want something from the kitchen? Another cup of tea, maybe?"

"How about a gin and tonic—hold the tonic?" She rubbed beneath her eyes. "Or a couple of hundred milliliters of serentol?"

I tried to pretend she'd made a joke. "You know the dinos won't let us open the bar for migrators. The scanner might misread your brain chemistry and your visit to Gend would be nothing but a three-year drunk."

"Don't you under*stand*?" She was right back at the edge of hysteria. "I am not *going*!" I didn't really blame her for the way she was acting but, at that moment, all I wanted was to get rid of Kamala Shastri. I didn't care if she went on to Gend or back to Lunex or over the rainbow to Oz, just as long as I didn't have to be in the same room with this miserable creature who was trying to make me feel guilty about an accident I had nothing to do with.

"I thought I could do it." She clamped hands to her ears as if to keep from hearing her own despair. "I wasted the last two years convincing myself that I could just lie there and not think and then suddenly I'd be far away. I was going someplace wonderful and strange." She made a strangled sound and let her hands drop into her lap. "I was going to help people see."

"You did it, Kamala. You did everything we asked."

She shook her head. "I couldn't *not* think. That was the problem. And then there she was, trying to touch me. In the dark. I had not thought of her since...." She shivered. "It's your fault for reminding me."

"Your secret friend," I said.

"Friend?" Kamala seemed puzzled by the word. "No, I wouldn't say she was a friend. I was always a little bit scared of her, because I was never quite sure what she wanted from me." She paused. "One day I went up to 10W after school. She was in her chair, staring down at Bloor Street. Her back was to me. I said, 'Hi, Ms. Ase.' I was going to show her a genie I had written, only she didn't say anything. I came around. Her skin was the color of ashes. I took her hand. It was like picking up something plastic. She was stiff, hard—not a person anymore. She had become a thing, like a feather or a bone. I ran; I had to get out of there. I went up to our apartment and I hid from her."

She squinted, as if observing—judging—her younger self through the lens of time. "I think I understand now what she wanted. I think she knew she was dying; she probably wanted me there with her at the end, or at least to find her body afterward and report it. Only I could *not*. If I told anyone she was dead, my parents would find out about us. Maybe people would suspect me of doing something to her—I don't know. I could have called security but I was only ten; I was afraid somehow they might trace me. A couple of weeks went by and still nobody had found her. By then it was too late to say anything. Everyone would have blamed me for keeping quiet for so long. At night I imagined her turning black and rotting into her chair like a banana. It made me sick; I couldn't sleep or eat. They had to put me in the hospital, because I had touched her. Touched *death*."

=Michael,= Silloin whispered, without any warning flash. =An impossibility has formed.=

"As soon as I was out of that building, I started to get better. Then they found her. After I came home, I worked hard to forget Ms. Ase. And I did, almost." Kamala wrapped her arms around herself. "But just now she was with me again, inside the marble...I couldn't see her but somehow I knew she was reaching for me."

=Michael, Parikkal is here with Linna.=

"Don't you see?" She gave a bitter laugh. "How can I go to Gend? I'm *hallucinating*."

=It has broken the harmony. Join us alone.=

I was tempted to swat at the annoying buzz in my ear.

"You know, I've never told anyone about her before."

"Well, maybe some good has come of this after all." I patted her on the knee. "Excuse me for a minute?" She seemed surprised that I would leave. I slipped into the hall and hardened the door bubble, sealing her in.

"What impossibility?" I said, heading for the control room.

=She is pleased to reopen the scanner?=

"Not pleased at all. More like scared shitless."

=This is Parikkal.= My earstone translated his skirring with a sizzling edge, like bacon frying. =The confusion was made elsewhere. No mishap can be connected to our station.=

I pushed through the bubble into the scan center. I could see the three dinos through the control window. Their heads were bobbing furiously. "Tell me," I said.

=Our communications with Gend were marred by a transient falsehood,= said Silloin. =Kamala Shastri has been received there and reconstructed.=

"She migrated?" I felt the deck shifting beneath my feet. "What about the one we've got here?"

=The simplicity is to load the redundant into the scanner and finalize....=

"I've got news for you. She's not going anywhere near that marble."

=Her equation is not in balance.= This was Linna, speaking for the first time. Linna was not exactly in charge of Tuulen Station; she was more like a senior partner. Parikkal and Silloin had overruled her before—at least I thought they had.

"What do you expect me to do? Wring her neck?"

There was a moment's silence—which was not as unnerving as watching them eye me through the window, their heads now perfectly still.

"No," I said.

The dinos were skirring at each other; their heads wove and dipped. At first they cut me cold and the comm was silent, but suddenly their debate crackled through my earstone.

=This is just as I have been telling,= said Linna. =These beings have no realization of harmony. It is wrongful to further unleash them on the many worlds.=

=You may have reason,= said Parikkal. =But that is a later discussion. The need is for the equation to be balanced.=

=There is no time. We will have to discard the redundant ourselves.= Silloin bared her long brown teeth. It would take her maybe five seconds to rip Kamala's throat out. And even though Silloin was the dino most sympathetic to us, I had no doubt she would enjoy the kill.

=I will argue that we adjourn human migration until this world has been rethought,= said Linna.

This was typical dino condescension. Even though they appeared to be arguing with each other, they were actually speaking to me, laying the situation out so that even the baby sapient would understand. They were informing me that I was jeopardizing the future of humanity in space. That the Kamala in reception D was dead whether I quit or not. That the equation had to be balanced and it had to be now.

"Wait," I said. "Maybe I can coax her back into the scanner." I had to get away from them. I pulled my earstone out and slid it into my pocket. I was in such a hurry to escape that I stumbled as I left the scan center and had to catch myself in the hallway. I stood there for a second, staring at the hand pressed against the bulkhead. I seemed to see the splayed fingers through the wrong end of a telescope. I was far away from myself.

She had curled into herself on the couch, arms clutching knees to her chest, as if trying to shrink so that nobody would notice her.

"We're all set," I said briskly. "You'll be in the marble for less than a minute, guaranteed."

"*No*, Michael."

I could actually feel myself receding from Tuulen Station. "Kamala, you're throwing away a huge part of your life."

"It is my right." Her eyes were shiny.

No, it wasn't. She was redundant; she had no rights. What had she said about the dead old lady? She had become a thing, like a bone.

"Okay, then," I jabbed at her shoulder with a stiff forefinger. "Let's go."

She recoiled. "Go where?"

"Back to Lunex. I'm holding the shuttle for you. It just dropped off my afternoon list; I should be helping them settle in, instead of having to deal with you."

She unfolded herself slowly.

"Come on." I jerked her roughly to her feet. "The dinos want you off Tuulen as soon as possible and so do I." I was so distant, I couldn't see Kamala Shastri anymore.

She nodded and let me march her to the bubble door.

"And if we meet anyone in the hall, keep your mouth shut."

"You're being so mean." Her whisper was thick.

"You're being such a baby."

When the inner door glided open, she realized immediately that there was no umbilical to the shuttle. She tried to twist out of my grip but I put my shoulder into her, hard. She flew across the airlock, slammed against the outer door and caromed onto her back. As I punched at the switch to close the inner door, I came back to myself. *I* was doing this terrible thing—me, Michael Burr. I couldn't help myself: I giggled. When I last saw her, Kamala was scrabbling across the deck toward me but she was too late. I was surprised that she wasn't screaming again; all I heard was her ferocious breathing.

As soon as the inner door sealed, I opened the outer door. After all, how many ways are there to kill someone on a space station? There were no guns. Maybe someone else could have stabbed or strangled her, but not me. Poison how? Besides, I wasn't thinking, I had been trying desperately not to think of what I was doing. I was a sapientologist, not a doctor. I always thought that exposure to space meant instantaneous death. Explosive decompression or something like. I didn't want her to suffer. I was trying to make it quick. Painless.

I heard the whoosh of escaping air and thought that was it; the body had been ejected into space. I had actually turned away when thumping started, frantic, like the beat of a racing heart. She must have found something to hold onto. *Thump, thump, thump*! It was too much. I sagged against the inner door—*thump, thump*—slid down it, laughing. Turns out that if you empty the lungs, it is possible to survive exposure to space for at least a minute, maybe two. I thought it was funny. *Thump*! Hilarious, actually. I had tried my best for her—risked my career—and this was how she repaid me? As I laid my cheek against the door, the *thumps* start to weaken. There were just a few centimeters between us, the difference between life and death. Now she knew all about balancing the equation. I was laughing so hard I could scarcely breathe. Just like the meat behind the door. Die already, you weepy bitch!

I don't know how long it took. The *thumping* slowed. Stopped. And then I was a hero. I had preserved harmony, kept our link to the stars open. I chuckled with pride; I could think like a dinosaur.

I popped through the bubble door into reception D. "It's time to board the shuttle."

Kamala had changed into a clingy and velcro slippers. There were at least ten windows open on the wall; the room filled with the murmur of talking heads. Friends and relatives had to be notified; their hero had returned, safe and sound. "I have to go," she said to the wall. "I will call you all when I land."

She gave me a smile that seemed stiff from disuse. "I want to thank you again, Michael." I wondered how long it took migrators to get used to being human. "You were such a help and I was such a…I was not myself." She glanced around the room one last time and then shivered. "I was really scared."

"You were."

She shook her head. "Was it that bad?"

I shrugged and led her out into the hall.

"I feel so silly now. I mean, I was in the marble for less than a minute and then —" she snapped her fingers —- "there I was on Gend, just like you said." She brushed up against me as we walked; her body was hard under the clingy. "Anyway, I am glad we got this chance to talk. I really *was* going to look you up when I got back. I certainly did not expect to see you here."

"I decided to stay on." The inner door to the airlock glided open. "It's a job that grows on you." The umbilical shivered as the pressure between Tuulen Station and the shuttle equalized.

"You have got migrators waiting," she said.

"Two."

"I envy them." She turned to me. "Have *you* ever thought about going to the stars?"

"No," I said.

Kamala put her hand to my face. "It changes everything." I could feel the prick of her long nails—claws, really. For a moment I thought she meant to scar my cheek the way she had been scarred.

"I know," I said.

Copyright © 1995 by James Patrick Kelly.

BOOK REVIEWS

by Paul Cook

Paul Cook is the author of eight books of science fiction, and is currently both a college instructor and the editor of the Phoenix Pick Science Fiction Classics line.

Count to a Trillion
by John C. Wright
Tor Science Fiction, 2012
Mass Market Paperback: 416 pages
ISBN 978-0765367457

John C. Wright earned his chops with his dazzling trilogy, *The Golden Age*. The individual novels were *The Golden Age* (2002), *The Phoenix Exultant* (2003), and *The Golden Transcendence* (2003). These novels depicted a future solar civilization on the verge of making the first leap to the nearest star. Wright demonstrated his prowess with clever writing and an inventive plot that kept the middle and final novels suspenseful and allowing for the creation of an organic whole by the time the story was over. It was a stellar achievement (no pun intended).

That said, we come to a new series, or trilogy, by Mr. Wright, the first book of which is *Count to a Trillion*, now out in paperback. With its brilliant cover by John Harris, *Count to a Trillion* follows Menelaus Illation Montrose, formerly a Texas gunslinger in a post-apocalyptic America, who also happens to be a genius at advanced mathematics, as he is enlisted for an interstellar mission to a star made of antimatter which is orbited by a very mysterious artifact called The Monument that is covered with cryptic mathematical symbols. His job is to decipher those symbols while the rest of the crew harvests the antimatter from the Diamond Star.

Before cryo-sleep, he injects himself with a serum that causes him to advance to a posthuman genius state, beyond what he already is. When he awakens he discovers his shipmates had sabotaged him and at the same time caused the Diamond Star to signal to its Makers that humans are prowling the vicinity, and we learn that the Makers are now "on their way" to check us out to see if we'd be worthwhile to conquer and make into slaves. Menelaus has to deal with that information (and what to do about it in 8000 years when the Makers will be arriving) as well as combating his best friend, a similarly transformed posthuman. There's a romantic triangle also in the brew, plus lots of talk about advanced mathematics (*de rigueur* for almost all science fiction novels these days). The novel doesn't so much end as drop off—not like *The Golden Age*, which had a satisfying conclusion. The next installment will be *The Hermetic Millennia*, which is now out in hardbound editions.

It would be unfair to compare *Count to a Trillion* to the opening novel in the Golden Age trilogy. This is a different beast. It's just as inventive and just as much fun to read, but here Wright uses less flamboyant language and he is much less nuanced in orchestrating his ideas (which also take the place for sub-plots, also common to most SF novels). Some readers might not like this. I actually found it rather engaging. Much science fiction these days, especially short fiction, is written in somber tones with a kind of dourness (or seriousness) that I can't explain. I think it comes from the idea that "literature" has to be serious and a lot of writers are doing this, if perhaps unconsciously. *Count to a Trillion* was actually a lot of fun to read and it bodes well for the quality of the novels to follow. It never flags and it's always interesting.

To be fair, however, *Count to a Trillion* doesn't work as a stand-alone novel the way Wright's earlier novel *The Golden Age* did in 2002. This is my only complaint about *Count to a Trillion*. Perhaps the next two can be combined into a giant three-volume single work that could be read straight through (such as James Blish's *Cities in Flight* books could or Asimov's *The Foundation Trilogy).* But probably not. (My cynicism sometimes gets the better of me.) Still, *Count to a Trillion* is a kick and it keeps the ideas coming. And I will read all the novels that follow.

Firebird (An Alex Benedict Novel)
by Jack McDevitt
Ace Science Fiction, 2012
Mass Market Paperback: 368 pages
ISBN 978-1937007805

Firebird is the sixth novel about Alex Benedict and his amanuensis (assistant, Gal Friday, co-conspirator) Chase Kolpath, who are both antiquities dealers in the far, far future—eight thousand years from now, to be exact. Chase is the narrator of these books, much in the same way that Dr. Watson records Sherlock Holmes' adventures. In *Firebird* Kolpath tells the story of how Alex Benedict becomes interested in the disappearance of a scientist, Christopher Robin (yes, that's his name; no Winnie the Pooh, though), who just might have figured out a path into another reality or the multiverse. Or he might have been murdered and his body "disappeared." Or he might have been sucked into a black hole since Robin was interested in one of their more unique quirks. These are the possibilities for Robin's disappearance that come up as Benedict and Kolpath conduct their investigation. Along the way, they come across a planet of helpless AIs who are

enslaved by some rather ruthless AIs who live in vehicles and homes left behind by the original inhabitants who do their best to kill both Benedict and Kolpath. Like the other novels in the Alex Benedict series, *Firebird* is structured like a mystery but it falls well within the mainstream tradition of hard science fiction. Anyone familiar with these books won't be disappointed by this release.

That said, *Firebird* has a major flaw, one that haunts all of the Benedict/Kolpath books. Chase Kolpath tells these stories, but the writing is rather flat and there is nothing particularly distinct about her character. That is to say, she's not a Dr. Watson. And Benedict certainly is no Sherlock Holmes. His character is rather flat, and so is his speech diction. More to the point: Kolpath writes like a 21st century white, middle-class American. Indeed, there is no real sense that these stories (and these characters) are products of a future eight thousand years distant. Read *Ilium* by Dan Simmons or the Golden Age trilogy by John C. Wright. Read the Long Sun saga by Gene Wolfe. Or *Dune.* These stories triumph because their authors have envisioned a future that is extremely different. There are no white, middle-class Americans in any of those books. McDevitt so concentrates on the mysteries to be solved in the Alex Benedict novels that he misses the bigger picture. There will be no white middle-class Americans eight thousand years from now. Whoever they will be, posthuman or not, they will not be speaking English with American inflections; they won't sound anything like us or have any of our concerns regarding politics, religion, or culture. And there won't be television talk shows like you can find on CNN or MSNBC or Fox.

And McDevitt knows this. Right in the middle of the novel, we have this exchange:

> "I'd be interested," said Alex, "in coming back in, say, ten thousand years to see what the human race is like."
>
> "We'll all be different by then," [Chase] said. "We'll probably have gotten rid of old age. We'll have a complete map of the Milky Way. Everybody will have a 200 IQ. And we'll all be impossibly good-looking."

With this bit of dialog McDevitt seems to be attempting to convince the reader that things won't change much by Alex Benedict's time but that they most certainly will eleven thousand years hence. Think of the visuals from the first *Dune* movie. Think of when they wheeled out the Third Stage Navigator in his hovering aquarium. Think of his mute assistants—their garb, their physical carriage, their demeanor. Whatever you think of the movie *Dune*, that one scene *is* the future. *That* was a posthuman ten thousand years from now.

Alex Benedict and Chase Kolpath are really no more than prosperous antiquities dealers living in Cincinnati or Miami right now. They speak like them, act like them, and the world around them isn't all that much transformed by any kind of cultural or sociological changes—except that it has FTL transportation.

McDevitt is missing a great opportunity here. He's a fine writer and has written some excellent fiction in the past. But his job is also to dazzle us. We know how his mind works. We really need to see his imagination take control and *soar*.

The Big Book of Adventure Stories
Edited by Otto Penzler
Vintage, 2011
Paperback: 896 pages
ISBN 978-0307474506

This is a must-have collection for all readers interested in the great pulp literature of the first half of the 20th century. Editor Penzler has chosen stories, novelettes, and whole novels from those magazines that gave us Tarzan, The Spider, Zorro, The Cisco Kid,

Hopalong Cassidy, and Bulldog Drummond. You'll find a Conan story, an entire Tarzan novel, epic stories by H. Rider Haggard, Alistair MacLean, Talbot Mundy, and the classic "The Most Dangerous Game" by Richard Connell. There are few science fiction stories in this collection, stories by Damon Knight and Philip José Farmer. But there is also the first Buck Rogers novel, *Armageddon 2419 A.D.*

Only two pulp characters are missing here (probably for copyright reasons): Doc Savage and Jules de Grandin. Doc Savage is represented, in a sense, with a short story by Lester Dent, Doc Savage's main writer. Dent's story will remind the reader of why he was so good at writing Doc Savage novels. It has all the Doc Savage elements for a good story: A mysteriously deserted island with dozens of shipwrecks, pirates, and *very* narrow escapes for our heroes.

This important collection is 896 pages in length and will provide the reader with weeks, if not months, of pleasurable reading. I highly recommend this anthology because science fiction did not arise out of nowhere. It came from a milieu of magazines that were published cheaply, magazines that allowed for a flourishing of brilliant storytelling. This collection belongs in every library.

Wool Omnibus
by Hugh Howey
Simon & Schuster, 2013
Mass Market Paperback: 528 pages
ISBN 978-1476735115

Wool by newcomer Hugh Howey is probably science fiction's first major self-publishing success story. Howey originally published this novel online in five smaller sequences, none of which, it turns out, really do stand on their own. Wisely, he put them together in the form it exists in now, which you can get in an electronic edition as well as a print-on-demand book of excellent quality. Professionally copyedited and proofread with a fine cover to boot, *Wool* is a terrific book, a great read from start to finish. (So successful has this book been this last year, that Simon & Schuster will publish it *officially* in March 2013. Talk about finding a publisher the hard way!)

Wool is a throwback to the after-the-apocalypse novels of the 1950s wherein humans have taken to caves or tunnels or the basements of bombed-out buildings waiting for the radioactive dust clouds above them to settle and for life to return to normal. Think Daniel Galouye's *Dark Universe* (1961), Philip Wylie's *Triumph* (1963) and scores of other stories that were products of the Cold War and the fear of nuclear war.

Wool chronicles the adventures of a small group of humans living in a very deep silo. Just where is never made clear. But something terrible had ruined the earth and its toxic residue still can be seen outside through a single camera lens. Their enclosed culture has several rigid rules in order to keep everyone alive. One rule is that anyone who even *thinks* about going outside is actually "invited" to leave. They're kicked out because simply having the thought of leaving is a crime. The novel opens with the silo's sheriff who has voluntarily opted to go outside. Earlier, his beloved wife had gone outside after a bout of extreme depression. So, he's finally reached the end of his emotional tether and decides to leave. It's a self-inflicted death sentence.

Those who go outside are provided with a protective suit (but no oxygen tanks) and a piece of wool to clean the lens of the only camera that allows an outside view. Wool, here, is an obvious metaphor. Nonetheless, the world outside is still caught in the grips of a staggering ecological disaster. The sun is barely visible during the day and only recently have a few stars been seen through the haze at night. The city in the distance still stands, but it's in ruins and thoroughly dark. This is how this brilliant adventure starts.

Howey's writing style is clean, crisp, and the story never lags as we learn about the silo and who keeps the humans in check within their barely pleasant prison. It's clear that Howey has done his homework and has avoided the usual clichés that crop up with this kind of story. The novel takes some unusual turns, but Howey never loses control of the story. It becomes more complicated as it evolves, particularly when a new sheriff, a woman named Juliette, seeks out the answer to the question as to why their first sheriff left on his own. I won't give away any more than that. Hugh Howey, an author unknown to me until now, has written an extraordinary post-apocalypse novel that actually adds something new to the literature. It's a keeper (and I'll bet you a quarter that there's a movie in Mr. Howey's future).

♈

Ready Player One
by Ernest Cline
Broadway, 2012
Paperback: 384 pages
ISBN 978-0765367457

Ready Player One takes place in or around 2045 where the world is an over-used, fuel-depleted, bombed-out, broken-down nightmare. There is little, if any, civil order. Kids still go to school and there are shards of a government manifesting here and there, but the protagonist of *Ready Player One* won't have any of it and has to get along the best he can.

Our hero, Wade Watts, is a pimply, overweight teenager who spends most of his spare time in an online world call OASIS. Watts, though alienated, is nonetheless resourceful, brilliant, and inventive. Thing is, he's cracked the secret "key" to OASIS left behind by its creator, James Halliday, the richest man in the world. As such, Watts stands to inherit the fortune Halliday left behind, and lots of people start chasing after Watts. The novel is rife with fanboy references to games and gaming and especially to the 1980s, the decade not only of cool music but the rise of video games. It's a thrill ride for any kid who's played any chase 'em and gun 'em down video, hated school, and was afraid of girls.

This book has received rave reviews for its depiction of a "novel" future (to quote one reviewer) and a uniquely resourceful hero (to reference another). These would be true if the customers who posted their reviews on *Ready Player One*'s Amazon page hadn't been at all aware of the last seventy years of science fiction literature and hadn't seen the *Matrix* movies (as well as *Blade Runner, Escape from New York,* and *12 Monkeys*).

Nothing in this book is even remotely new or inventive. The main character is every pre-pubescent hero or heroine that you've read about in science fiction. Think Podkayne of Mars. Think Ender. And of course Wade Watts survives by his wits (which are nothing more than PC gaming skills that in real life would be worthless). In Wade's world, the sky is polluted; the water is polluted; people's minds are polluted. And Ernest Cline writes all of this with clear élan as if neither he nor his readers have ever seen any of this before. I had a lot of trouble finishing this novel because every page had ideas and character types taken directly from other science fiction short stories and novels, especially since the 1980s. However, if you are under thirty and haven't read much science fiction and have never seen the *Matrix* movies or *Blade Runner,* or any movie where computer geeks save the world, then *Ready Player One* is for you.

After the Fall, Before the Fall, During the Fall by Nancy Kress
Tachyon Books, 2012
Paperback: 192 pages
ISBN 978-1616960650

Nebula- and Hugo-Award-winner Nancy Kress' short novel, *After the Fall, Before the Fall, During the Fall,* is a tightly controlled story in three alternating parts about a world in the midst of several ecological disasters, most of them manmade. The main plot concerns a young boy named Pete in the future who is tasked to "raid" our present era for children who are necessary to create a breeding population in the "Shell." The Shell is an enclosed structure built by aliens called the Tesslies who have imprisoned 26 humans and given them "Grab" technology to pull human babies out of the past in order to keep humankind going in the future.

The novel's main adult character, mathematician Julie Kahn, using her unique algorithms, has discovered a pattern to strange child kidnappings that keep occurring in the present era and sets out to find out why they are happening. In the midst of all this, bad microbes are mutating and eating at roots and plants, tectonic plates are shifting everywhere, especially in the Atlantic, and Yellowstone's supermassive magma dome is about to explode.

The novel is efficiently written with a careful balance between the sections of the novel that are the "before," the "during," and the "after." And all of it makes for an effortless read.

That said, the novel has several flaws. While Ms. Kress has created a number of sympathetic characters in this novel, especially Julie Kahn, the science itself is iffy. Kress wants a convergence of catastrophes that will wipe out humankind. But she also wants them to have been caused by Gaia, the Earth Goddess, in rebellion. But such tropes don't actually work here. Mutated germs and toxic pollution are one thing. But to have a super-volcano explode while a massive Atlantic tsunami (in an unrelated geologic action) destroys the coasts of Europe and America at the same time is a stretch. That is, having them *caused* by an Earth Goddess. It becomes something we have to take on faith—and that transcends science fiction.

In the end, one of the novel's characters lectures us on how bad we all are to the earth. I'm surprised at this because it breaks the first rule of writing which says, *show*, don't *tell*. Truly, we don't need a character telling us that we're horrible people because we shit where we eat (so to speak). We've already *seen* it throughout the novel.

Still, I loved the Tesslies, the aliens who resemble Nikola Tesla's electrical halo experiments, and I liked the Shell. I particularly loved the fact that Kress doesn't tell us who the Tesslies are or where they came from or why they're doing what they're doing with such a small breeding pool of 26 people. There is more here for Kress to play with, if she wishes. I'd love to see how Pete and his new family make use of the future the Tesslies have created for them.

SERIALIZATION

We'll be serializing a novel in each issue of Galaxy's Edge, and I'm incredibly proud to introduce Daniel F. Galouye's Dark Universe. Published in 1961, it was Dan's first novel, and it was nominated for a Hugo, which is almost unheard-of for debut novels.

But the real kicker came when I had lunch with him at the 1968 Worldcon, and he mentioned to me that he had voted for Robert A. Heinlein's Stranger in a Strange Land for the 1962 Hugo. I later found out that Dark Universe had lost by two votes. If Dan had voted for himself – which would be one vote less for Stranger, one more for Dark Universe – his very first novel would have tied one of the bestselling books of the decade by an acknowledged master of the field.

Dan wrote this book at a time when half the country expected a nuclear war with Russia to take place momentarily. There were thousands of prepared caves, sub-basements, and bomb shelters just waiting to protect us from the devastation. I'll say no more. Read on, and enjoy the opening of one of the field's classics.

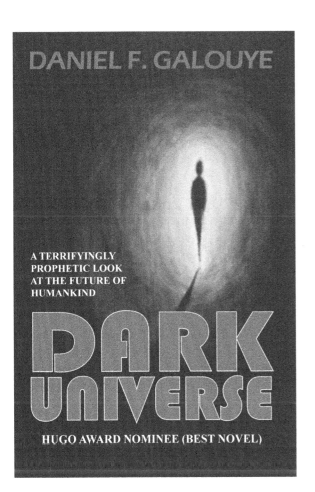

DARK UNIVERSE
by Daniel Galouye
Phoenix Pick, 2010
Trade Paperback: 182 pages. *Kindle, Nook, More*
ISBN: 978-1-60450-487-3

DARK UNIVERSE

by Daniel F. Galouye

CHAPTER ONE

Pausing beside the hanging needle of rock, Jared tapped it with his lance. Precise, staccato-like tones filled the passageway.

"Hear it?" he coaxed. "It's right up ahead."

"I don't hear a thing." Owen edged forward, stumbled and fell lightly against Jared's back. "Nothing but mud and hanging stones."

"No pits?"

"None that *I* can hear."

"There's one not twenty paces off. Better stick close to me."

Jared tapped the rock again, inclining an ear so he would miss none of the subtle echoes. There it was, all right—massive and evil as it clung to a nearby ledge listening to their advance.

Ahead were no more needles of rock he could conveniently tap. The last echoes had told him that much. So he produced a pair of clickstones from his pouch and brought them together sharply in the hollow of his hand, concentrating on the returning tones. To his right, his ears traced out great formations of rocks, folded one over the other and reflecting a confusing pattern of sound.

Owen clutched his shoulder as they pressed forward. "It's too smart. We'll never catch up with it."

"Of course we will. It'll get annoyed and attack sooner or later. Then there'll be one less soubat to contend with."

"But Radiation! It's pitch silent! I can't even hear where I'm going!"

"What do you think I'm using clickstones for?"

"I'm used to the central echo caster."

Jared laughed. "That's the trouble with you pre-Survivors. Depend too much on the familiar things."

Owen's sarcastic snort was justified. For Jared, at twenty-seven pregnancy periods of age, was not only his senior by less than two gestations, but also was still a pre-Survivor himself.

Drawing up beneath the ledge, Jared unslung his bow. Then he handed Owen the spear and stones.

"Stay here and click out some distinct tones—about a pulse apart."

He eased forward, arrow strung. Now the ledge was casting back sharp echoes. The soubat was stirring, folding and unfolding its immense, leathery wings. He paused and listened to the evil form, audibly outlined against the smooth, rock background. Furry, oval face—twice as large as his own. Alert ears, cupped and pointed. Clenched talons, sharp as the jagged rocks to which they clung. And twin *pings* of reflected sound brought the impression of bared fangs.

"Is it still there?" Owen whispered anxiously.

"Can't you hear it yet?"

"No, but I can sure smell the thing. It—"

Abruptly the soubat released its grip and dropped. Jared didn't need clickstones now. The furious flapping of wings was a direct, unmistakable target. He drew the bow, placing the feathered end of the arrow against his ear, and released the string.

The creature screamed—a piercing, ragged cry that reverberated in the passage.

"Good Light Almighty!" Owen exclaimed. "You got it!"

"Just punctured a wing." Jared reached for another arrow. "*Quick*—give me some more echoes!"

But it was too late. The thrashing of its wings was carrying the soubat off down a branch passage.

Listening to the retreating sound, Jared absently fingered his beard. Cropped close to his chin, it was a dense growth that projected bluntly forward, giving his face a self-confident tone. Taller than the span of a bowstring, he was lance-like in posture and his limbs were solidly corded. Although shoulder length in the back, his hair was trimmed in front, leaving ears unobstructed and face fully exposed. This accommodated his fondness for open eyes. It was a preference that wasn't based on religious belief, but rather on his dislike for the facial tautness which came with closed eyes.

Later, the side passage narrowed and received a river that flowed up out of the ground, leaving only a thin strip of slippery rock for them to tread.

Gripping his arm, Owen asked, "What's up ahead?"

Jared sounded the clickstones. "No low rocks. No pits. The stream flows off into the wall and the passage widens again."

He was listening more intently, though, to other, almost lost echoes—minor reflections from small things that slid into the river as they retreated from the disturbing noise of the stones.

"Make a note of this place," he said. "It's crawling with game."

"Salamanders?"

"Hundreds of them. That means decent-sized fish and hordes of crayfish."

Owen laughed. "I can just hear the Prime Survivor authorizing a hunting expedition *here*. Nobody's ever been *this* far before."

"*I* have."

"When?" the other asked skeptically.

They cleared the stream and were back on dry ground again.

"Eight or nine pregnancy periods ago."

"Radiation—but you were a child then! And you came *here*—*this* far from the Lower Level?"

"More than once."

"Why?"

"To hunt for something."

"What?"

"Darkness."

Owen chuckled. "You don't *find* Darkness. You *commit* it."

"So the Guardian says. He shouts, 'Darkness abounds in the worlds of men!' And he says that means sin and evil prevail. But I don't believe it means that."

"What *do* you believe?"

"Darkness must be something real. Only, we can't recognize it."

Again Owen laughed. "If you can't recognize it, then how do you expect to find it?"

Jared disregarded the other's skepticism. "There's a clue. We know that in the Original World—the first world that man inhabited after he left Paradise—we were closer to Light Almighty. In other words, it was a good world. Now let's suppose there's some sort of connection between sin and evil and this Darkness stuff. That means there must be *less* Darkness in the Original World. Right?"

"I suppose so."

"Then all I have to do is find something there's less of in the Original World."

Clickstone echoes traced out a massive obstruction ahead and Jared slowed his pace. He reached the barricade and explored it with his fingers. Rocks, piled one upon the other, stretched completely across the passage, rearing up to his shoulder.

"Here it is," he announced, "—the Barrier."

Owen's grip firmed on his arm. "*The* Barrier?"

"We can make it over the top easily."

"But—the law! We can't go past the Barrier!"

Jared dragged him along. "Come on. There are *no* monsters. Nothing to be afraid of—except maybe a soubat or two."

"But they say it's worse than Radiation itself!"

"That's what they *tell* you." By now Jared had him halfway up the mound. "They even say you'll find the Twin Devils Cobalt and Strontium waiting to carry you off to the depths of Radiation. Rot! Compost!"

"But the Punishment Pit!"

Scrambling down the other side, Jared rattled his clickstones with more than one purpose in mind. Besides drowning out Owen's protests, the clatter also plumbed the passage before them. Owen had somehow gotten in front and the close-quarter echoes were clearly transmitting sonic impressions of a stocky body, alert with tension and protected by outstretched, groping arms.

"For Light's sake!" Jared rebuked. "Get your hands down! I'll tell you if you're going to bump into anything."

The next echo crest caught the other's shrug. "So I'm no good with clickstones," he gruffed, stepping off in a resentful stride.

Jared followed, appreciating Owen's pluck. Cautious and hesitant, he took things reluctantly. But when the final *click* fetched its impression of an unavoidable situation with natural foe or Zivver, there wasn't a more determined fighter around.

Zivvers and soubats and bottomless pits, Jared reflected—those were the challenges of existence. If it weren't for them the Lower Level World and its passages would be as safe as Paradise itself was before man turned his back on Light Almighty and, as the legend had it, came to the various worlds that men and Zivvers now inhabited.

At the moment, though, only the soubats held his concern. One in particular—a vicious, marauding creature that had winged furiously into the Lower Level and snatched away a sheep.

He spat in disgust, recalling the venomous expletives his archery instructor had muttered long ago: "Stinking, Light damned things from the bowels of Radiation!"

"What *are* soubats?" one of the young archers had asked.

"They started off like the inoffensive little bats whose manure we collect for the plants. But they had truck with the Devils somewhere along the way. Either Cobalt or Strontium took one of them down to Radiation and made it over into a supercreature. From that one came all the soubats we have to contend with now."

Jared filled the passage with anxious, probing echoes. Owen, stubbornly maintaining the lead, was advancing more cautiously now, sending his feet out in sliding motions rather than pronounced steps.

The other's closed-eyes preference brought a smile to Jared's lips. It was a habit that would never be broken. It accommodated the belief that the eyes themselves should be protected and preserved for feeling the Great Light Almighty's presence on His Return.

But there wasn't anything objectionable about Owen, Jared assured himself, except that he was too susceptible to literal acceptance of the legends. Like the one which held that Light had resented man's invention of the manna plant and had cast him out of Paradise and into eternal Darkness, whatever that was.

One *click* and Owen was there—several paces ahead. Another and he was gone. In the interim there had been a distressed shout and the sound of flesh impacting on rock. Then:

"For Light's sake! Get me out of here!"

More echoes disclosed the presence of the shallow pit which had, until then, lurked in the echo void ahead of Owen.

Standing on the lip of the cavity, Jared lowered his lance. The other grabbed hold and started to pull himself out. But Jared tensed, wrenched the spear free and cast himself on the ground. He barely escaped clawing talons as the soubat swooped down.

"We're going to get a soubat!" he shouted exultantly.

By its shrieks, he tracked the animal as it made a ranging turn, gaining altitude, then dived down in a second, screaming attack. Jared lunged up, anchored the spear in a crevice and braced himself along the shaft, aiming it at the onrushing fury.

All Radiation broke loose as three hundred pounds of wrath hit Jared in a single, violent blast and bowled him over. He rose and felt the warmth of blood on his arm where talon had laid open flesh.

"Jared! You all right?"

"Stay down! It might come back!" He ran a hand over the ground and retrieved his bow.

But all was silent. The soubat had retreated once more, this time possibly with a spear wound added to its distress.

Owen climbed out of the pit. "You hurt?"

"Just a couple of scratches."

"Did you get it?"

"Radiation no! But I know where it is."

"I'm not even asking where. Let's go home."

Jared tapped the ground with his bow and listened. "It turned off into the Original World—up ahead."

"Let's go back, Jared!"

"Not until I get that thing's tusks in my pouch."

"You're going to get them *somewhere else*!"

But Jared went on. And, reluctantly, Owen followed.

Later he asked, "Are you *really* determined to find Darkness?"

"I'm going to find it if it takes the rest of my life."

"Why bother with hunting evil?"

"Because I'm really listening for something else. And Darkness may be just a step along the way."

"What *are* you hunting for?"

"Light."

"The Great Light Almighty," Owen reminded, reciting one of the tenets, "is present in the souls of good men and—"

"Suppose," Jared broke in boldly, "Light isn't God, but something else?"

The other's religious sensitivity was shocked. Jared could tell by his breathless silence, by the slight acceleration of his pulse.

"What else *could* Light Almighty be?" Owen asked finally.

"I don't know. But I'm sure it's something good. And if I can find it, life will be better for all mankind."

"What makes you think that?"

"If Darkness is connected with evil, and if Light is its opposite, then Light must be good. And if I find Darkness, then I may have some kind of idea as to the nature of Light."

Owen snorted. "That's ridiculous! You mean you think our beliefs are wrong?"

"Not altogether. Maybe just twisted around. You know what happens when a story passes from mouth to mouth. Just think what *could* happen to it passing from generation to generation."

Jared returned his attention to the passage as the clickstone echoes betrayed a great hollow space in the wall on his right.

They stood in the vaulted entrance to the Original World and Jared's *clicks* lost themselves in the silence of a vast expanse. He substituted his largest, hardest pair of sounding rocks. These he had to clap together with considerable force to produce reports loud enough to carry to the farthest recesses and back.

First—the soubat. Its lingering stench verified that the thing was somewhere in here. But none of the returning echoes carried with it the textural impression of leathery wings or soft, furry body.

"The soubat?" Owen asked anxiously.

"It's hiding," Jared said between *clicks*. Then, to take his friend's mind off the danger, "How good are you? What do you hear?"

"A Radiation of a big world."

"Right. Go on."

"In the space just ahead—softness. A clump or two of—"

"Manna plants. Growing close around a single hot spring. I can hear scores of empty pits too—pits where boiling water used to feed the energy hunger of *thousands* of plants. But, go ahead."

"Over there on the left, a pool—a big one."

"Good!" Jared complimented. "Fed by a stream. What else?"

"I—Radiation! Something queer. A lot of queer things."

Jared advanced. "Those are living quarters—stretched all around the wall."

"But I don't understand." Owen, confused, followed along. "They're out in the open!"

"When the people lived here they didn't have to find their privacy in grottoes. They *built* walls around spaces out in the open."

"*Square* walls?"

"They had a flair for geometry, I suppose."

Owen pulled back. "Let's get out of here! They say Radiation isn't too far from the Original World!"

"Maybe they say that just to keep us out."

"I'm beginning to think that you don't believe *anything*."

"Of course I do—whatever I can hear, feel, taste, or smell." Jared changed position and the echoes from his stones aligned themselves with an opening in one of the living quarters.

"Soubat!" he whispered as the stream of *clicks* brought back an impression of the thing hanging inside the cubicle. "You take the spear. We'll be ready for it this time!"

Cautiously, he approached within arrow range of the structure, securing his stones. He didn't need them now—not with the sound of the thing's breathing as clear as the snorting of an angry bull.

He strung an arrow and wedged a second under his belt where it would be within convenient reach. Behind him, he heard Owen dig the spear shaft into the ground. Then he asked, "Ready?"

"Let it fly," Owen urged. And there was no quaver in his voice. The last *click* had sounded. The lines were drawn.

Aiming at the hissing breath, he released the bowstring.

The arrow screamed through the air and thudded into something solid—too solid to be animal flesh. Screeching its rage, the soubat hurtled toward them. Jared strung the second arrow, taking his lead in advance of the winged fury.

He let it fly and ducked.

The beast shrieked in agony as it zipped by overhead. Then there was a *thud* and a final rush of air from the great lungs.

"For Light's sake!" came the familiar exclamation. "Get this stinking thing off me!"

Grinning, Jared tapped his bow on the solid rock underfoot and, in return, picked up the sonic effects of a disheveled heap—soubat, human, broken lance, and protruding arrow shaft.

Owen squirmed out finally. "Well, we got the damned thing. *Now* can we go home?"

"As soon as I finish." Jared was already cutting out the tusks.

Soubats and Zivvers. One by one, the Lower and Upper Level people could hope to eliminate the former. But what would prevail against the latter? What *could* prevail against creatures who used no clickstones but who, nevertheless, knew everything about their surroundings? It was an uncanny ability nobody could explain, except to say they were possessed of Cobalt or Strontium.

Oh, well, Jared mused, prophecy held that man would vanquish all his foes. He supposed that included the Zivvers also, although to him it had always seemed that Zivvers were human too—after a fashion.

He finished prying out the first tusk and some remote recess of his mind dredged up memories of childhood teachings:

What is Light?
Light is a Spirit.
Where is Light?
If it weren't for the evil in man, Light would be everywhere.
Can we feel or hear Light?
No, but in the hereafter we shall all see Him.

Rubbish! Anyway, no one could explain the word *see*. What did you do to the Almighty when you *seed* Him?

He secured the tusks in his pouch and stood up, listening all around. There was *something* here that there might be less of than in the other worlds—something man called "Darkness" and defined as sin and evil. But what was it?

"Jared, come here!"

He used clickstones to establish Owen's location. The echoes brought an impression of his friend standing by a thick pole that was leaning over at such an angle as to be almost lying on the ground. He was feeling an object dangling from the upthrust end—something round and brittle that hurled back distinct, ringing tones.

"It's a *Bulb*!" Owen exclaimed. "Just like the Guardian's relic of Light Almighty!"

Jared's memory resurrected more of the beliefs:

So compassionate was the Almighty (it was the Guardian of the Way's voice that came back now) *that when He banished man from Paradise, He sent parts of Himself to be with us for a while. And He dwelled in many little vessels like this Holy Bulb.*

There was a noise somewhere among the living quarters.

"Light!" Owen swore. "Do you smell *that*?"

Indeed Jared did smell it. It was so offensively alien that it made the hair bristle on his neck. He rattled his clickstones desperately, backing off all the while.

The echoes brought an incredible, jumbled pattern of sound—impressions of something human, but not human; unbelievably evil because it was different, yet arresting because it seemed to have a pair of arms and legs and a head and stood more or less upright. It was advancing, trying to take them by surprise.

Jared reached into his quiver. But there were no more arrows. Then, terrified, he cast his bow away and turned to flee.

"Oh, Light!" Owen moaned, scrambling back toward the exit. "What in Radiation *is* it?"

But Jared couldn't answer. He had all he could do trying to find the way out while keeping his ears on the unholy menace. It was reeking more terribly than a thousand soubats.

"It's Strontium himself!" Owen decided. "The legends are true! The Twin Devils *are* here!" He turned and bolted for the exit, his own bewildered shouts providing the guiding echoes.

Jared only stood there, paralyzed by a sensation altogether beyond comprehension. His auditory impression of the monstrous form was clear: it seemed the thing's entire body was made up of fluttering sheets of flesh. But there was something else—a vague yet vivid bridge of *noiseless* echoes that spanned the distance from the creature and boiled down into the depths of his conscious.

Sounds, odors, tastes, the pressure of the rocks and material things around him—all seemed to pour into his being, bringing pain. He clamped his hands over his face and raced after Owen.

A *zip-hiss* cleaved the air above his head and a moment later Owen's voice rose in a cry of anguished terror. Then Jared heard his friend collapse, falling at the entrance to the Original World.

He reached the spot where Owen lay, slung the unconscious form over his shoulder and plunged on. *Zip-hiss.*

Something grazed his arm, leaving droplets of moisture clinging to the flesh. In the next instant he was tripping, falling, picking himself up and racing on under the burden of Owen's dead weight. And he was seized by a sudden grogginess he couldn't explain.

Deaf now, he staggered against the piled boulders that formed the passage's left wall and groped his way around one of the huge rocks. Then he stumbled into a crevice between two outcroppings and fell with Owen on top of him, lapsing into unconsciousness.

CHAPTER TWO

"**G**ood Light! Let's get out of here!" Owen's whisper jarred him awake and Jared struggled erect. Then, remembering the Original World and its terror, he lurched back.

"It's gone now," the other assured.

"You certain?"

"Yes. I heard it listening all around out there. Then it left. What in Radiation was it—Cobalt? Strontium?"

Jared crawled from among the boulders and reached for a pair of clickstones. But then he thought better of making any noise.

Owen shuddered. "That smell! The sound of its shape!"

"And that other sensation!" Jared swore. "It was like something—psychic!"

He snapped his fingers softly, evaluating the reflected sounds, and continued around a great hanging stone that cascaded in graceful folds, flowing into a mound which strained up from the floor like a rearing giant.

"What other sensation?" Owen asked.

"Like all Radiation breaking loose in your head. Something that wasn't sound or smell or touch."

"I didn't hear anything like that."

"It wasn't hearing—I don't think."

"What made us pass out?"

"I don't know."

They went around a bend in the passage. Now that they had put some distance behind them, Jared began using his clickstones. "Light!" he exclaimed, relieved. "But I'd welcome even a soubat now!"

"Not without weapons you wouldn't."

And, as they crossed the Barrier and continued on alongside the wide river, Jared wondered why his friend hadn't experienced the same uncanny sensation he had. As far as he was concerned, that phase of the incident was even more frightening than the monster itself.

Then his lips grew grimly taut as an alarming possibility suggested itself: Suppose his Original World experience had been a punishment from the Great Almighty for his blasphemous belief that Light was something less than God?

They headed into more familiar territory and he announced, "We've got to report this to the Prime Survivor."

"We can't!" Owen protested. "We broke the law in coming here!"

Which was a complication Jared hadn't considered. Owen, to be sure, was in enough trouble as it was, having let the cattle get in the manna orchard last period.

Several hundred breaths later, Jared led the way around the final major hazard—a huge pit without bottom. He put his pebbles away. Not long afterward he hissed for silence, then drew Owen over to a recess in the wall.

"What's wrong?" the other demanded.

"Zivvers!" he whispered.

"I don't hear anything."

"You will in a few heartbeats. They're going down the Main Passage ahead. If they turn this way we may have to run for it."

The sounds in the other tunnel were more audible now. A sheep bleated and Jared recognized the pitch. "That's one of *our* animals. They raided the *Lower Level.*"

The Zivver voices reached maximum volume as the pillagers passed the corridor intersection, then fell off.

"Come on," Jared urged. "They can't ziv us now."

He went not more than thirty paces, however, before he drew up and cautioned in his lowest voice, "Quiet!"

He held his breath and listened. Besides his own pounding heartbeat and Owen's fainter one, there was yet a third—not too far away, weak, but pumping violently with fright.

"What is it?" Owen asked.

"A Zivver."

"You're just getting the scent from that raiding party."

But Jared edged forward, weighing the auditory impressions, sniffing out other clues. The scent of the Zivver was unmistakable, but it was of minor proportions—that of a child! He drew in another whiff and detained it in his nasal chamber.

A girl Zivver!

Her heartbeat was distinct as he clicked his pebbles once to sound out the details of the cleft in which she was hiding. She stiffened at the noise, but didn't try to escape. Instead, she started crying—plaintively.

Owen relaxed. "It's only a child!"

"What's the matter?" Jared asked solicitously, but got no reply.

"What are you doing out here?" Owen tried.

"We're not going to hurt you," Jared promised. "What's wrong?"

"I—I can't ziv," she finally managed between sobs.

Jared knelt beside her. "You're a Zivver, aren't you?"

"Yes. I mean—no, I'm not. That is—"

She was perhaps thirteen gestations old. No older, certainly.

He led her out into the passageway. "Now—what's your name?"

"Estel."

"And why are you hiding out here, Estel?"

"I heard Mogan and the others coming. I ran in here so they wouldn't ziv me."

"Why don't you want them to find you?"

"So they won't take me back to the Zivver World."

"But that's where you belong, isn't it?"

She sniffled and Jared heard her wiping her cheeks dry.

"No," she said despondently. "Everybody there can ziv except me. And when I'm ready to become a Survivoress there won't be any Zivver Survivors who'll want me."

She began sobbing again. "I want to go to your world."

"You can't Estel," Owen tried to explain. "You don't understand what the sentiment is against—I mean—oh, you tell her, Jared."

Jared brushed the hair off her face when the reflection of his voice told him it was hanging there. "Once in the Lower Level we had a little girl—just about your age. She was sad because she couldn't hear. She wanted to run away. Then, one period, all of a sudden she could hear! And she was glad she had been smart enough *not* to run away and get lost before then."

"She was a Different One, wasn't she?" the girl asked.

"No. That's just the point. We only *thought* she was Different. And if she'd run away we never would have found out she wasn't."

Estel was silent as Jared led her toward the Main Passage.

"You mean," she asked after a while, "you think *I* might start *zivving*?"

He laughed and halted in the larger corridor beside a gurgling hot spring that sent its moist warmth swirling all around them. "I'm sure you'll start zivving—when you least expect it. And you'll be just as happy as that other little girl."

He listened in the direction of the Zivver raiders and readily picked up the sound of their receding voices. "What do you say, Estel—want to go home?"

"Well, all right—if you say so."

"Good girl!" He gave her a pat and propelled her in the direction of the other Zivvers. Then he cupped his hands and filled the passage with his voice. "There's one of your children back here!"

Owen shifted nervously. "Let's get out of here before we get stomped."

But Jared only laughed softly. "We'll be safe long enough to make sure they pick her up." He listened to the girl groping toward the returning Zivvers. "Anyway, they can't ziv us now."

"Why not?"

"We're standing right by this hot spring. They can't ziv anything too close to a boiling pit. That's something I learned on my own, gestations ago."

"What's a hot spring got to do with it?"

"I don't know. But it works."

"Well, if they can't ziv us, then they'll hear us."

"Point Number Two about Zivvers: they rely too much on zivving. Can't hear or smell worth a damned."

Soon they reached the entrance to the Lower Level World. Jared listened to Owen strike off for his own quarters, then he headed toward the Administration Grotto. He had made up his mind to report the Original World menace without implicating his friend.

Everything seemed normal—too normal, considering that Zivvers had just staged a raid. But then, the attacks were not so infrequent that the Survivors couldn't take them in stride when they did come.

Off to his left he caught Randel's scent and traced his climb up the pole to rewind the echo caster's pulley. Presently there was a speed-up in the mechanical *clacking* of the stones. And Jared listened to the more complete impressions the accelerated echoes provided. He made out the details of a work party spreading compost in the manna orchard, another digging out a new public grotto. Against the distant wall women were washing cloths in the river.

What struck him most, though, was the relative silence, which testified that *something* had happened. Even the children were drawn into small, voiceless clusters in front of the residential recesses.

There was a groan on his right—from the Injury Treatment Grotto—and he altered course. The central caster's reflected *clacks* told him someone was in front of the entrance. When he got closer he heard the feminine outline of Zelda.

"Trouble?" he asked.

"Zivvers," she said tersely. "Where were you?"

"Out after a soubat. Any casualties?"

"Alban and Survivor Bridley. Just roughed up though." Her voice filtered through hair that protectively draped her face.

"Any *Zivvers* get hurt?"

She laughed—a bitter outburst, like the twang of a bowstring. "You kidding? The Prime Survivor's been listening for you."

"Where is he?"

"Meeting with the Elders."

Jared continued on over to the Administration Grotto, but quieted his steps as he neared the entrance. Elder Haverty had the floor. His high-pitched, faltering voice was easily recognizable.

"We'll close up the entrance!" Haverty pounded the slab. "Then we won't have to worry about either the Zivvers *or* the soubats!"

"Sit down, Elder," came the authoritative voice of the Prime Survivor. "You're not making sense."

"Eh? How so?"

"We're told that was tried long ago. It only choked off the circulation and ran the heat up into the sweltering range."

"Least we could do," Haverty persisted, "is close it up *some*."

"Ought to be bigger as it is."

Jared eased up to the grotto entrance, but stood to one side so he wouldn't block any of the direct sounds from the caster. That would betray his presence even to the most insensitive ears.

The Prime Survivor was absently tapping the meeting slab with his fingernail, producing unobtrusive echoes.

"However," he said, "there *is* something we can do."

"Eh? What's that?" Elder Haverty asked.

"We couldn't do it by ourselves. It's too big a project. But we might undertake it as a joint enterprise with the Upper Level."

"We never had any joint enterprises with them before." It was Elder Maxwell's voice that entered the discussion.

"No, but they know we're going to have to pool our resources."

"What's the pitch?" asked Haverty.

"There's one *passageway* we might seal off. It wouldn't disturb the circulation in either the Upper or Lower Level. But, still, it would block us off from the Zivver World, as far as we know."

"The Main Passage," Maxwell guessed.

"Right. It'd be quite a job. But with both Levels working at it, we could do it in maybe half a pregnancy period."

"What about the Zivvers?" Haverty wanted to know. "Won't *they* have anything to say about that?"

Jared heard the Prime Survivor shrug his shoulders before continuing: "The two Levels far outnumber the Zivvers. We could keep adding material to this side of the barricade faster than they could haul it away from the other side. Eventually they'd give up."

Silence around the slab.

"Sounds good," Maxwell said. "Now all we got to do is sell the Upper Level on the idea."

"I think we can do that." The Prime Survivor cleared his throat. "Jared, come on in. We've been waiting for you."

The Prime Survivor might be getting old, Jared conceded, entering. But his ears and nose hadn't aged any. From the uninterrupted fingernail tapping, Jared received a composite impression of all the faces at the slab turned in his direction. There was a figure standing behind the Prime Survivor, he sensed.

The man moved into the clear and Jared picked up his features—short and somewhat stooped despite the comparative youthfulness his breathing suggested; hair flowing down past his forehead and around the sides of his face, with irregular openings to accommodate his ears and nose-mouth region. The fullest fuzzy-face in the Lower Level—Romel Fenton-Spur, his brother.

After the amenity of Reasonable Time for Recognition and Reflection had been observed, the Prime Survivor cleared his throat. "Jared, it's about time to apply for your Survivorship, don't you think?"

Jared's impulse was to brush aside the prosaic matter and launch into his revelation of the menace lurking in the Original World. But his presentation would have to be rational, so he decided to put it off a while. "I suppose so."

"Ever think of Unification?"

"Radiation no!" Then he pinched his tongue. "No, I haven't given it any thought."

"You realize, of course, that every man must become a Survivor and that the principal obligation of a Survivor is to survive."

"That's what I've been told."

"And surviving doesn't mean merely preserving your own life, but also passing it down through the generations."

"I'm aware of that."

"And you've found no one with whom you'd like to Unify?"

There was Zelda; but she was a fuzzy-face. There was Luise, who was both open-eyed and bare-faced

to the clickstones. But she was always tittering. "No, Your Survivorship."

Romel snickered in anticipation of something or other and reproachful gestures were audible around the slab. For Jared, the sardonic giggle was reminiscent of earlier days when Romel's malicious pranks usually took the form of a swish-rope that would lash out from behind a boulder, twine around his ankles and snatch him off his feet. The fraternal antagonism was still there. Only, now it managed to find other adult—well, almost adult—forms of expression.

"Good!" the Prime Survivor enthused, rising. "I think we've found a Unification partner for you."

Jared sputtered a moment, then shed his respect with an oath. "Not for *me* you haven't!"

How could he tell them he had no time for Unification? That he had to be free to continue what he had started out to do long pregnancy periods ago? That he doubted their religious beliefs? That he wanted to spend his life proving Light was something physical, attainable in this existence—not something restricted to the afterlife?

Romel laughed and said, "That's for the Elders to decide."

"You're no Elder!"

"Neither are you. And, Jared, you're forgetting the Eminence of Seniority Code."

"To Radiation with the code!"

"That'll be enough," interrupted the Prime Survivor. "As Romel suggests, your Unification is for us to decide. Elders?"

Maxwell proposed, "Let's hear more about this arrangement first."

"Very well," the Prime Survivor went on. "Neither I nor the Wheel have let this get out yet, but we're both sold on the idea of joining hands between the two worlds. The Wheel thinks that end can be helped along by Unification between Jared and his niece."

"I won't do it!" Jared vowed. "The Wheel's just trying to pass off some spook of a relative!"

"Have you ever heard her?" the Prime Survivor asked.

"No! Have you?"

"No, but the Wheel says—"

"I don't care *what* the Wheel says!"

Jared drew back and listened. The Elders were rumbling impatiently. They weren't too happy over his stubbornness. If he didn't do something—*any-thing*—soon, they'd have him hooked!

"There's a monster in the Original World," he blurted, "I was out chasing a soubat and—"

"The Original World?" asked Elder Maxwell incredulously.

"Yes! And this thing—it reeked like Radiation and—"

"Do you realize what you've done?" the Prime Survivor demanded severely. "Crossing the Barrier is the worst possible offense, besides Murder and Misplacement of Bulky Objects!"

"But this creature! I'm trying to tell you I heard something *evil!*"

The Prime Survivor's voice drowned out even the central caster's *clacks*. "What in the name of Light Almighty did you *expect* to find in the Original World? Why do you think we have laws, the Barrier?"

"This calls for severe punishment," Romel suggested.

"You keep out of it!" snapped the Prime Survivor.

"The Punishment Pit?" Maxwell prompted.

"Eh? What?" clipped Haverty. "I imagine not. Not with a Unification arrangement pending."

Jared tried again. "This thing—it—"

"How about Seven Activity Periods of Detachment and Servility?" Haverty went on. "If he does it again—two gestations in the Pit."

"Lenient enough," Maxwell agreed. But he left unexpressed the general knowledge that only one prisoner had ever spent more than ten activity periods in the Pit and that he had had to be tied down for a whole gestation before he became harmless.

The Prime Survivor spoke up. "We'll make Jared's token punishment contingent on his accepting Unification."

The Elders eagerly smote the slab in approval.

"While serving your sentence," the Prime Survivor told Jared, "you can condition yourself for a visit to the Upper Level for the Five Periods Preparatory to Declaration of Unification Intentions."

Still snickering, Romel Fenton-Spur followed the Elders out.

When they were alone, Jared told the Prime Survivor, "That was a Radiation of a trick to play on *your own son!*"

The elder Fenton gave an expressionless shrug.

"Why tie in with that bunch up there?" Jared went on querulously. "We've fought Zivvers on our own this long, haven't we?"

"But they're multiplying, outgrowing their food supply."

"We'll set traps! We'll produce more food!"

Jared listened to the other shaking his head dourly. "On the contrary. We're going to produce *less*. You forget those three hot springs that dried up not thirty periods ago. That means dead manna plants—not as much food for the animals and ourselves."

Jared felt a touch of concern for the Prime Survivor. They were standing in the entrance to the grotto now and the sounds his father was reflecting conveyed their impressions of thinning limbs that had reluctantly yielded ample muscular development of a more active era. His hair was thin, but still swept proudly back over his head, evidencing an obstinate rejection of facial protection.

"It didn't have to be me," Jared grumbled. "Why not Romel?"

"He's a spur."

Jared didn't understand why the accident of illegitimate birth should make any difference in this situation. But he let the point go. "Well, anybody else then! There's Randel and Many and—"

"The Wheel and I have been discussing closer relations since you were hip high. And I've been building *you* up in his estimation until he thinks you're almost the equal of a Zivver."

Silence was perhaps the severest penalty of Jared's punishment.

Silence and drudgery.

Hauling manure from the world of the small bats, trudging to the cricket domain to collect insect bodies as compost for the manna orchard. Rechanneling overflow from the boiling pits and getting steam-shriveled flesh in the process. Tending livestock and hand-feeding chicks until they could feel around for their own food.

And all the while never to be allowed a word. Never a word spoken to him except in direction-giving. No clickstones for fine hearing. Completely isolated from contact with others.

The first period lasted an eternity; the second, a dozen. The third he spent tending the orchard and consigning to Radiation everyone who approached because they came only to give orders—all but one.

That was Owen, who relayed instructions to begin excavating a public grotto. And Jared heard the troubled lines on his face. "If you think you ought to be working alongside me," Jared said, violating Vocal Detachment, "you'd better forget it. I *made* you cross the Barrier."

"I've been worrying about that too," Owen admitted distantly. "But not nearly as much as about something else."

"What?" Jared spread more compost around the manna plant stalk.

"I'm not worthy of being a Survivor. Not after the way I acted out there in the Original World."

"Forget the Original World."

"I can't." Owen's voice was filled with self-reproach as he moved off. "Whatever courage I had I left beyond the Barrier."

"Damned fool!" Jared called softly. "Keep away from there!"

He spent the fourth period languishing in solitude, without even a single person bringing instructions. The fifth he tried congratulating himself on at least having escaped the Pit. But throughout the sixth, as he bemoaned aching muscles and insufferable fatigue, he realized he might as well have gotten the more severe punishment. And before the final stint of exhausting drudgery ended, he wished to Radiation he *had* been sentenced to the Pit!

He finished wresting a final slab into place for one of the new grottoes, then pegged the echo caster into silence for the sleep period. Numb with weariness, he dragged himself to the Fenton recess.

Romel was asleep, but the Prime Survivor was still lying awake. "I'm glad it's over, son," he comforted. "Now get some rest. Tomorrow you'll be escorted to the Upper Level for the Five Periods Preparatory to Declaration of Unification Intentions."

Lacking strength to argue, Jared collapsed on his ledge.

"There's something you ought to know," his father went on soberly. "The Zivvers may be taking cap-

tives again. Owen went out to collect mushrooms four periods ago. He hasn't been heard from since."

Suddenly wide awake, Jared wasn't as exhausted as he had imagined. When the Prime Survivor fell asleep, he retrieved his clickstones and stole out of the Lower Level World, tempering condemnation of Owen's addleheaded pride with concern for his safety.

Fighting the impulse to drop in his tracks and sleep there forever, he pushed on past the place where he had encountered the Zivver child, along the bank beside the swift stream and into the smaller tunnel. Sounding the depths of each pit along the way, he reached the Barrier and dragged himself over it. On the other side his foot brushed across something familiar—Owen's quiver!

Beside it were a broken lance and two arrows. The bow, his clickstones told him, lay against the wall, cracked almost in half. Sniffing what might have been the lingering scent of the Original World creature, he backed off toward the Barrier.

Owen didn't even have a chance to use his weapons.

CHAPTER THREE

At the entrance to the Upper Level, the unfamiliar tones of the central echo caster brought Jared crude impressions of a world much like his own, with grottoes, activity areas, and livestock compounds. In addition it had a natural ledge running along the right wall and sloping down to the ground nearby.

Waiting for his reception escort, he turned his thoughts grimly back to the discovery of Owen's weapons on the other side of the Barrier. All he could think of then was that the evil creature had been a punishment sent by Light Himself for his sacrilegious rejection of established beliefs. Certainly he had been wrong. The Barrier *had,* after all, been erected solely to protect man from monster. Yet, he knew he would not forfeit his quest for Darkness. Nor would he let the uncertainty surrounding Owen's fate rest for very long.

"Jared Fenton?"

The voice, coming from behind a boulder on his left, took him by surprise. Stepping out into the full sound of the central caster, the man said. "I'm Lorenz, Adviser to Wheel Anselm."

Lorenz's voice suggested a person of short stature, small lung capacity, depressed chest. Added to this composite was the indirect sonic impression of a face whose audible features were rough with creases and lacked the soft, moist prominences of exposed eyeballs.

"Ten Touches of Familiarization?" Jared offered formally.

But the Adviser declined. "My faculties are adequate. I never forget audible effects." He struck off down a path that coursed through the hot-springs area.

Jared followed. "The Wheel expecting me?" Which was an unnecessary question, since a runner had come ahead.

"I wouldn't be out here to meet you if he wasn't."

Detecting hostility in the Adviser's blunt responses, Jared turned his attention fully on the man. The caster tones were being harshly modulated by his expression of resentful determination.

"You don't want me up here, do you?" Jared asked frankly.

"I've advised against it. I don't hear where we can gain anything through close association with your world."

The Adviser's sullen attitude puzzled him for a moment—until he realized unification between the Upper and Lower Level would certainly affect Lorenz's established status.

The well-worn path had straightened and was now taking them along the right wall. Residential recesses cast back muffled gaps in the reflected sound pattern. And Jared sensed rather than clearly heard the knots of inquisitive people who were listening to him pass.

Presently the Adviser caught his shoulders and spun him to the right. "This is the Wheel's grotto."

Jared hesitated, getting his bearings. The recess was a deep one with many storage shelves. In the space before the entrance there was a large slab with adequate leg room carved in its sides. From its surface came the symmetrical sounds of empty manna shell bowls, giving the over-all impression of an orderly arrangement for a meal that would accommodate many persons.

"Welcome to the Upper Level! I'm Noris Anselm, the Wheel."

Jared listened to his more than amply proportioned host advance around the slab with arm extended. That the hand found his on first thrust spoke well for the Wheel's perceptive ability.

"I've heard a lot about you, my boy!" He pumped Jared's arm. "Ten Touches?"

"Of course." Jared submitted to exploring fingers that swept methodically across his face and chest and along his arms.

"Well," said Anselm approvingly. "Clean-cut features—erect posture—agility—strength. I don't guess the Prime Survivor exaggerated too much. Feel away."

Jared's hands Familiarized themselves with a stout but not flaccid physique. Absence of a chest cloth, clipped hair and beard, suggested resistance to the aging process. And lids that flicked their protest to his touch signified abiding rejection of closed eyes.

Anselm laughed. "So you've come with Declaration of Unification Intentions in mind?" He led Jared to a bench beside the slab.

"Yes. The Prime Survivor says—"

"Ah—Prime Survivor Fenton. Haven't heard him in some time."

"He sends—"

"Good old Evan!" the Wheel declared expansively. "He's got a likely idea—wanting the two Levels closer. What do you think?"

"At first I—"

"Of course you do. It doesn't take much imagination to hear the advantages, does it?"

Abandoning hope of completing a sentence, Jared accepted the question as rhetorical while he concentrated on faint impressions coming from the mouth of the grotto behind him. Someone had moved out into the entrance and was silently listening on. Reflected *clacks* fetched the outline of a youthful, feminine form.

"I said," Anselm repeated, "it doesn't take much imagination to hear the benefits of uniting the Levels."

Jared drew attentively erect. "Not at all. The Prime Survivor says there's a lot to be gained. He—"

"About this Unification. Figure you're ready for it?"

At least Jared had managed to finish *one* answer. But there was no point in pushing his success, so he simply said, "Yes."

"Good boy! Della's going to make a fine Survivoress. A little headstrong, perhaps. But you take my own Unification…"

The Wheel embarked on a lengthy dissertation while Jared's attention went back to the furtive girl. At least he knew who she was. At the mention of the name "Della," her breathing had faltered and he had heard a subjective quickening of her pulse.

The brisk, clear tones of the Wheel's voice produced sharp-sounding echoes. And Jared took note of the girl's precise, smooth profile. High cheekbones accentuated the self-confident tilt of her chin. Her eyes were wide open and her hair was arranged in a style he hadn't heard before. Swept tightly away from her face, it was banded in the back and went streaming bushily down her spine. His imagination provided him with a pleasing echo composite of Della racing down a windy passageway, long tresses fluttering behind.

"…But Lydia and I never had a son." His garrulous host had gone on to another subject by now. "Still, I think it would be best if the Wheelship remained in the Anselm line, don't you?"

"To be sure." Jared had lost track of the conversation.

"And the only way that can come about without complications is through Unification between you and my niece."

This, Jared reasoned, should be the cue for the girl to step from concealment. But she didn't budge.

The Upper Level had recovered from his arrival and now he listened to the sounds of a normal world—children shouting at play, women grotto-cleaning, men busy at their chores, a game of clatterball in progress on the field beyond the livestock pens.

The Wheel gripped his arm and said, "Well, we'll get better acquainted later on. There'll be a formal dinner this period where you'll Familiarize yourself with Della. But, first, I've had a recess prepared for your convenience."

Jared was led off along the row of residential grottoes. But they hadn't gone far when he was drawn to a halt.

"The Prime Survivor says you have a remarkable pair of ears, my boy. Let's hear how good they are."

Somewhat embarrassed, Jared turned his attention to the things about him. After a moment his ears were drawn to the ridge running along the far wall.

"I hear something on that ledge," he said. "There's a boy lying up there listening out over the world."

Anselm drew in a surprised breath. Then he shouted, "Myra, your child up on that shelf again?"

A woman nearby called out, "Timmy! Timmy, where are you?"

And a slight, remote voice answered, "Up here, Mother."

"Incredible!" exclaimed the Wheel. "Utterly incredible!"

As the formal dinner neared its end, Anselm thudded his drinking shell down on the slab and assured the other guests, "It was quite remarkable! There was the lad, *all the way across the world*. But Jared heard him anyway. How'd you do it, my boy?"

Jared would have let the matter drop. He'd had his fill of uneasiness, each guest having taken the full Ten Touches.

"There's a smooth dome behind the ledge," he explained wearily. "It magnifies the tones from the central caster."

"Nonsense, my boy! It was an amazing feat!"

The slab came alive with murmurs of respect.

Adviser Lorenz laughed. "Listening to the Wheel tell about it, I'd almost suspect our visitor might be a Zivver."

An uncomfortable hush followed. Jared could hear the Adviser's complacent smile. "It was remarkable," Anselm insisted.

There was a lull in the conversation and Jared steered the talk away from himself. "I enjoyed the crayfish, but the salamander was especially good. I've never tasted anything like it before."

"Indeed you haven't," Anselm boasted. "And we have Survivoress Bates to thank. Tell our guest how you manage it, Survivoress."

A stout woman across the slab said, "I had an idea meat would taste better if we could get away from soaking it directly in boiling water. So we tried putting the cuts in watertight shells and sinking them in the hot springs. This way the meat's *dry* cooked."

On the edge of his hearing, Jared sensed that Della was listening to his slight movements.

"The Survivoress used to prepare salamander even better," offered Lorenz.

"When we still had the big boiling pit," the woman said.

"When you *still* had it?" Jared asked, interested.

"It dried up a while back, along with a couple of others," Anselm explained. "But I suppose we'll be able to do without them."

The other guests had begun drifting off toward their grottoes—all except Della. But still she ignored Jared.

The Wheel gripped his shoulder, whispered "Good luck, my boy!" and headed for his own recess.

Someone turned off the echo caster, ending the activity period, and Jared sat listening to the girl's even breathing. He casually tapped the slab with a fingernail and studied the reflected impressions of a creased feminine brow and full lips compressed with concern.

He moved closer. "Ten Touches?"

There was a sharp alteration in the sound pattern as she faced the other way. But she offered no protest to Familiarization.

His probing fingers traced out her profile first, then verified the firmness of her cheekbones. He explored further the odd hair style and her level shoulders. The skin there was warm and full, its smoothness harshly broken by the overlay of halter straps.

She drew back. "I'm sure you'll recognize me the next time."

If he was going to be stuck with Unification, Jared decided, he could fare worse by way of a partner.

He waited for the feel of her fingers. But none came. Instead, she slid off the bench and walked casually toward a natural grotto whose emptiness reflected her footfalls. He followed.

"How does it feel," she asked finally, "to have Unification forced on you?" Her words bore more than a trace of bitter indignation.

"I don't much care for it."

"Then why don't you refuse?" She sat on a ledge in the grotto.

He paused outside, tracing the details of the recess as relayed by her rebounding words. "Why don't *you?*"

"I don't have much of a choice. The Wheel's made up his mind."

"That's tough." Her attitude suggested that the whole arrangement was his idea. But he supposed she did have a right to be indignant. So he added, "I guess we could both do worse."

"Maybe *you* could. But I might have my pick of a dozen Upper Level men I'd prefer."

He bristled. "How do you know? You haven't even had Ten Touches."

She scooped up a stone and tossed it. *Kerplunk.*

"I didn't ask for them," she said. "And I don't want them."

He wondered whether a few swats in the right place wouldn't soften her tongue. "I'm not *that* objectionable!"

"You—objectionable? Paradise no!" she returned. "You're *Jared Fenton* of the Lower Level!"

Another pebble went *kerplunk.*

"'I hear something on that ledge'," she mocked his earlier words. "'There's a boy lying up there listening out over the world'."

Della threw several more stones while he stood there with his ears trained severely on her. They all went *kerplunk.*

"That demonstration was your uncle's idea," he reminded her.

Instead of answering, she continued tossing rocks into the water. She had him on the defensive. And if he chose to strike back it would only seem he was in favor of their Unification, which couldn't be further from the truth. Unification and the obligations it brought would mean an end to his search for Light.

Della rose and went to the grotto wall where a group of slender stones hung needlelike from the ceiling. She stroked them lightly, and melodious tones filled the recess with vibrant softness. It was a wistful tune that sang of pleasant things with deep, tender meaning. He was stirred by the girl's sensitive talent as he was by the sharp contrasts the music showed in her nature.

She slapped several of the stones in an impulsive burst of temperament, then scooped up another pebble. Whispering through the air, her arm arched out to toss the rock as she turned and strode defiantly from the grotto.

Kerplunk.

Curious, he went over to explore for the puddle. He was concerned over the fact that he hadn't detected the liquid softness of water in the recess. He found the pool a moment later, however. A deep, almost still spring, it had a surface area no larger than his palm.

Yet, over a distance of thirty paces, Della had casually cast more than a dozen stones—detecting and hitting her target with each one!

Through much of the ceremony the next period, Jared found his thoughts returning to the girl. He wasn't as much disturbed by her arrogance as he was by the possibility that her pebble-throwing demonstration may have been calculated. Was she merely belittling his ability? Or was the performance really as casual as it had seemed? In either case, the capacity itself remained unexplained.

Wheel Anselm moved closer to him on the Bench of Honor and slapped his back. "That Drake's plenty good, don't you think?"

Jared had to agree, although there were several Lower Level Survivors who could hit more than three out of nine arrow targets.

He concentrated on the reflected *clacks* of the central caster and listened to Drake draw another arrow. An anxious silence fell over the gallery and Jared tried unsuccessfully to pick out Della's breathing and heartbeat.

Drake's bowstring *twanged* and the arrow whistled across the range. But the muffled *thud* of its impact revealed that it had missed the target and dug into earth.

After a moment the Official Scorer called out, "Two hand widths to the right. Score: three out of ten."

There was a burst of applause.

"Good, isn't he?" Anselm boasted.

Jared became more aware of Lorenz's breathing as the Adviser turned toward him and said, "I should think you'd be eager to get in on these contests."

Still smarting from Della's insinuation that he was conceited, Jared said noncommittally, "I'm prepared for anything."

The Wheel overheard and exclaimed, "That's fine, my boy!" He rose and announced, "Our visitor's going to lead off the spear-throwing competition!"

More applause. Jared wondered, though, whether he had detected a feminine breath escaping in contempt.

Lorenz brought him over to the spear rack and he spent some time selecting his lances.

"What's the target?" he asked.

"Woven husk discs—two hand spans wide—at fifty paces." The Adviser caught his arm and pointed it. "They're against that bank."

"I can hear them," Jared assured. "But I want *my* targets thrown up in the air."

Lorenz drew back. "You must want to hear how big a fool you can make of yourself."

"It's my party." Jared gathered up his spears. "You just toss the discs."

So Della was certain he had an exaggerated opinion of himself, was she? Riled, he broke out his clickstones and retreated to the fringe of the hot-springs area. Then he began a steady, brisk beat with the pebbles in his left hand. The familiar, refined tones supplemented those of the echo caster. And now he could clearly hear the things about him—the ledge on his right, the hollowness of the passageway behind him, Lorenz standing ready to cast the discs.

"Target up!" he shouted at the Adviser.

The first manna husk disc *swished* through the air and he let a spear fly. Wicker crunched under the impact of pointed shaft, then disc and lance clattered to the ground together.

Momentarily, he sensed something was out of place. But he couldn't decide what it was. "Target up!"

Another direct hit. And then another.

Exclamations from the gallery distracted him and he missed his fourth shot. He waited for silence before ordering more discs into the air. The next five shots found their mark. Then he paused and listened intensely around him. Somehow he couldn't ignore the vague suspicion that something wasn't as it should be.

"That was the last target," the Adviser shouted.

"Get another," Jared called back, letting his remaining spear lie on the ground.

An awed silence hung over the gallery. Then Anselm laughed and bellowed, "By Light! Eight out of nine!"

"With *that* kind of ability," Lorenz added from the distance, "he *must* be a Zivver."

Jared spun around. That was it—*Zivvers!* He realized that for heartbeats now he had been catching their scent!

Just then someone shouted, "Zivvers! Up on the ledge!"

Disorder swept the world. Women screamed and scrambled for their children while Survivors bolted for the weapons rack.

Jared heard a spear *zip* down from the height and clatter against the Bench of Honor. The Wheel swore apprehensively.

"Everybody stay where you are!" boomed a voice Jared had not forgotten from previous raids—that of Mogan, the Zivver leader. "Or the Wheel gets a shaft in the chest!"

By now Jared had pieced together a more or less complete auditory composite of the situation. Mogan and a score of Zivvers were spaced along the ledge, the central caster's tones rebounding clearly against their raised lances. A lone Zivver guarded the entrance, standing next to the large boulder.

As gingerly as he could, Jared stooped to retrieve his spear. But a lance *hissed* down and stabbed into the ground in front of him.

"I said *nobody* moves!" Mogan's menacing voice poured down.

Even if he could get his hand on the spear, Jared realized, the ledge would be out of range. The rear guard at the entrance, however, was a different matter. And there was nothing but boiling pits and manna plants between him and the man. If he could make it to the first spring, none of the raiders would be able to ziv his progress through the heated area.

He traced the flight of another spear from the ledge. It sank into the echo caster's shaft, wedging itself against the pulley. And the Upper Level was thrown into stark silence.

"Take what you want," the Wheel quavered, "and leave us alone."

Jared sidled toward the first hot spring.

"What do you know about a Zivver who's been missing for the past twenty periods?" Mogan demanded.

"Nothing at all!" Anselm assured him.

"Like Radiation you don't! But we'll find out for ourselves before we leave."

Moist warmth swirled against Jared's chest and he lunged the rest of the way into the vapors.

"We don't know anything about it!" the Wheel reiterated. "We've had a Survivor missing too—for over fifty periods!"

Clicking his teeth faintly to produce echoes as he crept through the hot-springs area, Jared pulled up sharply. A Zivver missing? One of the Upper Level men too? Could there be any connection between those two occurrences and what had happened to Owen? Had the Original World monster crossed the Barrier after all?

Mogan barked, "Norton, Sellers—go search their grottoes!"

Jared cleared the last boiling pit and stepped soundlessly over to the boulder. Now only the big rock stood between him and the raider guarding the entrance. And the man's breathing and heartbeat clearly divulged his exact location. No one had ever enjoyed such an advantage of potential surprise over a lone Zivver! But he had to strike fast. Norton and Sellers were already trotting down the incline and would, in the next three or four breaths, pass within a few paces of the boulder.

More things than he could keep track of happened in the next instant. Even as he started his lunge around the rock, he caught the horrible stench of the thing from the Original World. It was too late, however, to check his charge.

Then, as he broke around the boulder, a great cone of roaring silence screamed out of the passageway. The incredible sensation struck him squarely in the face with deafening force. It was as though obscure regions were being opened in his mind—as though thousands of sensitive nerves that had never been stimulated before were suddenly flooding his brain with alien impulses.

In that same instant he heard the *zip-hiss* that had sounded in the Original World just before Owen collapsed. And he listened first to the Zivver crumpling before him and then to the frantic cries of distress rising from his rear.

Whirling to flee before the monster and the terrifying noise that he could neither hear nor feel, Jared was only vaguely aware of the Zivver spear that was screeching in his direction.

He tried to duck at the last heartbeat.

But he was too late.

CHAPTER FOUR

Guided by clickstones, Jared went cautiously down the passageway. The inconsistencies before him were distressing. The corridor itself was both familiar and strange. He was certain he had been here before. There was that slender stone dripping cold water into the puddle below with melodious monotony, for instance. He had stood beside it many times, running his hands over its slick moistness and listening to the beauty of the drops.

Yet, even as he aimed his clicks *directly* at it now, it changed like a living thing, growing until its tip actually touched the water, then shrinking back into the ceiling. Nearby, the mouth of a pit opened and closed menacingly. And the passage itself contracted and expanded as though it were a giant's lung.

"Don't be afraid, Jared." A gentle, feminine voice stirred the deep silence. "It's just that we've forgotten how to keep things in place."

Her tone was soothing and familiar, yet unfamiliar and disturbing at the same time. He sent out precise clicks. The impression returning from nearby was like a silhouette—as though he were hearing the woman only with back sounding. Her features were blank. And when he reached out, she wasn't there. Yet she spoke:

"It's been so long, Jared! The details are all gone."

He went hesitantly forward. "Kind Survivoress?"

And he sensed her amusement. "You make it sound so stiff."

Instantly, an entire flight of misplaced childhood memories rushed back. "But you—weren't even real! You and Little Listener and the Forever Man—how can you be anything but a dream?"

"Listen around you, Jared, Does any of this sound real?"

The hanging stone was still squirming. Rock brushed against his arm as the right wall closed in, then pulled away again.

Then he was only dreaming—just as he had dreamed, oh, so many times, so many gestations ago. He remembered with a pang of nostalgia how Kind Survivoress would take him by the hand and lead him off. It wasn't a hand he could always feel. And she didn't really take him anywhere, because he would be asleep on his ledge all the while.

Yet, suddenly he would be scampering in the familiar passage or in a nearby world with Little Listener, the boy who heard only the inaudible sounds of the minor insects. And Kind Survivoress would explain, "You and I, Jared, can keep the Listener from being lonesome. Just think how awful his world is—all pitch silent! But I can bring him into this passage, as I can bring you. When I do, it's as though he wasn't deaf anymore. And the two of you can play together."

Jared was fully back in the familiar-strange passageway now.

And Kind Survivoress offered, "Little Listener's a grown man. You wouldn't know him."

Confused, Jared said, "Dream things don't grow!"

"We're *special* dream things."

"Where's the Listener?" he asked skeptically. "Let me hear him."

"He and the Forever Man are fine. The Forever Man's old now, though. He's not really a Forever Man, you know—just almost. But there's no time to hear them. I'm worried about you, Jared. You've got to wake up!"

For a moment he almost felt as though he were going to break out of the dream. But then his thoughts went calmly back to his childhood. He remembered how Kind Survivoress had said he was the only one she could reach—and, even then, only when he was asleep. But he wouldn't stop telling people about her. And she was afraid because she knew others were beginning to wonder whether he might be a Different One. She didn't want the fate that befell all the Different Ones to befall him. So she had quit coming.

"You *must* wake up, Jared!" She interrupted his reminiscences. "You're hurt and you've been unconscious too long!"

"Is that all you came back for—just to wake me up?"

"No. I want to warn you about the monsters and about all the dreams I've heard you have—dreams of hunting *for Light. The monsters are hideous and evil! I reached out and touched one's mind. It was so full of horrible, strange things that I couldn't stay in it for more than a fraction of a heartbeat!"*

"There's more than one monster?"

"There are many of them."

"What about hunting Light?"

"Don't you hear, Jared, you're only chasing more dream stuff? There's no such thing as Darkness and Light, as you think of them. You're just trying to escape responsibility. There's Survivorship to think of, Unification—things that really mean something!"

He had always been sure that if his mother had lived she would have been quite like Kind Survivoress.

He started to answer her. But she was no longer there.

Jared rolled against the softness of a manna fiber mattress and felt the bandage on his head.

From somewhere in the distance, rising above the audible background, came a reassuring paternal voice pacing itself through the monotonous patter of the Familiarization Routine:

"…Here we are under the echo caster, son. Hear how loud it sounds? Notice the direction of the *clacks*—straight up. We're in the center of the world. Listen to how the echoes come back from all the walls at practically the same time. This way, boy…"

Jared elevated himself on an unsteady elbow and someone caught his shoulders, easing him down again.

It was Adviser Lorenz, who turned his head the other way and urged, "Go tell the Wheel he's coming around."

Jared caught Della's receding scent as she left the recess. It had to struggle through the heavier odors clinging to everything around him—odors that identified Wheel Anselm's grotto.

From outside, the tutoring father's spiel bore back in on Jared's conscious, complicating his attempts to reorient himself.

"…There, directly before you, son—can you hear that empty space in the sound pattern? That's the entrance to our world. Now we're going over to the poultry yard. Watch it, boy! There's an outcropping about five paces in front of you. Let's stop here. Feel it. Get an idea of its size and shape. Try to hear it.

Remember *exactly* where it is. And you'll save yourself many a bruised shin…"

Jared tried to banish the distracting voice and compose his thoughts. But the effects of his recent dream lay heavily upon him.

It was most odd that Kind Survivoress should emerge from his forgotten fantasies all of a sudden, as though he had reached back into the abyss of his past and brought forward a warm, memorable slice of childhood. But he recognized the manifestation for what it was—no more than a wistful yearning for the security he hadn't known since his own father had taken him by the hand and Familiarized him with his world, as that attentive father outside was doing now.

"What in Radiation happened?" he managed.

"You took a lance broadside on the temple," Lorenz reminded. "You've been out like an echo caster for a whole period."

Suddenly he remembered—everything. And he lurched up. "The monsters! The Zivvers!"

"They're gone—all of them."

"What happened?"

"Best we could make out was that the monster seized a Zivver at the entrance. Two other Zivvers tried to save him. But they just collapsed in their tracks."

Clacks from the central caster entered through parted curtains and bounced off the Adviser's face, carrying away a composite of his apprehensive expression. Something else was hidden among the wrinkles, adding further tautness to his closed eyelids—an uneasy hesitancy. The Adviser appeared to be deciding whether to say something.

Jared, however, was more concerned over the monster's having invaded the Upper Level. Until now, he had been certain the Barrier was adequate to keep the creature on the other side. He felt that he and Owen deserved whatever they had gotten for violating the taboos. But it didn't end there. Rather, the monster had crossed the Barrier to enter one of the worlds of man. And once more Jared wondered whether he might not be responsible. He had invaded the Original World first, hadn't he? And hadn't the monster picked a most convincing time to strike again—just when he was beginning to compound blasphemy by giving thought to resuming his search for Light?

The Adviser drew in a decisive breath. "What were you doing when you got hit by that spear?"

"Trying to reach the Zivver on guard at the entrance."

Lorenz stiffened audibly. "Then you *admit* it?"

"What's there to admit? I heard a chance to carry off a hostage."

"Oh." The word was shaded with disappointment. Then the Adviser added dubiously, "The Wheel will be glad to learn that. A lot of us wondered why you stole away."

Jared swung his legs over the side of the ledge. "I don't hear what you're trying to prove. You mean you think—"

But the other continued, "So you were going to *attack* a Zivver? That's a little hard to believe."

First there had been Lorenz's open hostility. Then there was his jestful—or perhaps only superficially jestful—suggestion that Jared's abilities were Zivverlike. Now this latest obscure insinuation. It all added up to *something*.

He caught the man's wrist. "What *do* you suspect?"

But just then Wheel Anselm swept the curtain aside and strode in. "What's all this about attacking a Zivver?"

Della followed him inside and Jared listened to her almost soundless motions as she came over to the slumber ledge.

"That's what he was trying to do when he made his way over to the entrance," Lorenz explained skeptically.

But Anselm missed the inflection. "Isn't that what I said he had in mind? How are you feeling, Jared my boy?"

"Like I was clouted with a lance."

The Wheel laughed patronizingly, then became serious. "You were closer to that thing than any of us. What in Radiation was it?"

Jared considered telling them about his previous experience with the monster. But the Law of the Barrier applied as rigidly here as in the Lower Level. "I don't know. I didn't have much time to listen to it before I took that lance."

"Cobalt," Adviser Lorenz murmured. "Must have been Cobalt."

"Might have been Cobalt *and* Strontium," Della suggested distantly. "Some got the impression there were *two* monsters."

Jared stiffened. Hadn't his dream, too, intimated there were more than one of the incredible creatures?

"Light—it was awful!" Anselm agreed. "It *must* have been the Twin Devils. What else could throw such uncanny things into your head like that?"

"It didn't, as you say, 'throw things' into everybody's head," the Adviser reminded officiously.

"True. Not all felt what I felt. For instance, none of the fuzzy-faces remember anything *that* odd."

"I don't either, and I'm not a fuzzy-face."

"There were a few *besides* the fuzzy-faces who didn't feel the sensations. How about you, my boy?"

"I don't know what you're talking about," Jared lied, sparing himself the necessity of going into details.

Anselm and Lorenz fell silent while Della laid a hand gently on Jared's forehead. "We're preparing something for you to eat. Is there anything else I can do?"

Confused, he trained an ear on the girl. She'd never spoken that charitably before!

"Well, my boy," Anselm said, backing off, "you take it easy for the rest of your stay—until you're ready to return home for Withdrawal and Contemplation Against Unwise Unification."

The curtains swished as he and the Adviser left.

"I'll hear about that food," Della said, and followed them out.

Jared lay back on the ledge, exploring the soreness beneath the bandage. Still fresh in memory was his encounter with the monster—or monsters. In their presence, he had experienced the identical sensation he had felt in the Original World. For a moment, as he recalled the impression of uncanny pressure on his face, it seemed as though his *eyes* had received most of the force. But why? And he was still puzzled that Owen hadn't experienced the peculiar feeling. Could his friend's closed-eyes preference possibly have had anything to do with his not having sensed the psychic pressure?

Della returned and he heard that she was carrying a shell filled with—he listened to the consistency of the liquid and sniffed its faint aroma—manna tuber broth. But he sensed more than that. There was something he couldn't identify in her other hand.

"Feel well enough for some of this?" She extended the bowl.

Her words had been feather-edged with concern and he was at a loss to explain her sudden change of heart.

Something warm dripped on his hand. "The broth," he cautioned, "you're spilling it."

"Oh." She leveled the bowl. "I'm sorry."

But he listened sharply at the girl. She hadn't even *heard* the liquid running down the outside of the shell. It was as though she were practically deaf!

Improvising a test, he whispered almost subvocally, "What kind of broth is this?"

There was no response. She had no fine hearing at all! Yet, after the formal dinner, she had heard well enough to use as a target the swirling fluidity of a pool so small and so silent that he hadn't even been aware of its presence.

She put the bowl on a nearby shelf and extended the object in her other hand. "What do you think of this, Jared?"

He inspected the thing. Clinging to it was the scent of the monster. It was tubular, like a manna stalk, but cut off on both ends. The smooth face of the larger end, however, was shattered. He ran a finger into the break and felt a hard, round object within. Withdrawing his finger, he cut it against something sharp.

"What is it?"

"I don't know. I found it at the entrance. I'm sure one of the monsters dropped it."

Again he felt the round thing behind the broken surface. It reminded him of—something.

"The big end was—warm when I picked it up," she disclosed.

He cast his ears warily on the girl. Why had she hesitated before the word "warm"? Did she know it was heat that Zivvers zivved? Was she furtively bringing up the subject so she could hear his reaction—perhaps even trying to test the Adviser's insinuation that he might be a Zivver? If that was her intention, it was well hidden.

Then he jolted erect. *Now* he remembered what the round object in the broken end of the tube reminded him of! It was a miniature version of the Holy Bulb used during religious services!

And he shook his head in bewilderment. What sense did *that* fool paradox make? Wasn't the Holy Bulb associated with Light—with goodness and virtue—rather than with hideous, evil monsters?

His remaining periods in the Upper Level were uneventful to the point of monotony. He found the people not at all friendly. Their experience with the monsters had left them apprehensive and distant. More than once his words had gone unheard while quickened heartbeats reflected lingering fear.

If it hadn't been for Della's presence, he might have returned home before his scheduled departure. As it was, though, the girl was a challenging enigma.

She stuck close by all the while. And the friendship she extended was so profuse that he often felt her hand slipping into his as she took him about the world acquainting him with the people.

On one occasion Della added to the mystery when she paused and whispered, "Jared, are you hiding something?"

"I don't know what you mean."

"I'm a pretty good marksman myself, don't you think?"

"With rocks—yes." He decided to nudge her on.

"And I'm the one who found that thing the monsters left behind."

"So?"

Her face was turned eagerly toward his and he studied her in the sound of the central caster. When he said nothing more, he heard her breathing become heavy with exasperation.

She turned to walk away but he caught her arm. "What do you *think* I'm hiding, Della?"

But her mood had changed. "Whether or not you've decided to Declare Unification Intentions."

That she was lying had been obvious.

Yet, throughout the final two periods she seemed to hang onto everything he said, as though his next words might be the very ones she wanted to hear. Even up to the moment of his departure her disposition was one of restrained expectancy.

They were standing by the manna orchard, with his escort party waiting at the entrance, when she said reproachfully:

"Jared, it isn't fair to hold anything back."

"Like what?"

"Like why you can—hear so well."

"The Prime Survivor spent all his time training me to—"

"You've told me all about that," she reminded impatiently. "Jared, if we're of the same mind after Withdrawal and Contemplation, we'll be Unified. It wouldn't be right to keep secrets then."

Just when he was at the point of demanding to know what she was driving at, Lorenz walked up with a bow slung over his shoulder.

"Before you leave," he said, "I thought you might give me a few pointers on archery."

Jared accepted the bow and quiver, wondering why Lorenz should suddenly want to improve his marksmanship. "Very well, I don't hear anybody over on the range."

"Oh, but the children will be playing there in a few beats," the Adviser dissented. "Listen at the orchard. Can you hear that tall manna plant right in front of you, about forty paces off?"

"I hear it."

"There's a fruit shell on the highest stalk. It ought to make a good enough target."

Backing well away from the vapors of the nearest boiling pit, Jared rattled a pair of clickstones. "With a stationary target," he explained, "you first have to sound it out clearly. The central caster doesn't give a precise impression."

He strung an arrow. "Then it's important not to move your feet, since you're oriented only in your original position."

Releasing the bowstring, he listened to the arrow pass more than two arm lengths above the shell.

Surprised that he should miss by that much, he sounded the stones again. But from the corner of his hearing he caught Lorenz's reaction. The Adviser's expression was one of nearly irrepressible excitement. Della, too, wore an almost ecstatic tone on her face.

Why should they be overjoyed because he had failed to hit the shell? Bewildered, he strung another arrow and let it fly.

It went astray by the same distance.

Now the Adviser and the girl sounded even more jubilant. But Lorenz exuded triumph, whereas Della seemed intensely gratified.

He missed with two more shots before he wearied of their incomprehensible game. Annoyed, he dropped the bow and quiver and headed for the exit where the escort party awaited. After he had gone several paces he realized why his aim had been off. Standard bowstring tension here was greater than in his world! It was that simple. He even remembered now that the string had felt stiffer.

Then he stopped short. Abruptly he heard everything clearly. He *knew* why Lorenz had reacted as he had when the arrows missed—even why the archery exhibition had been arranged in the first place.

In order to protect his status as Adviser, Lorenz was intent on disqualifying him from Unification with Della. What better way than to prove him a Zivver?

The Adviser must have known Zivvers couldn't ziv in the heat of an orchard-hot springs area. And, since Jared had consistently missed the target there, Lorenz must now be *certain* he was a Zivver.

But what was the girl's interest? Evidently she also knew of the Zivvers' limitation. And she had recognized what the test might prove, even though she may not have known it was contrived specifically for that purpose.

But, then, she had actually been *elated* over his failure to hit the shell. Why?

"Jared! Jared!"

He listened to Della running forward to overtake him.

She caught his arm. "You don't have to tell me now. I know. Oh, Jared, Jared! I never dreamed anything like this would happen!"

She drew his head down and kissed him.

"You know—what?" he asked, drawing her out.

She went on effusively, "Don't you hear I suspected it all along—from the moment you threw the spears? And when I brought you that tube the monster dropped I all but said I had found it by its *heat*. I couldn't make the first move, though—not until I was certain you were a Zivver too."

From the depths of his astonishment, he managed to ask, *"Too?"*

"Yes, Jared. I'm a Zivver—just like you."

The Captain of the Official Escort came over from the entrance. "We're ready whenever you are."

CHAPTER FIVE

Rigid self-discipline was customary in Withdrawal and Contemplation. So crucial a decision called for searching introspection. For Unification automatically meant full Survivorship—a double measure of responsibility. Then too, one so dedicated also had to concern himself with the demanding obligations of Procreating and Familiarization of Progeny.

These considerations were far from Jared's mind over the next few periods, however, as he meditated in the silence of his heavily curtained grotto. He thought of Della—yes. But certainly not in the sound of normal Unification. Rather, his speculation centered on the significance of her being a Zivver. How had she managed to conceal that fact? And what were her intentions?

At that, though, the situation was not without humor. There was Lorenz—on a Zivver hunt. And all the while he had one right beside his ear! As far as Jared was concerned, the girl would be conveniently available for counteraccusation should the Adviser ever decide to accuse *him* of being a Zivver.

If he so chose, he could expose her any time he wanted. But what would he gain? Anyway, the fact that *she* thought *he* was a Zivver made for an interesting situation and he was anxious to hear what would come of it.

This line of thought invariably led to conjecture on the nature of zivving. What magical power was it that permitted one to know where things were in total silence and in the absence of odors? Or, like his imaginary Little Listener, did Zivvers hear some sort of soundless noise made by all things, animate and inanimate alike? Then he remembered it wasn't sound at all, but heat that they zivved.

Each time his attention wandered to these irrelevant matters, he knew he was not rendering full service to the spirit of Withdrawal and Contemplation. Yet, he supposed all of these subjects deserved exploration under the special conditions of his Unification.

He spared himself one possible distraction, though, in not telling the Prime Survivor about the monsters' invasion of the Upper Level. That would only have revived condemnation of his trip to the Original World.

On the fourth period of retreat he was jolted from meditation by a commotion in the world outside. At first he thought the monsters had reached the Lower Level. But there was not so much consternation as dismay in the voices of those streaming toward the orchard.

They had all abandoned the residential area by the time he decided on interrupting Withdrawal. He started after them. But halfway across the world, the central caster fetched impressions of the Prime Survivor and Elder Haverty coming in his direction.

"How long did you *expect* to keep it a secret?" Haverty was asking.

"Until I could decide what to do about it, at least," the Prime Survivor answered glumly.

"Eh? What? I mean, what *can* you do about something like that?"

But the other had detected Jared. "So you broke Withdrawal," he observed. "I suppose it's just as well."

Haverty excused himself, explaining that he was going to hear if Elder Maxwell had any ideas on how to cope with the situation.

"What happened?" Jared asked after the other had gone.

"We've just had nine hot springs go dry." The Prime Survivor led the way toward their grotto.

Jared was relieved. "Oh, I thought it might be soubats, or maybe Zivvers."

"I wish to Light that's *all* it was."

In the curtain-shielded privacy of their recess, the Prime Survivor paced aimlessly. "This is a critical situation, Jared!"

"Maybe the springs will start flowing again."

"The other three that dried up haven't started again. I'm afraid they're out for good."

Jared shrugged. "So we'll have to do without them."

"Don't you hear the seriousness of this thing? We have a tight, delicate balance here. What's happened might well mean some of us *won't be able to survive!*"

Jared started to offer further encouragement. But suddenly he was preoccupied with self-concern. Was this part of the pattern of punishment he had brought on by provoking the Original World monster? Hot springs going dry in both the Upper and

SIMULACRON-3

DANIEL F. GALOUYE

Afterword by
Mike Resnick

Lower Level, evil beings pushing past the Barrier—were they all actually strokes of vengeance by an offended Light Almighty?

"What do you mean—'some of us won't be able to survive'?"

"Figure it out yourself. Each hot spring feeds the tendrils of a hundred and twenty-five manna plants at the most. Nine dead boiling pits means almost twelve hundred fewer plants."

"But that's just a fraction—"

"Any fraction that reduces the survival potential is a critical factor. If we apply the formula, we hear that with nine less hot springs we can support only thirty-four head of cattle instead of forty. All the other livestock will have to be reduced proportionately. In the long run it will mean seventeen less people can exist here!"

"Well make up the difference with more game."

"There'll be *less* game—with more soubats than ever flying the passageways."

The Prime Survivor stopped pacing and stood there breathing heavily. Clickstone echoes weren't needed to tell that he was crestfallen, that the creases in his face were etched even more deeply.

Jared couldn't escape a sense of helplessness as he thought of man's absolute dependence on the manna plants. Actually, they stood between the Survivors and death, providing as they did food for humans and livestock alike; rich juices; fibers for the women to twist into cloths, ropes and fishing nets; shells that could be split in half and used as containers; stalks that could be dried out sufficiently for sharpening into a spear or arrow.

Now, almost bitterly, he could recall his father's voice finding new depths of respect and thoughtfulness gestations ago in reciting one of the legends:

"Our manna trees are a copy of the magnificent plants created by Light in Paradise—but a poor copy indeed. Light's creation was topped by thousands of gracious, lacy things that swayed in the breeze and made whispering noises while they enjoyed constant communion with the Almighty. They drank of His energy and used it in such a manner as to mix the water they drank with bits of soil and with the air that men and animals breathed out. And they transformed these things into food and pure air for man and animal alike.

"But Light's plant wasn't *good enough*. It seems we had to fashion a tree without the graceful, whispering things at the top—one which has, instead, great masses of awkward feelers that grow deep into the boiling pits. There they draw energy from the water's heat and use it to transform the foul air of the worlds and passageways and the elements from compost into fibers and tubers, fruit and fresh air."

That was the manna plant.

"What are we going to do about the hot-springs situation?" Jared asked finally.

"How are you coming along with Contemplation?"

"I suppose I've just about exhausted the subject."

"That helps." The Prime Survivor lodged a hand on his shoulder. "I've an idea there's going to be drastic need for help from the Upper Level before long. You realize, of course, that you don't have much of a choice in Contemplation. Under the circumstances, this Unification couldn't *possibly* be Unwise."

"No. I don't suppose it could."

The Prime Survivor cuffed his arm warmly. "I'm sure you'll be ready to return to the Upper Level just as soon as the Seven Periods of Withdrawal are over."

Outside, a deep silence that had fallen over the world was interrupted by the first phrases of the Litany of Light. The Guardian of the Way's fervent voice cracked with veneration as he shouted out the Recitations. More subdued but no less reverent were the Responses by the worshippers.

Recalling that Revitalization Ceremonies had failed after the first three springs had gone dry, Jared brushed the curtain aside and headed for the Assembly Area to join the services. That it would be a novel experience added little to his enthusiasm.

He stayed on the fringe of the Congregation. To have gone up front at the first ceremony he had attended in gestations would have distracted Guardian and Survivors alike. And he felt even more self-conscious when he heard a sharp-eared child nearby grip his mother's arm and exclaim, "It's Jared, Mother! It's Jared Fenton!"

"Hush and listen to the Guardian!" the woman reproved.

Guardian Philar was circulating among them, his words rebounding clearly from the object he clutched against his chest.

"Feel this Holy Bulb," he exhorted. "Be inspired along the passageway of virtue. Let us hurl back Darkness. Only by renouncing evil can we discharge our obligations as Survivors and listen ahead to that great period when we will be Reunited with Light Almighty!"

If the Guardian of the Way wasn't the gauntest man in the Lower Level, Jared felt certain, then he was at least in close running for the distinction. Bouncing off his body, central caster echoes picked up the harsh bluntness of bones that threatened to erupt through skin. His beard was sparse to the extreme of being fully inaudible. But the most prominent features of his haggard face were eyes set deep in their sockets and lids squeezed so firmly together that it was doubtful whether they had ever been open.

He reached Jared and paused, his voice stooping for but not quite finding a bass fervor. "Among all the things in this world, our Holy Bulb is the only one that has ever been in contact with Light. Feel it." And, when Jared hesitated, *Feel it!*

His hand went out reluctantly and touched its cold, round surface. In exaggerated proportion, it had the same properties as the miniature Bulb in the object the monsters had left in the Upper Level. And he wondered…

But he banished the thought. Wasn't it his own curiosity—over the Bulb and many other things—that had gotten the worlds into their present predicament?

The Guardian moved on, swaying, almost chanting. "There are those who would deny that Light ever dwelt in this relic. To them goes the blame for having provoked the Almighty's wrath."

Jared lowered his head, aware that many around him would have no trouble identifying the person for whom the accusation was intended.

"So the spiritual challenge we face on this Revitalization Period," the Guardian concluded, "is a personal one. The echoes from the wall are clear. Unless we atone individually for our misdeeds, we may expect to find that the same Light Almighty who banished Survivor from His presence has it in His power to destroy Survivor completely!"

He replaced the Holy Bulb in its niche and faced the Congregation, arms outstretched. An elderly woman went and stood humbly before him and Jared listened to Philar's hands performing the final ritual.

"Do you feel Him?" the Guardian demanded.

The woman grunted a disappointed negative reply and moved on.

"Patience, daughter. Effective Excitation comes to all those who persevere against Darkness."

Another Survivoress, two children and a Survivor humbled themselves in front of Guardian Philar before the first positive response was evoked in the Excitation of the Optic Nerve Ceremony. It was elicited from a young woman. As soon as the Guardian brushed aside the veil of hair that hung in front of her face and applied fingertips to her eyelids she cried out ecstatically:

"I feel Him! Oh, I feel Him!"

The stark emotion in the woman's voice made Jared's flesh tingle.

Patting her head approvingly, the Guardian turned to the next person.

Jared lagged behind the last in line, not letting himself imagine those who were Effectively Excited might actually be feeling nothing more than a special pressure from the Guardian's hands. Rather, he tried to keep his thoughts receptive, so that his first participation in the ritual would not be thwarted by long-standing prejudice.

By the time his turn arrived, the others had gone from the Assembly Area leaving only him and the Guardian. Waiting with his head lowered, he listened to Philar's severe expression. The Guardian was not concealing his belief that Jared's flagrant disrespect for the Barrier had brought on the Lower Level's misfortunes.

Bony hands reached out to Jared's face. They explored their way along his cheeks to his eyes. Then fingernails pressed into the soft recesses beneath the lower lids.

At first there was—nothing. Then the Guardian applied an almost painful pressure.

"Do you feel Him!" he demanded.

But Jared only stood there confounded. *Two fuzzy half rings of silent sound were dancing around in his head.* He could feel them *not* where the Guardian was pressing, but somewhere near the upper area of his eyeballs. Effective Excitation was the same sort of sensation he had twice experienced in the presence of the monsters!

Was he actually supposed to be feeling a part of Light Himself? If so, then why should he be aware of the presence of the Almighty, in a slightly different way, whenever he was near the Twin Devils? If Light was good, then why should He also be associated with the evil creatures?

Jared repressed the profane thoughts, chasing them completely out of his mind, together with the memory of ever having entertained them.

Fascinated, he listened to the dancing rings. They became more or less vivid as the Guardian varied the pressure of his fingernails.

"Are you feeling Him?"

"I feel Him," Jared admitted weakly.

"I didn't expect you would," the other said, somewhat disappointed. "But I'm glad to hear there's still hope for you."

He went over and sat on a ledge below the Holy Bulb niche and his voice lost some of its sharpness. "We haven't heard too much of you over here, Jared. Your father's been concerned about that and I can understand why. Some period the destiny of this world will be in your hands. Will they be *good* hands?"

Jared lowered himself on the ledge and sat there with his head bowed. "I *felt* Him," he mumbled. "I *felt* Him."

"Of course you did, son." The Guardian laid a sympathetic hand on his arm. "You could have felt Him sooner than this, you know. And things would have been different for you—different, perhaps, for the whole world."

"Did *I* cause the hot springs to dry up?"

"I can think of nothing that would enrage the Almighty more than violation of the Barrier taboo."

Jared's hands clutched each other in distress. "What can I do?"

"You can atone. Then we'll hear what happens afterward."

"But you don't understand. It may be more than just violating the Barrier! I've thought Light might not be Almighty, that He—"

"I do understand, son. You've had your doubts, like other Survivors from time to time. But remember—in the long run, one isn't to be judged by his skepticism. The true measure of a reconverted Survivor is the sincerity with which he renounces his disbeliefs."

"Do you think I can find the right amount of sincerity?"

"I'm sure you can—now that we've had this talk. And I've no doubt that should promised Reunion with Light come during your time, you'll be prepared for it."

The Guardian trained his ears on infinity. "What a beautiful period that will be, Jared—Light all around us, touching everything, a Constant Communion, with the Almighty bringing man total knowledge of all things about him. And Darkness will be erased completely."

Jared spent the rest of that period in the seclusion of his grotto. Unification, however, was not the subject of his Contemplation. Instead, he reviewed his new persuasions, careful not to entertain any thoughts that might be offensive to the Almighty.

In that single quarter period he renounced his dedicated search for Darkness and Light, denying himself any regret over having done so. And he resolved he would never again go beyond the Barrier.

New convictions firmly implanted, he relaxed in the assurance that everything would be all right—spiritually and physically. So certain did it seem he had done the proper thing that he wouldn't have been at all surprised to hear the twelve dry springs had begun running again. It was as though he had entered into a covenant with Light.

He was still reaffirming his resolution when the Prime Survivor entered. "The Guardian just told me you'd heard the sound, son."

"I hear a lot of things I didn't hear before." The earnest words bathed his father's face and carried back with them the outline of a smile that was warm with approval and pride.

"I've been waiting for you to speak like this for a long time, Jared. It means I can now go ahead with my plans."

"What plans?"

"This world should have young, vital leadership. It lacked that even *before* the springs went dry. With this challenge facing us, we need the imagination of a youthful leader all the more."

"You want me to become Prime Survivor?"

"As soon as possible. It'll take plenty of preparation. But I'll give you all the help I can."

A half-dozen periods earlier, Jared would have had no part of this development. But now it seemed only a minor enlargement of the life of dedicated purpose to which he had pledged himself.

"I don't hear any arguments," the Prime Survivor said gratefully.

"You won't. Not if this is the way you want it."

"Good! Over the next couple of periods I'll tell you some of the things that have to be done. Then, when you get back from the Upper Level, we'll start our formal training."

"How are the Elders going to take this?"

"After they heard what went on between you and Guardian Philar, they didn't have any objections at all."

Early the next period—even before the central echo caster had been turned on—Jared was shaken roughly from his sleep.

"Wake up! Something's happened!"

It was Elder Averyman. And whatever had happened must have been serious, indeed, for him to have burst into a private grotto.

Jared bounded to his feet, conscious of his brother's restless stirring on the next ledge. "What is it?" he demanded.

"The Prime Survivor!" Averyman broke for the exit. "Come—quick!"

Jared raced off after him, hearing both that Romel was awakening and that his father's ledge was empty. He overtook the Elder near the entrance to the world. "Where are we going?"

But Averyman only huffed more erratically. And the rush of air into and out of his lungs was chopped into discontinuous sound by the motion of the hair that hung down over his face.

That something was seriously amiss was evidenced by more than the Elder's behavior. Indistinct voices, muffled in apprehension, could be heard in small, scattered groups. And Jared listened to several other persons, who had evidently been up and about soon enough to hear what had happened, racing toward the entrance.

"It's the Prime Survivor!" Averyman managed between gasps. "We were out for our early walk. And he was saying how he was going to let you take over. When we passed by the entrance—" He stumbled and Jared crashed into his flailing form.

Someone turned on the central caster and Jared oriented himself as the details of his world sprang into audibility all around him. Among the impressions came that of Romel plodding along after them.

Elder Averyman brought his breathing under control. "It was awful! This thing came rushing from the passage, all fluttering and foul smelling! Your father and I could only stand there terrified—"

The smell of the monster still clung to the air. Detecting it, Jared raced ahead.

"Then there was this hissing sound," Averyman's laboring voice receded. "And the Prime Survivor fell where he stood. He didn't move—not even when the thing came for him!"

Jared reached the entrance and elbowed his way past several Survivors who were asking one another what had happened.

The odor was even more offensive in the Passageway, growing stronger in the direction of the Original World. Mingled with it was the familiar scent of the Prime Survivor. There seemed to be an accumulation of the stench a short distance away. Jared followed his nose to the spot, reaching down to pick up something soft and limp.

About twice the size of his hand, it felt like manna cloth. Only, the texture was incomparably finer. And from each corner dangled a ribbon of the same material.

It was something that certainly required further study. But, as long as it reeked with the smell of the monster, he couldn't bring it into the world without causing commotion. So he put it down and scraped dirt over it, fixing the location of the spot in his mind.

On the way back he almost collided with his brother, who was groping along the passageway.

"It sounds like you'll be Prime Survivor sooner than you expected," Romel said, not without a trace of envy in his voice.

To be continued in Issue Two

Views expressed by guest or resident columnists are entirely their own.

SOMETHING DIFFERENT

by Horace E. Cocroft

Horace Cocroft, an avid student of military history, thinks about off things like the economic engine of Middle Earth and other such matters…

Economics in SF

A few months ago, an unusual Paul Krugman blog entry caught my attention. He'd been asked to write the introduction to a new edition of Isaac Asimov's "Foundation" trilogy. In it, he discusses his youthful fascination with the idea of psychohistory, a science that can predict human behavior through mathematical formulas. "I didn't grow up wanting to be a square-jawed individualist or join a heroic quest; I grew up wanting to be Hari Seldon, using my understanding of the mathematics of human behavior to save civilization." Unfortunately for Krugman, the closest he could manage was economics.

Economic conditions, as the last few years have proven, and as the residents of Greece or Spain could attest, directly affect all aspects of life. The well-being of individuals, their ability to achieve their hopes and dreams, and the obstacles and frustrations that oppose them are all dependent on the state of the economy. This is true of fictional people as well. Novels such as *The Great Gatsby* or *The Grapes of Wrath* are shaped by the economic conditions and economic systems prevalent in the novel. Of course contemporary works don't need to explain the world that they are set in, as readers are familiar with the world around them. Even historical works can get by with little explanation. Most people know that conditions during the Great Depression were hard, but that the Roaring Twenties were prosper-

ous. Wholly invented worlds, however, require a bit more description.

In the world of *Star Trek*, to take a particularly annoying example, economics are simply done away with. Apparently there's no money in the Federation, almost no economic transactions whatsoever. How the characters at *Deep Space Nine* pay for drinks at Quark's Bar is a mystery. Worries about finances and money are sneeringly left to less progressive species like the Ferengi. More importantly, the allocation of resources in the Federation is equally mysterious. I suppose in a world with replicators, unlimited resources might be possible, but even then the question of labor raises its head. How do you get people to do work that they're not personally thrilled with? There are an awful lot of waiters in the world of *Star Trek*. I can see taking the time and effort to become a member of Starfleet and explore the galaxy, but if you're not getting paid to do it, who would show up for work as a waiter? Or even, say, a lawyer? There are many people who are genuinely interested in the practice of law, but the fact that it is very well compensated has more to do with its popularity as a profession. It's difficult to say that the economics in *Star Trek* are nonsense, because there just aren't any.

An example of a fictional world that handles its economic realities very well is the "Novels of the Change," by S.M. Stirling. His world, a post-apocalyptic world where electricity and other advanced forms of power generation no longer work, is one stuck at a medieval technological level. In it, characters have to make a living, and have economic concerns. "Should I sell this flock of sheep at Corvallis, or can I get a better price in Portland?" It's not the primary concern of the main characters, but you're always aware that it's something they have to deal with. It makes the world feel more realistic and lived in. (As an aside, does anyone else think the producers of the NBC show *Revolution* owe some money to Stirling? He came up with that electricity failing plot years ago.)

Of course, not every exercise in world building needs a detailed economic structure. Nobody reads Tolkien expecting to find a discussion of the trade policies of the Shire. Still, I've always been curious about how Bilbo supported himself before his share of Smaug's loot. He was obviously a gentleman of leisure, to be able to take a trip of several months on short notice. And exactly how did the Dúnedain Rangers support themselves? Were they hunter-gatherers? Did they live off the largesse of the elves at Rivendell? Apparently, the only economic agents in Middle-earth are the Dwarf Lords, in their houses of stone.

Not all fantastic worlds need realistic economics. Authors such as Philip K. Dick, and, to a lesser extent, Ray Bradbury, are more concerned with ideas and images than with making a world feel lived in and realistic. An unconcern for economic and material realities is almost a part of their writing style. The Amber novels of Roger Zelazny go in the other direction. They're so big and sprawling that economic concerns seem trivial in comparison. The universes these authors construct have their own strengths, and aren't dependent on realistic-feeling settings to draw in readers.

The Lord of The Rings aside, the novels that seem to do the best job at establishing a realistic economic setting for the worlds their characters inhabit are the ones that persist for more than one book. The short stories and novels of Lois McMaster Bujold's Vorkosigan books have a fine economic foundation. There is competition between social classes for economic and political power on individual worlds, trade between worlds, and at the individual level, the pursuit of profit, or in some cases, the simple struggle to keep one's head above water. Most of her books (at least the ones that don't deal with Jackson's Whole) aren't focused on economic matters, but you are aware that these are characters and societies with economic concerns and desires. Similarly, David Drake's RCN series shows a universe where both individuals and governments pursue their economic interests, and where economic worries often provide a check on ambition. The larger scope and broader view of a multi-book series gives authors more room to give their universes both depth and detail. Even a space opera (and I mean that in the best sense of the phrase) such as David Weber's Honor Harrington series is very explicit about the way economic strength translates into military power.

An area where science fiction is traditionally very strong is depicting the effects that newly developed technologies have on an economic system. Tech growth usually leads to increases in productivity, which generally feeds economic growth. However, tech growth can also cause dislocations in an economy, as newer ways of doing things leave workers and whole industries behind. Science fiction often does a good job of depicting both the positive and negative aspects of how technological advancement affects society.

Sound economics is a useful world-building tool, even if it is just part of the background. Economic conditions can provide motivation for characters, provide challenges for characters, or simply make a world feel more realistic. And economic flavoring can be something as simple as describing the barter system in a post-apocalyptic world.

♈